SHARON SALA

Deep in the Heart

HarperTorch
An Imprint of HarperCollins*Publishers*

This is a work of fiction. Names, characters, places, and incidents are products of the author's imagination or are used fictitiously and are not to be construed as real. Any resemblance to actual events, locales, organizations, or persons, living or dead, is entirely coincidental.

HARPERTORCH
An Imprint of HarperCollins*Publishers*
10 East 53rd Street
New York, New York 10022-5299

Copyright © 1996 by Sharon Sala
ISBN: 0-06-108326-7

First HarperTorch paperback printing: January 2003
First HarperCollins paperback printing: February 1996

HarperCollins ®, HarperTorch™, and ◈ ™ are trademarks of HarperCollins Publishers Inc.

Printed in the United States of America

Visit HarperTorch on the World Wide Web at www.harpercollins.com

10 9 8 7 6 5 4 3 2

First love is sweetest, because it is new.
When it goes the distance, it is rare.

This book is dedicated to first loves,
and to the lucky few
who kept theirs alive.

Prologue

FOR ALL INTENTS AND PURPOSES, Samantha Jean Carlyle was dead. It was just the when and how of it that had yet to happen.

The floor of her latest apartment was no softer than the last one, but it was where she felt safest. After all that she'd gone through during the last three months, below window level was the closest thing to heaven that she could find.

The proof of her fate lay in a circle on the floor around her, encompassing her with the evil that it contained. The hate mail and answering machine message tapes overflowed with warnings and promises from a stalker who wanted her dead.

Her face was blank. The light in her eyes had been out for weeks. When hope finally died, it had taken Samantha's will to survive with it. The police had all but accused her of making up the entire story. Her boss had sent her home to get herself and her act together before she was permitted to return. Her friends were gone . . . and so was her faith in her fellow man.

Samantha's breath caught at the back of her throat and came up on a sob.

"Oh God, I need help," she whispered. Her head hit the wall as she slumped against it. "There's no one on this earth who will believe me. My parents are dead. My so-called friends have abandoned me. If only there was someone left who would . . ."

The words froze on her tongue. She shuddered as a memory suddenly surfaced—of a boy she'd known, and the man that he'd become—of the vows they'd traded and the promises that they'd made to each other. She traced an old scar on the inside of her wrist and wondered if she'd finally lost her mind.

But the thought wouldn't go away. Long hours passed while she remembered a young man who'd sworn an allegiance that she thought never would be broken. But as she crawled to her feet and made her way through the shadows in her apartment to the phone, she kept thinking, "What if he's no longer there? What if he doesn't even remember me?" Another sob slipped from her lips as she dialed with trembling fingers.

A phone call later, she had the assurance of knowing that there was a number listed in his name. And Cotton, Texas, was so small that a name on an envelope would be all that was needed to get a letter delivered to a resident

If he was the man she remembered him to be . . . if time hadn't changed Johnny Knight to the extent that he'd lost all value for an old promise made, then maybe there *was* still one person left who cared if she lived or died.

"Dear God, let him come," she whispered, and began to write the letter, knowing full well it might be her last.

1

JOHN THOMAS KNIGHT always knew he was going to hell. He just never expected to get there in a yellow cab.

Since his plane set down in Los Angeles two hours ago he'd prayed more than he'd prayed in his entire life, and he still wasn't certain he was going to ever see home again. From where he was sitting, Cherokee County, Texas, was looking better all the time. Here in L.A., traffic didn't flow, it snarled and jammed, and the people who drove in it wore equally snarled expressions.

People have to be crazy to live here, he thought.

As his cab stopped for a red light, a tall, thin man wearing combat fatigues appeared in the median of the busy thoroughfare, seemingly out of nowhere, and proceeded to execute a perfect somersault. He landed on his knees and then began chanting in a language John Thomas couldn't understand.

"Crazy fool," he muttered, and tried to imagine the Sam he had known living in a place like this.

The thought of Sam reminded him of why he was here, and of the last time he'd seen his childhood playmate who'd become his first love.

He'd been eighteen and hurting, trying to be a man and not cry as he kissed her good-bye at the bus stop. Samantha Carlyle had been sixteen and so full of their love that he could still remember the sheen of tears in her eyes as the bus pulled away.

He frowned, remembering also that the next time he'd come home—ten weeks later for his father's funeral—her family had already moved to California without a by your leave or a forwarding address to help him find her.

He traced the thin, hairline scar across his wrist, remembering late summer nights, and blood oaths taken and promises given. Swearing a "cross my heart and hope to die" friendship forever. Nights when the extreme heat of slow summer days had lessened to an acceptable simmer and the only witnesses to their meeting were locusts buzzing a crazy cacophony in the mimosa trees overhead.

His gut tightened as the cab took a turn, and he wondered if it was from fear of traffic, or the pain of remembering the night of her sixteenth birthday, when they'd exchanged a different kind of oath. A promise that ended with them wrapped in each other's arms beneath the same mimosa trees. He shuddered and shut his eyes, trying to call back the memory of the expression on Samantha's face as he'd taken her undying pledge of love, as well as her virginity, all in one night. They'd been so happy . . . and so sure.

And it had ended so swiftly that thinking about it still made him ache.

His mouth curved in a wry smile as he thought back to the dreams of callow youth. Then the smile died when he remembered the letter he'd received at home two days ago. The letter that had sent him flying across the country from Cherokee County, Texas, to L.A. with his heart in his throat. The letter that had him praying he wouldn't be too late to keep the promise he'd made all those years ago.

He won't leave me alone, she'd written. *And I have nowhere left to run. Johnny . . . please come get me! Don't let me die!*

The lingering resentment of her unexplained disappearance, and the old, unanswered questions from their youth were not enough to make him ignore her cry for help. Not after all they'd been through together. It was The least he could do for someone who'd been his best friend for the first half of his life thus far.

He shifted in the seat and then frowned, jamming his Stetson tighter on his head as the cabby took a corner like a piss ant hunting dry ground. He wondered if the man drove this way out of repressed aggression, or if it was because he didn't know enough of the English language to understand the road signs.

"Either slow the hell down or pay attention to what you're doing," he growled, flashing his badge across the front seat for good measure. A Texas sheriff's badge carried no authority in California, but John Thomas was too fed up to care about details.

The cabby's shocked expression did little toward appeasing the nervous twitch John Thomas felt low in his belly, and he knew that the sinking feeling he'd lived with for the last forty-eight hours had nothing to do with California traffic.

Minutes later the cabby pulled up in front of a pink stucco apartment complex surrounded by palms. The black wrought-iron fence and ornate gate standing ajar told him in no uncertain terms that he was definitely in laid-back L.A.

He crawled out of the cab with his bag in one hand and his hat in the other, then tossed some bills through the open window opposite the driver.

"My God," he muttered, and jammed his Stetson back on his head. "Pink houses! Back home they'd either slap on some whitewash or burn 'em all down and put them out of their misery."

"Vat you say to me?" the cabby yelled.

John Thomas just shook his head and waved the cabdriver away. Then he took a slow, deep breath and stepped up onto the sidewalk. He stared straight up into the underside of a towering palm tree and back at the odd, almost garish blending of color and cultures surrounding him. Readjusting his Stetson, he picked up his bag and headed toward what he hoped was the vicinity of Apartment 214.

By the time he reached the second floor of the complex, he'd encountered two sets of men holding hands, a woman with purple hair who was wearing a tight, pink bodysuit, a teenager walking four dogs—none above the size of a half-grown armadillo—and had been propositioned by a preteen girl young enough to be his daughter.

But when he arrived at the door to Apartment 214, he no longer worried about where he was, but who he was going to see.

He and Samantha were no longer teenagers. But they'd been friends long before they'd been lovers, and in spite of the painful and dramatic way in which they'd parted, he still considered her more than a friend. The twenty-plus years of friendship that lay between them were still as strong as it had been on the night their blood had mixed and their promises had slipped into the silence of the night.

He dropped his bag beside the door, threw back his shoulders and knocked. It was, after all, why he'd come.

There were no tears left to cry. Unmitigated terror had become commonplace for Samantha Carlyle. She was waiting for the inevitable. Day by day the stalker came closer, and there was nothing she could do to stop him.

She could barely remember her life three months

ago when she'd been a highly valued member of a Hollywood casting agency, calmly and competently going
about the business of fitting the famous and the not-so-
famous into starring and supporting roles.

She had thrived on the constant pressure and excitement of finding just the right actor or actress for the
part in question. And although she'd been in the business over seven years, she had never gotten used to
being the one who also doled out the bad news to the
ones who didn't make the cut. Most of the times the
actors and actresses took the rejections in stride. But
now and then, there would be one who was devastated
by the news. Those were the times that she wished
she'd been checking groceries in some supermarket,
not ruining someone's hopes and dreams.

"And look at you now," Samantha whispered to her
own reflection as she stood in the window overlooking
the courtyard below. "You have no job. You're running
from the devil and your own shadow. You're just hiding . . . and waiting to die."

Until now, she'd never considered what it meant to
be "living on borrowed time." She looked again at her
reflection and wondered what there was about her that
could drive a man to insane threats of vengeance.

Her face was no different from many others—
heartshaped, but a bit too thin, and framed by a mane
of thick, black hair. Her nose was still small and turned
up at the world, but there was no longer a jut to her
chin. It only trembled. Her lips were full but colorless,

and the life that had once shone from her eyes seemed dim . . . almost gone. She shuddered and dropped the drapes, rearranging them to shut the sun out and herself in from prying eyes.

When the harassment had gone from hate mail to phone calls with spine-chilling messages left in an unrecognizable voice, she'd nearly lost her mind and, soon after, she did lose her so-called friends.

As if that wasn't enough, she'd moved her residence twice, certain each time she would outwit the culprit. And then came the day that she realized she was being stalked. But by then going back to the police was out of the question. They had convinced themselves that she was concocting the incidents herself. In fact, they had almost convinced her.

Her anger at their accusations had quickly turned to disbelief when they had proved to her, without doubt, that the hate letters she'd been receiving had been typed on her own office typewriter, and that the calls left on her answering machine were traced to an empty apartment that had been rented in the name of Samantha Jean Carlyle. It was enough said. When LAPD reminded her that perpetrating fraud was a crime, she'd taken her letters and her tapes and gone home, having decided to hire a personal bodyguard. Then she'd reconsidered her financial situation and given up on that idea.

That was the day her boss put her on indefinite leave of absence, after reminding her, of course, that when she got her act together she would be welcomed back.

The victim had become the accused. At first she'd been furious over everyone's lack of sympathy for her situation or concern for her life. Then she'd become too busy trying to stay alive.

It was the constant frustration and the growing fear that no one was going to save her, let alone believe her, that made her remember Johnny Knight.

Until the call she'd made in the middle of the night last week, she hadn't known if he was still in Cherokee County . . . or if he was even alive. Their last link had been severed years ago when her family had moved away from Cotton. At sixteen, she'd loved him enough for two lifetimes, and it had still not been enough to keep their connection intact after her family moved to California.

But the bond of their lifelong friendship was burned deep within her memory and was strong enough to prompt the letter she'd written. He was her last and only hope.

Her stomach growled now, reminding her that, once again, she'd forgotten to eat. And then she remembered the reason she had not: there was no food in the house, and she was too afraid of the maniac who might be lurking outside to go buy any.

A sharp knock at the door sent her spinning around. She clasped her hand to her throat, felt the blood leave her face, and fought the wave of nausea that hit her belly. Transfixed, she stood in the middle of the room and listened.

*   *   *

For some reason, John Thomas had expected an instant answer to his summons. When it was not forthcoming, he rechecked the address and then frowned as he looked back at the number on the apartment door. They matched.

A picture flashed in his mind of opening the door and finding that he'd come this far only to be too late. Of her lifeless body flung out across the room in careless abandon, left there by the man who'd entered her world uninvited. It made him shake, and it made him angry. The unexpected emotion made his second attempt at knocking sound more like a frontal attack.

But all it did was frighten Samantha into the thought of making one last call to LAPD, knowing full well that they would only blame her for crying wolf.

John Thomas was at the point of looking for the apartment manager when he heard a woman's voice. It was faint, and a little shaky, and it hit him belly first as he tried to connect the soft, husky sound with the teenager that he'd known.

"Who is it?" she said.

"Sam? Is that you? Let me in."

Samantha gasped. She didn't recognize the voice. It was deep and gravelly and echoed beneath the overhanging roof under which he was standing. But there was only one person left alive on the face of the earth who'd ever called her Sam. She ran to the door and peered through the peephole, afraid to look, but afraid not to take the chance.

He didn't look the way she'd expected, but from the distorted view through the hole, neither would her own parents had they still been alive.

"Who is it?" she asked again, and watched the man on the other side of the door stuff his hands in his pockets in a gesture of frustration.

"It's me. . . . It's . . ." He almost said John Thomas. But it wouldn't have been how she'd known him. She'd been long gone by the time he'd decided that being called Johnny wouldn't do for a fresh-faced marine home on his first leave.

"It's Johnny. I got your letter. Let me in." His voice softened as he realized how frightened she must be if what she'd claimed was true.

"Do you swear?" he heard her ask, and then he smiled. He knew what he needed to say to assure her of who he was.

"Cross my heart and hope to die," he said quietly.

It was what she'd been waiting to hear. Tears came softly. Tears that she thought were lost forever. They came with the relief that flooded through her as she reached for the locks lining the door.

Tumblers turned and chains clinked, and then the door cracked . . . just enough so that he saw, for the first time in fifteen years, the clear, perfect blue of Samantha Carlyle's eyes. And then the door swung back, and she stood framed in the opening, and he forgot to breathe.

Woman! She'd turned into a woman! And my

God . . . what a woman! She was beautiful. In his mind he'd known it had happened. But his heart hadn't been ready for the shock.

"Johnny?"

Samantha stared long and hard at the towering, broad-shouldered cowboy, trying to see a hint of the boy that she'd known and loved in the black hair and sharp cheekbones of the big man standing at her door. The eyes looked familiar and only a little stunned. They were still a rich, warm shade of brown. His mouth was firm, his chin stubborn. But his appearance had changed so much that Samantha knew he could have passed her on the street unrecognized. And then she remembered! The telling proof should still be visible. She reached for his wrist.

At the touch of her hand, he shuddered. And when he realized that she was moving aside the band of his watch, he knew what she was looking for. He stilled, and then waited, letting her call the shots.

Samantha held her breath as she looked down. Intent on her search, she didn't see his expression darken. When her fingers felt and then traced the hard ridge of tissue beneath his watchband, all the breath went out of her body in a long, slow sigh. She had found the scar.

The pale, thin reminder of their childhood pledge was still there. It had to be him! She looked up and smiled. It was her first smile in months, and its rarity made it all the more precious.

"It is you!" she whispered. "You came!"

Within his next heartbeat she was in his arms. John Thomas felt himself losing a grip on reality as he held her close. And when he would have loosened his hold, he felt her arms tighten in a desperate response. It had been so long—too long. Although he remembered her rejection of him years ago, he wondered if it had been long enough.

When he could think past the soft, womanly body pressed intimately against him, he realized that the last time he'd held her like this, she'd given herself completely and then within weeks had disappeared without a word. A draft of hot air circled around the back of his neck like demon's breath.

He remembered why he'd come.

"Wait a minute, Sam."

He grunted, then shoved his bag through the open door of her apartment with the toe of his boot as he kicked it shut behind him. She didn't speak, and he didn't want to. Well aware of her desperation, he let her cling to him. There would be time later to talk, but for now, remembering was all they could do.

2

Cotton, Texas, 1974

"SAMANTHA JEAN, where are you going?"

Sam rolled her eyes and sighed. *Darn!* If Daddy would only have oiled that hinge on the back door, Mama wouldn't be able to hear her.

"Just outside," she answered vaguely.

"It's nearly dark," her mother warned.

"I know, but I'll be with Johnny."

She missed hearing her mother's snort of exasperation, and even if she hadn't, she wouldn't have been swayed by the fact that her mother thought Johnny Knight was too big and tough for an eight-year-old girl. At the ripe old age of ten, he'd already gained a reputation in their tiny town as a "street kid."

His old man had been a widower for several years, and had long since left Johnny's caretaking up to whoever cared to notice. By the time Johnny Knight was eight, he'd earned the respect of older boys in the neighborhood by taking none of their guff. But what had stunned the entire community was the strange friendship that had sprung up between the school principal's little girl and Cotton's only truant.

Samantha's small bare feet pounded against the dry, dusty earth as she flew down the alley toward the town park. A dog barked in a yard two houses over and a cat darted across her path, but nothing slowed her down. She patted the pocket of her dusty jeans just to make sure that she had everything Johnny had told her to bring. This was too important a night to mess up. And Johnny's approval was too important for her to lose.

Long, blue shadows slipped across the wooded area of the grassy square. Samantha dodged a night moth as it swooped across her line of vision. She didn't gasp or squeal, although the urge to do so was strong. It was nearly dark, and without Johnny's presence, Samantha wasn't as brave as she might have been.

And then he was there, stepping out of a line of trees and jogging toward her with a smile on his face and his shaggy black hair in forgotten disarray. He waved as she swerved and turned in his direction.

"Did you bring the stuff?" he asked.

Samantha nodded and pulled nervously at her faded T-shirt, her elfin face oddly solemn.

"You still wanna do this?"

She nodded again.

He slapped her on the back, and grinned. "Then

come on, Sam. Injun Tommy told me how this was done. So if we're gonna do it, we gotta do it right."

Dusk was upon them as Johnny led the way into a bank of trees hidden deep within the town park. He'd already cleared a place beneath a heavily flowering mimosa and Samantha's belly flopped nervously as she knelt and began emptying her pockets.

Darkness enveloped them as nightfall began to emerge. Johnny worked swiftly, spreading the assorted tools he would need to work their magic before Sam's mom began yelling her name, calling out into the darkness as she did every evening for her little girl to come home. It had never occurred to Johnny to be sad that no one ever called his name, that no one seemed concerned that darkness was upon him. At ten, he was a most self-sufficient little man.

"Okay," he said, looking down into Sam's wide blue eyes, and peering closely just to assure himself there were no tears showing. "I'm ready."

"Me too," she said, and offered her arm.

"You want to go first?" Johnny asked, surprised by Sam's unexpected show of courage.

She nodded.

He shrugged. "Here goes." He took her wrist and held it firmly. "You can close your eyes if you wanna."

Although the urge to do so was strong, she shook her head no.

The slice across her wrist was quick, and little more than a sting. She gasped, and looked down in time to

see Johnny work a similar cut into his own wrist below
the base of his thumb.

A small stream of bright red blood seeped and then
began to flow down her arm. Samantha's heart knocked
against her rib cage, but she willed herself not to cry.
This was too serious for squeamish bellies and crybabies.

"Now," Johnny said softly, and grasped her arm
once again. As their wrists met and their blood mingled, he spoke. "Repeat after me." And she did.

"Friends forever in need and in deed."

"Friends forever in need and in deed."

Samantha echoed his pledge in a soft whisper,
shocked by the sticky feel of their blood mixing and
running across each other's hands.

"Secrets are kept and no promises broken."

"Secrets are kept and no promises broken."

The locusts in the tree beneath which they were sitting broke into a crazy humming buzz, a cacophony of
ecstasy that made Samantha jump with fright.

Suddenly what had begun as a game became more
than the children could comprehend. That night, a
bond was formed between them that would take more
years than they had at this moment to understand.

"I do so swear."

"I do so swear."

"Cross my heart and hope to die."

"Cross my heart and hope to die."

They looked at each other and then smiled. It was
done.

Johnny's dark brown eyes and thick hair—always in need of a cut—were comfortably familiar to Samantha, as was the square, angry thrust to his jaw. Yet she knew that tonight their relationship had changed. Now she was no longer the little kid he let tag long. Now she belonged. She belonged to Johnny Knight . . . and he belonged to her.

Johnny saw Sam's blue eyes widen apprehensively as their arms separated. Even he felt a twinge of panic at the sight of all of the blood on both their wrists. Nervously, he swiped at her arm with the tail of his shirt to clean a spot, then tore open a Band-Aid and quickly applied it to the cut on her wrist. He opened another Band-Aid, and then handed it to Sam, watching closely as she applied it to his own cut.

He felt silent satisfaction that she had yet to bawl. And when he remembered a grimy handkerchief in his pocket, he yanked it out and began swiping at the remaining blood on their hands and arms until there was nothing left to show what they'd been up to except a couple of empty Band-Aid wrappers on the ground at their feet.

"Samantha! It's time to come home!"

The cry was faint, but it was sure. At the sound of her mother's voice, Sam jerked, clasped her hand over her bandaged wrist, and looked around nervously.

Johnny sighed. It never failed. Her mother always called just when things were getting good.

"I guess you'd better go," he said, and helped her to her feet, checking the place on her arm once again in the thick Texas darkness to assure himself that the blood had stopped flowing. He couldn't be sending Sam back home now, only to bleed to death later in the night.

She sighed, oddly reluctant to break the tenuous bond she felt between them.

"Samantha Jean!" her mother called again.

When her mother used both names, she meant business.

"I've got to go," she said, and started to run when Johnny's voice stopped her.

"Sam! Wait!"

She turned and stared, peering anxiously into the darkness beneath the mimosa, unwilling to leave him, yet afraid to anger her mother.

"Remember, you can't tell. If you tell, then the spell is broken," he warned.

"I promise," she whispered. "Cross my heart and hope to die." And then she was gone.

Four years later he punched the boy across the street for teasing Samantha Carlyle and making her cry. And four years after that, on her sixteenth birthday, she gave Johnny more than her word of honor.

Johnny Knight stood beneath the thick stand of mimosa trees, hidden from prying eyes as he waited in the darkness for Samantha to come. And he knew that she would. She'd promised.

He shivered. Partly from nervous excitement, partly from need. He wanted Samantha in the worst way possible for an eighteen-year-old boy to want. But he loved her too much to push her. Tonight he had some news to give her that she wasn't going to like.

Today he had joined the marines. The armed services had been his only hope. His grades wouldn't get him a scholarship to any collage, and his job barely kept him alive. His father had been in prison now for nearly a year, so there was no one around to help him better his life. He had to do for himself . . . as well as for Samantha. He had so many dreams for his future. And she was in every one of them.

And then he heard footsteps, and when she burst through the thicket and flew into his arms, his heart swelled with such love that words were impossible. For the moment, all he could do was hold her.

"I didn't think I would make it," she cried, and fell into his arms, laughing and shaking at the same time from the excitement of slipping away. "What's the big secret? You nearly scared me to death when you called."

Johnny frowned. Ever since his father had gone to prison, Samantha had been forbidden to see him or talk to him. He knew he'd taken a big chance by calling her house, but it had been necessary. Johnny hated Samantha's father for keeping them apart. It wasn't fair. He hadn't committed the crimes, but he was paying all the same, and in a way that was nearly killing him. Giving up Samantha had been impossible. Ever since her father's ultimatum, they'd been sneaking out just to be together.

He took her in his arms, nuzzling the soft spot at the base of her ear that always made her shiver and giggle. She responded just as he'd expected.

"Oh God, Sam, I'm going to miss you." He found it hard to talk and not cry, and yet there was no way he could let her know how much it hurt him to say this.

She grew still. "Miss me? Why? Where are you going?"

Johnny hugged her close. He couldn't look at her. If she cried, he might find himself crying right along, and *men* of eighteen did not cry.

"The marines. I joined today."

"No!"

Her cry pierced his heart. She clutched his shirt in a desperate reaction to the news.

"Johnny! Why?"

But as soon as she looked at his face, she knew the answer. The only way he could make a life for himself was to get away. Everyone looked at Johnny and thought of his father. The townspeople had all made their own silent calculations as to how long it would be before the son became a thief too.

She buried her face against his shirt. Just as he feared, she started to cry.

"When?"

He bit his lip and dug his fingers into her hair as she shifted within his embrace. Somehow the words finally came.

"Day after tomorrow, 8 A.M."

"You'll forget me," she whispered, and lifted her face for his kiss. "You'll go away, and never come back."

"I couldn't forget you if I tried," he said, aching in so many places he couldn't think. "And I *will* come back. I will come back for you. Cross my heart and hope to die."

She laughed through her sobs. It was a repeat of their childhood pledge that she remembered all too well.

Johnny tilted her face to his. He only meant to kiss her. But their mutual consolation became a desperate coupling. A need to prove to each other where their true feelings lay.

"Ah God, Samantha. I love you, so much," Johnny whispered. "I love you so much I hurt."

Sam hid her face. She was embarrassed, and at the same time, thrilled. She knew where he hurt . . . and how bad. The proof of it was pressing hard against her belly. And she was scared. Scared of loving Johnny. And scared not to.

Just as she had on a night long ago when they'd made a blood oath to be friends for life, Samantha made a decision. And once again, she made the first move.

She stepped out of Johnny's arms and started unbuttoning her blouse. One button after the other came undone, and all the while, Samantha was shaking, unable to look at him and face what he must be thinking.

Johnny was dumbfounded, and at the same time, on

fire. He couldn't believe what she was doing. And yet, he knew he wouldn't have stopped her, even if he could.

"Sammy?"

She paused. Slowly, she looked up into his face. Night shadows hid all but the strongest portions of his features. But she could see those dark Texas eyes staring back at her through the shadows. She reached out and took his hand, then gently but firmly, placed it upon her breast.

"Oh God, Sammy, are you sure?"

She nodded. "Love me, Johnny. I can't let you go, without giving you a reason to come back."

A groan of submission was his only response.

And there beneath the mimosa tree, they fell into each other's arms in a tangle of teenage arms and legs and love. And before the night was over, Samantha had given Johnny the only thing she had left to give. Herself.

Two days later she'd kissed him good-bye at the bus stop with his promises ringing in her ears.

Two weeks later, Samantha Carlyle and her parents unexpectedly moved to California. Samantha never realized that her father knew more than he should about their relationship. He'd hated the boy, and at the same time, feared their devotion to each other, knowing that it was rooted in too many years of friendship for him to fight.

He'd done what he thought was right by removing

his only daughter from temptation. He'd moved them a half a country away, and unknown to Samantha, purposely did not leave a forwarding address.

And for months on end, when no letters followed their move and his daughter had cried herself to sleep, he'd told himself that it was all for the best. That someday she would understand.

The someday had never come.

Samantha shuddered now as John Thomas's arms tightened around her. Obviously she wasn't the only one who hadn't forgotten their special bond.

He'd come through for her. He was here in L.A.

She sighed as his hands gently stroked the hair away from her face.

"Oh, Johnny," Samantha sobbed. "I can't believe you're here."

John Thomas couldn't believe it either. But he *was* in L.A., holding Sam Carlyle in his arms and wondering what to do next. He'd known the girl as well as he'd known himself. It was the woman who was making him nervous.

He hugged her once more for good measure, and then handed her a handkerchief from his hip pocket.

"Wipe," he said.

She did.

"Now, blow."

She grinned, and once again followed his order.

"One thing's for darn sure," she said, as she handed

the slightly used linen back to him. "You haven't changed. You're still as bossy as ever."

He grinned slightly. She had that right. John Thomas liked things done his own way.

Samantha stared at his face and knew that she was in the presence of a real heartbreaker. She recognized the type. She just wasn't sure if her Johnny—the streetwise boy she'd known with an attitude a yard wide—was still somewhere inside him, waiting to erupt within a moment's notice. This big man looked full of charm and was too sexy for his own good.

"So, Sam . . . Why am I here?" John Thomas asked. "What's the deal with the letter?"

The smile slid off her face as she stepped back and out of his arms. "The deal," she said, "is that some nut wishes me into the next level of cosmic consciousness."

John Thomas frowned. "What the hell does that mean?"

"It means someone hates me enough to want me dead."

The words were even uglier said aloud than written on paper.

"I don't get it. Can't the police catch him? How long has this been going on?"

Samantha sighed and led him toward the table. "It's a long story, Johnny. How long do you have?"

The look he gave her sent her old panic reeling, replacing it with a new, undefined fear. It was dark and solemn, and the touch of his hand as it cupped her cheek said more than any words could have done.

"Once upon a time, I would have said the rest of my life. But that was before you left Cotton." John Thomas couldn't and wouldn't say more about the old ache he still nursed. Time hadn't healed the devastation of her betrayal. "Right now, I want you to talk to me."

A pent-up sigh escaped her lips. His answer was more than she'd hoped for. And yet, she couldn't help resenting the fact that he'd been so blasé about their parting. Obviously it hadn't hurt him as badly as it had her. She still remembered the sleepless nights and the tears. Even after all these years, his lack of compassion for her broken heart made her wary. But she had more pressing problems to worry about than an old boy-friend who'd dumped her. At least he'd come to help. It was more than anyone else had done.

She pointed toward the table piled high with letters and packets that held more than one lifetime's worth of hate.

"Take a seat," she said. "Enjoy. I've got enough there to give you something to sleep on."

The bitter twist of her lips hurt his heart. He sat and stared at the mound of paper before him, wondering where to begin.

"Don't worry," she said, unwittingly answering his unspoken question. "It doesn't matter where you start. Ultimately they all say the same thing. Someone hates me. Someone wants me dead."

Then she turned away, suddenly embarrassed for this tall, handsome stranger to see so deeply into her life.

John Thomas took one look at the hurt on her face and made a decision. He stood up and pushed the stacks of papers away.

"Time enough for this stuff later," he said. "I've been on a plane for too long, and in this god-awful traffic even longer. I'm hungry. You pick the place. It's my treat."

"No!" Samantha paled and clutched at his arm. "You don't understand, Johnny. I can't go out. What if he sees me? What if he finds me again?" She looked back at the papers on the table. "What if the next time he says it in person? What if—"

"What if you let me worry about the son of a bitch for a while? Isn't that why you sent for me? After all, it's not like I've never seen a bad guy, Sam. If he does show his face, I'll know what to do."

The deadly anger in his voice seeped through her terror. She felt herself relaxing. Samantha stared long and hard into the face of the man standing before her.

"Johnny, exactly what do you *do* for a living?"

He grinned. "You don't know? You really don't know?"

She shook her head.

He stuck his hand in his pocket and what he pulled out made Samantha's eyes widen in shock. Then a slow, uncertain smile fell into place on her mouth.

"The bad boy of Cotton, Texas, is a cop?"

"A sheriff," he corrected, "of Cherokee County to be exact." He shook his head. "I thought you knew. I thought that's why you sent for me."

Samantha stared. "No, not at all," she whispered, absently rubbing the tiny scar on her wrist. "I was just grasping for straws—and hope—and thought of you."

All these years had passed and still, when the chips were down, she'd called and he'd come. That, in itself, said a lot for promises made and for secrets kept.

The jolt in his belly had nothing to do with hunger, but he had to change the subject.

"Remember, I don't eat green stuff," he warned. "At least, not much. I like meat, red meat. I don't eat anything that isn't cooked and I—"

Samantha laughed. "Oh my Lord," she said, and poked her finger playfully in his midsection. "I get the picture. You're one tough dude. You take your meat well done and—"

"My women over easy," he drawled.

Her face flushed and for the first time in months Samantha looked at a man with something other than fear. Thinking about Johnny Knight and love didn't come easy. She was still locked into the image she'd had of him at eighteen. This big man with a go-to-hell jaw and come-hither eyes took some getting used to.

"Are you coming?" he asked softly, well aware of what his sexy teasing had evoked.

"I think so," she finally answered, not completely certain of what he'd just asked her to attend. Was it dinner . . . or something else? Subtlety and Johnny Knight took a stretch of the imagination.

"Don't think, Sam. Know. Either we do, or we don't. It's all up to you."

This time, she knew for certain that he was slipping double entendres into the conversation. It did everything for her low spirits and self-esteem.

"Okay, cowboy, it's me and you, all the way. But don't push your luck. I'll let you know when . . . and how far. Okay?"

John Thomas heard her warning, though he certainly didn't need it. He'd gotten the message years ago, when her letters had all come back, marked *Returned to sender.*

3

THE RESTAURANT WAS CROWDED, which, in Samantha's case, made everything worse. She felt like a sitting duck plastered against the back of the booth. Every time the door opened, she flinched as if she'd already been shot.

Reading the menu was impossible. With each influx of new customers, or an exit of old, she felt compelled to watch. The horror of the situation was that if the stalker walked in and sat down beside her, she would not know him.

"Sam, I know good and well your mama told you it was rude to stare."

His slow Texas drawl, as well as the wry look in his eyes, distracted her, but only for a moment.

"She also told me, 'thou shalt not kill.' Unfortunately my nutcase and I didn't have the same mother. Otherwise we probably would not be having this conversation."

John Thomas looked down at the menu. But the
words had suddenly blurred across the page. When he
looked back at her, Samantha had a sensation of *déjà
vu*. It was the same look he'd had years ago when he'd
punched Hank Carver in the nose for making her cry.
In Johnny's eyes was something between anger and
annihilation.

"I told you, you don't need to worry any longer," he
said quietly. "That's why I came."

She nodded and blinked, then looked down at the
menu, suddenly intent on making a choice. But it was
hard to see through tears.

"Where are your folks, now?" he asked, for lack of
anything else to say. He didn't really care where they
were. They'd hated his guts and told him so on more
than one occasion.

The question took her unawares. It was a long way
from the subject of murder. And then again . . . not so
far at all.

"Dead. Nearly seven years now. Car accident. You
know what they say." She waved toward the traffic.
"It's murder out there."

Remembering what his taxi had driven through, his
response came out abrupt and angry. "I can believe
that." Then he dropped the menu onto the table.
"Sam . . . why do you stay?"

She stared out the window onto the street, blind to
the melee of humanity that was passing them by. She
was remembering the shock of losing both parents in

the space of a heartbeat, and the empty sensation of trying to belong when there was no one to belong to.

"I guess it was because I was already here, and I had nowhere else to go," she finally answered.

"You could have come home," he said.

She smiled. Slowly.

John Thomas caught his breath. He could have sworn that he just saw a light come on in the back of her eyes and shine out through that pure, clear blue.

Samantha wanted to laugh, but she knew it would hurt too much to make the effort. Something strange was happening inside of her. She was beginning to hope again. And while it was wonderful to know that she'd retained the ability, it was, at the same time, frightening. She knew only too well how quickly hope could be taken away. The fact that Johnny Knight still considered her a part of home was overwhelming. It had been years since she'd felt like she belonged anywhere.

"I was so young when we left," she said.

"You were sixteen," he answered. "Nearly grown."

She slid her fingers across his knuckles, rubbing gently at a nearly healed scrape on the third knuckle of his left hand, remembering that after the love that they'd shared, she'd felt like a woman, but at heart she had still been a scared child.

"For you, Johnny Knight, maybe sixteen was nearly grown." She smiled to soften her words. "The Sam you knew had no clue about life. Only passion . . . and young love."

He flushed at her casual reference to what had been the most important night of his life. And then he frowned as she continued.

"That awareness came later with a knock on my door in the middle of the night. I buried my parents alone. And waited for the world to stop." She took a deep breath. "But it didn't, and I somehow managed to find a foothold on sanity, and gradually made a secure niche for myself in life."

The play of emotions on her face was vivid. He could almost feel the old pain and the new fears swamp her.

"So tell me more about your job at the casting agency. I guess it's a good one?"

Then she did laugh, but only once. And it was a short, harsh bark of anger, not joy.

"Oh, but yes! I am—I was—one of the best casting agents in the business. Our agency has the reputation of having cast several Oscar-winning films. I have—had—a very good reputation." She grimaced to hide the pain. "That was before I lost my status as an asset, and became a liability they didn't want to fix."

A waitress appeared to take their order.

"I'll have crow," Samantha said, and then smiled grimly at the shock on the lady's face.

John Thomas frowned. This angry, bitter woman was not the Sam he'd expected to find. And then he wondered, what *had* he expected? How else should she be acting? If this had happened to him, he'd be fighting mad, too.

He interrupted before Samantha said anything else extraordinary.

"She'll have a cheeseburger, well done, uh . . . fries, and a strawberry malt," he said shortly. "Repeat it for me, only make my burger a double and leave off the fries."

The waitress nodded and hurried away.

Her eyebrows rose. "Well thank you very much for making up my mind," she drawled.

"Someone had to," he said.

Her eyebrows arched. "You aren't having fries?"

"I'll eat yours."

She caught her breath at the grin on his face and knew that the smartest thing she'd done since she'd moved to this godforsaken city had been mailing that letter to Texas.

Later, Samantha paced the floor in her apartment, alternating between staring at the broad back of the man sitting at her table poring over the stack of hate mail, and wondering how he'd gone from being a town truant to arresting them instead.

"Johnny, where is your father?"

Her question was as unexpected as the old pain he felt in the pit of his stomach. These days he rarely thought of his father, and when he did, he was hard-pressed to remember what he'd looked like.

He dropped a handful of papers, shoved back the chair he was sitting in, and stood. It took a lot of guts, but he had to be looking at her when he said it. If he wasn't, he'd always wonder what her first real reaction had been.

"He died in prison."

Samantha was quiet. The expression on her face never wavered, nor did the look in her eyes. It was still steadfast and sure. He exhaled, slowly.

"When?"

"Ten weeks after I left Cotton." He laughed once, but it was harsh and filled with pain.

"I didn't know," she whispered.

"How could you?" he said bitterly. "When I came back for the funeral, you were already gone."

Before he knew what was happening, Samantha had walked into his arms and wrapped herself around his heart.

"I'm sorry," she said. "I didn't mean to open up old wounds." Her voice was faint, a mere whisper. "I didn't know."

John Thomas rested his chin on her head, wrapped his hands in the long fall of black hair hanging down her back, and hugged her with a desperation that surprised him.

"It doesn't matter," he said.

"Yes. It mattered. It still does. And I wish I'd known."

"What would you have done, Sam, cried at the funeral? You were scared to death of him and you know it."

"I would have cried for you," she said softly.

Oh God, Samantha! And I would have let you, be-

*cause I damn sure couldn't cry for myself. And why—
why did you send my letters back? What the hell did I
do that was so bad you wouldn't even keep them to
read?*

"I see a pattern," he said, and stepped out of her
arms before he made fools of them both.

"Pattern?" She was lost until he pointed to the letters. "Oh, the letters."

The abrupt change of subject surprised her. Obviously she'd gotten too close to something he didn't
want to explore.

He drew her toward the table, and then began moving from one side to the other, thinking aloud as he
went.

"These seem angry. Just angry." He pointed to the
stack of mail closest to him. "But these," he pointed to
a stack in the middle, "these blame." He moved to the
stack at the farthest end. "These are the ones that scare
the hell out of me. These are the ones with the promises. These are the ones that hate."

She wrapped her arms around herself and shuddered.

"I'd never really thought of them in those terms. I
was too busy running from shadows to decipher their
contents."

"What did the police say?" Then he thought of
something. "Wait a minute. Why the hell do you have
these instead of the police? This is evidence, Samantha. Didn't you show it to them?"

His anger enveloped her. She began to shake. And because the fear had returned, it made her answer sharper than she'd intended.

"Hell yes, Johnny! They saw it. They saw it all."

"Then why didn't they act on it?"

"Because ultimately, they decided it was a put-up job. That I was faking my own threats for some unnamed reason."

"Why would they think that?"

She wilted before his eyes, and he had an unreasonable urge to comfort her. But he stayed the thought. He needed to get to the bottom of the story, and emotion would just get in the way.

"Because all of the early calls could be traced to a phone in an empty apartment taken out in my name, and most of the letters were typed on the typewriter in my office, that's why," she said. "Before you ask, I have no explanation as to how that could be. I damn sure didn't write them to myself." She started to shake. "And I'm not crazy. Do you hear me, Johnny? I'm not!"

He shoved his fingers through his hair, ruffling the even black lengths into wild disarray. Once again, he resisted the urge to touch her. She seemed so desperate and so small.

His lips narrowed into a hard, thin line. "But I still don't get it. What the hell are *you* doing with the actual clues to your case? They should be on file as evidence. It should have been checked for fingerprints, possible sources of—"

"It was. According to the detective in charge, they doubt that the threats were valid. No one ever made a move to harm me physically. I never saw anyone. And they'd checked and ruled out practically everyone I've ever met as a possible suspect. All that did was enforce their belief that I'd created the monster who was after me all by myself. When they suggested I see a psychiatrist, I got angry and demanded it all back."

"And they handed it over, just like that?"

She laughed harshly; the bitterness in her voice was unmistakable as she continued. "Why not? After all, it wouldn't be the first time someone in Hollywood staged a stunt to promote themselves. Remember, Johnny, this is the land of make-believe. This is California, home of Disneyland, of Hollywood, of Sunset and Vine, and Rodeo Drive. This is where the Peter Pans of the world come to stay. Don't you know that, Johnny? Don't you . . ." Tears poured down her cheeks, but her anger was alive. It was the first time since his arrival that he'd seen even a glimmer of the old Sam he once knew.

"Stop! Dammit to hell, stop it, Sam! I wasn't blaming you." He grabbed her by the arms and shook her, rougher than he'd intended. His voice softened as he slowly released his grip and cupped his hand against her cheek instead. "I wasn't blaming you."

"Well they did," she said, and yanked away from his touch. She couldn't let his sympathy envelop her as much as she wanted or she'd never get a grip on reality again. It would be too easy to just let go in the presence of someone stronger than herself.

"What's the detective's name? Who was in charge of your case?" he asked.

"Pulaski. Mike Pulaski."

"Get your purse," he ordered.

"Where are we going now?"

"LAPD. To pay a visit to Detective Pulaski. He's going to tell me what he told you. And I can promise you, Sam, when we leave, I'll have answers."

She grabbed her purse and headed for the door. "We'd better call a cab."

"Hell, no," he said, remembering his last cab ride in L.A. "We'll take your car."

She nodded. "The police station is a long way from here. I haven't driven much since all this began because I didn't want to be caught out alone in the car."

"Give me the keys. You point, I'll steer. I'm not getting in another damned cab again."

In spite of her fears, in spite of the knot in the pit of her stomach, she smiled.

The room at the police station was just as Samantha remembered. Rows of desks decorated with everything from stacks of files to three-day-old cups of coffee. There was a sign on the wall that read, *No smoking*. She grimaced as a thick veil of cigarette smoke drifted past her nose. Obviously, someone besides Johnny Knight didn't like being told what to do.

"Where to?" he asked shortly.

She pointed.

He took her by the hand and started across the room, his gaze fixed on a small cubicle that obviously passed as an office, although what went on inside would hardly have been secret, as the walls were glass.

Mike Pulaski sat behind a cluttered desk, a phone in one hand and a pen in the other. He waved the pen in the air to make his point as he shouted obscenities into the mouthpiece. One could feel his anger, even through the glass partition. His face turned a mottled shade of red as he slammed the receiver down in disgust. When he looked and saw the familiar face of Samantha Carlyle, his expression did not improve.

"Oh great," he muttered.

Then he noticed she was not alone. The man who was with her didn't fit the mold of an ordinary run-of-the-mill Californian. The fabric of his blue Levi's looked soft, well worn and faded. The stark white shirt he was wearing stretched tautly across a flat belly, and his dove-gray jacket was definitely western-cut.

Pulaski's gaze followed a long length of legs down to boots that were obviously not of Rodeo Drive. They were plain black, in need of polish, bore numerous nicks and scratches, and turned up just the tiniest bit at the toes. The strong stubborn features on the big man's face were shadowed by the wide brim of a gray Stetson that rode his head with familiarity.

"Just what I need. A cowboy."

The cowboy came in without being invited.

Mike Pulaski sat back in his chair, leaning as far as he dared without toppling over, and locked his hands across his ample belly in what he hoped was a gesture of disdain. He didn't like pushy people.

"You're in, now what can I do for you?" He frowned as the big man ushered Samantha Carlyle to a seat without answering him.

John Thomas briefly touched Samantha's shoulder and then turned and gave the cop a long look before pulling his badge. He held it over the desk between them.

"Sheriff John Thomas Knight, Cherokee County."

Mike Pulaski's feet hit the floor. It was reflex that made him stand and extend his hand before he'd even thought. Professional courtesy to another law enforcement official was ingrained in everyone on the force.

"Sheriff! Pleased to meet you! But I can't say that I'm familiar with Cherokee County. What department are you out of?"

"Texas."

Pulaski was staring. He knew it. He just couldn't seem to stop. "Texas? You're from Cherokee County, Texas?" He grinned and scratched his head. "Then what, may I ask, are you doing all the way out here? Chasing outlaws?"

"No." John Thomas's answer was short and sharp. "I came to see why the hell you're not."

Samantha inhaled sharply. Johnny hadn't changed a

bit. He still didn't pull punches. She smiled to herself. And since when did he call himself John Thomas? She'd always called him Johnny, and he had let her, even today.

"Excuse me?" Pulaski asked, and glared at Samantha Carlyle. This was bound to be her fault.

"I don't think I'm ready to," John Thomas said shortly. He leaned forward, bracing himself on Pulaski's desk, and stared straight into the detective's face "I want some answers, Pulaski. I want to know why the hell Samantha Carlyle has no police protection. I want to know why someone hasn't ordered a phone tap and tried to trace calls. I want to know why you have chosen to blow off a woman's cry for help. You convince me first, then I might be willing to excuse you. Got it?"

Pulaski's face turned bright red. "You have no right coming into my office, in my department, and trying to tell me how to do my job."

"I'm not trying to tell you how to do it. I just want to know why the hell you aren't. And I do have that right."

"By whose authority?" Pulaski demanded.

John Thomas turned to Samantha, saw the frightened expression in her eyes, and pointed.

"Hers." He smiled at Samantha and winked. "We're old friends." He looked back at Pulaski, daring him to argue.

Samantha shivered. *Old friends?* They were much

more than that. Old friends didn't do what Johnny had done. Old friends sent letters of sympathy, or even money. But they didn't put their lives on hold and come halfway across the country for someone they hadn't seen in fifteen years.

She stared at the back of his head, catching a glimpse now and then of the battle of wills going on between the two policemen, and wondered: if Johnny Knight isn't an old friend, then what is he?

"Old friends. I see," Pulaski said, and tried not to sneer.

John Thomas caught the innuendo. It made him mad as hell.

"Yes. *Old* friends." It had been years since he'd had to explain himself and it didn't sit easy on an already frazzled temperament. Anger was thick in his voice. "I haven't seen her in fifteen years, but I've known her for as long as I can remember. Her father was my grade school principal. We were childhood playmates. We climbed goddamned trees together. I even taught her how to clean fish." *I'm the first man she ever made love to,* he added silently to himself.

He turned and looked at Sam and knew she could read what he was thinking. At that moment, he didn't care.

She swallowed her panic as she saw the look on his face. If she only dared believe what she was seeing. But she didn't. She couldn't. She'd been hurt too badly once to trust him again. Besides, she was too busy trying not to die to worry about making love.

Pulaski blanched and held up his hands. "I get the message," he said. "But you've got to understand the situation from my point of view. Out here people do crazy things. I deal with druggies and—"

"Samantha Jean, did you ever do drugs?" John Thomas interrupted. He turned and fixed her with a piercing stare.

She gulped and jumped to her feet. The tone of voice was so like the one her mother would have used that the motion was instinctive.

"No! Of course not," she said quickly, and then sank limply back into her chair.

He nodded, satisfied with her answer, and turned back to Pulaski.

"She doesn't do drugs. What you're saying now doesn't pertain. I want answers to my questions."

Pulaski sank into his chair and knew that he'd long since lost control of the situation. All he could do was hang on for the ride.

"Just like that? You just turned and asked her and you believe her that easy? I thought you told me you haven't seen her in years? How do you know she's telling you the truth?"

"I told you we're old friends. Besides, Sam doesn't lie."

Samantha blinked at the conviction in his voice. The tears behind her eyes burned. The lump in her throat was huge, but the hard knot in the pit of her stomach had just loosened another hitch. She thought she'd long since given up hoping someone would believe her. Hearing the words, from Johnny's lips, was nearly overwhelming.

Pulaski nodded. It didn't matter what he said. Obviously the big man wasn't going to swallow it.

"Look," Pulaski said. "It's not so much that we didn't believe her. It's just that the facts pointed to a hoax." He shrugged. If they didn't like the truth, they shouldn't have come.

"So your stalker is smarter than you are? That's not news, Detective. I'm a cop, too, remember? There are plenty of brilliant criminals on the loose and you and I both know it. As for your reasoning, Sam told me about the phone business, as well as her typewriter being used to write the hate mail. Was she the only person who had access to it?" John Thomas asked.

Pulaski frowned. He didn't like being cross-examined. "Hell no," he said shortly. "We're not fools, Sheriff. We checked everyone out."

"You had to have missed someone."

Pulaski's chin jutted. "Well, we didn't. And she didn't give us much to work with. A few letters, possibly self-inflicted threats, a few phone calls, always left on a machine, which, for all intents and purposes, indicates she sent them to herself."

"You never assigned surveillance?"

"We did have someone assigned to watch her. But the whole time he was on the case, nothing happened. We don't have unlimited manpower."

"As for *her* not giving *you* enough stuff to work with, Detective. I thought that was your department. I thought that all a citizen had to do was report a crime."

Pulaski flushed. "That didn't come out exactly like I meant it," he said. "I meant that we didn't have much to go on."

John Thomas glared. "At my last count, you had twenty-nine separate pieces of hate mail, which, I might add, you handed back to her without blinking an eye. The last of which promised death in various forms and degrees. Where I come from, mister, that constitutes a viable threat."

"Well, you're not in Texas," Pulaski said shortly.

John Thomas straightened and stared. "No, but I'm damned sure going to be soon." He pulled a card from his pocket and tossed it onto Pulaski's desk. "If there's anything further you need of Miss Carlyle, you can reach her through me, at that number."

"You're taking her back to Texas?" Pulaski hadn't expected to feel an impact from the words, but he did. What he also felt, he suspected, was a little bit of guilty conscience.

"I'm taking her home," John Thomas said.

Samantha's shock was no less than Pulaski's. *Texas? I'm going back to Texas? With Johnny?* The implications of that overwhelmed her. And this time, in spite of her determination, tears fell. *Oh God. I'm going home.*

John Thomas touched his finger to the brim of his

hat, grabbed Samantha's hand, and together they exited Pulaski's office without looking back.

When the door flew back against the glass wall with a loud bang, several people looked up with a start in time to see the big cowboy and Samantha Carlyle make their exit.

"What the hell was that all about? And who is that man with the Carlyle woman?" another detective asked.

Pulaski rolled his eyes as he fingered the card John Thomas had tossed on his desk. He began to grin.

"That, I think, is how the West was won. That man was a sheriff. A genuine, pissed-off, Texas sheriff. And if there really is some crazy stalker after Samantha Carlyle and he runs into," he looked down at the card to refresh his memory, "John Thomas Knight, then I pity him."

He shook his head, walked into his office, and closed the door, suddenly in need of some peace and quiet.

The traffic and the drive home had done nothing for John Thomas's patience, nor did the message on Samantha's answering machine.

The moment they entered the room, her face paled at the sight of the flashing red light. Sensing the ominous threat waiting to be heard, she froze. Then in a useless but frantic display of panic, she began running through the apartment, checking locks and doors as though it would prevent her from hearing what was on the tape. But it was too late to stop what had already been sent. It was there as always. Waiting. Warning. Promising.

She ran, and John Thomas caught her, and for a heartbeat held her gently within his embrace.

"Don't, Sam. It might not be from him."

She shuddered and hid her face against his chest. "Oh Johnny. You don't understand. It's always from him."

A shared pain enveloped him at the lifeless tone of her voice.

"Then let's listen to what the bastard has to say, okay? Only this time, you won't be hearing it alone."

She nodded, walked to the machine, pressed the message button, and then leaned against him and stood motionless within his arms as the words slapped and the promises threatened.

I saw you with him. He can't help you, Samantha. You can run—and you can hide—but you'll never get away. Not from me. You must pay with your life. Don't you understand yet? Why do you fight me? Why don't you just wait and let it come? Blood cleanses as it flows.

The voice had been electronically altered. That was obvious by the computerized sound of the message.

John Thomas felt helpless. He felt rage. And he felt Samantha coming apart in his arms. He reached over and unplugged the entire answering machine without waiting for it to finish, then made her face him.

"Look at me, Sam." Her body quivered beneath his

hands as the blue in her eyes turned a dull, lifeless gray. "Dammit, look at me!" he yelled.

She slowly complied.

"Don't! Don't let that sick bastard kill you with nothing but words. That's all they are, Sam, words! He hasn't touched you yet, and so help me God, he's not going to get the chance. Do you understand?" He shook her gently to punctuate his promise.

She bit her lower lip to keep from screaming, drawing desperately on Johnny's strength because at the moment, she had none of her own.

"Good!" He hugged her once then set her firmly aside.

He could sense how close she was to breaking, and knew that too much sympathy could be all it would take to push her over the edge.

Besides, he had no intention of getting emotionally involved with her again. He'd protect her, but he wouldn't love her. Not a woman who didn't know how to say good-bye.

She watched as he began pacing back and forth across the floor. Samantha had a momentary vision of a mountain lion hovering, waiting to pounce.

"We can't take much," he said. "We don't want him to know that you're leaving. We just want him to think that when we leave, it's for no more than a day's outing."

"What? Take where?" Samantha said, lost for the moment at the turn of the conversation.

"To Texas. Don't you remember? I'm taking you home."

Her chin quivered and in spite of the sharp bite she gave the inside of her jaw, the tears still came.

"Well, hell," he said softly, and pulled her back into his arms. "You don't have to be so damned happy about it."

Many hours later, Samantha stirred as the wheels of John Thomas's truck turned off the highway onto a rough, graveled road. She blinked and opened her eyes only to see darkness all around.

The trip from L.A. to Dallas had been frantic. Storing her car in a rental unit had been Johnny's idea. They'd gone from there to a bank for Samantha to withdraw money, and then on to a restaurant, where they stunned the hostess by refusing a table, calling another cab, and disappearing out the back door of the same restaurant on their way to the airport.

Once in Dallas, John Thomas had dumped her and her small bag of belongings into his truck, paid the airport parking attendant for services rendered, and headed east out of the city with the sun low at their backs.

Somewhere between Terrell and Tyler, she'd fallen asleep. She never noticed when they passed through Cotton on their way to Johnny's place. But she did notice, after all sense of sound and motion had stopped, that they were in front of a small frame house.

The darker outline of the building silhouetted

against the abundance of trees around it was visible,
even though the moonlight was nearly nonexistent.
The tension of the last few hours began to seep out of
her body as the trees surrounded and protected. The silence of the country enveloped her. Samantha's heart
expanded from the newfound peace.

"Where are we?" she asked.

"Home."

She'd never heard a more beautiful word. She
crawled stiffly from his truck and then stopped and inhaled. Tears sprang quickly as memories overwhelmed
her. It might have been years since she'd been here, but
forgetting East Texas would have been impossible.

The scent of pine, sharp and tangy, filled the air.
Samantha smiled as she also recognized the faint,
sweet odors of dogwood and honeysuckle. They had
grown outside the bedroom window at her home in
Cotton when she was a child, when Johnny Knight had
been the Alpha and Omega of her world.

"Come on, Sam. We're both dead tired. There'll
be plenty of time tomorrow to look around. Right
now the only thing I want to see is the underside of
my pillow."

She let him lead her across the darkened yard and up
onto the porch, then stood aside while he fumbled in
the lack of light, trying to get the key in the hole.

"Can't you get it in?" she asked sleepily.

He stopped, his hand suspended in midair, and
thanked God for the anonymity of night. What she'd

asked had instantly imprinted another set of images
into his mind, and it had nothing to do with keys and
keyholes.

"Oh, I've got pretty good aim. Eventually, I get it
right. I've had *some* practice since we . . ." His voice
ended on a harsh grunt.

As sleepy as she was, Samantha heard the pain in
his voice and wondered where it had come from. He
was the one who'd scored the hit and run. He was the
one who hadn't written or called.

"I don't need a reminder of what we once shared,
Johnny, and you'd do well to remember it. I'm not
some floozy you're bringing home. I'm thirty-one
years old, and you damn well know it."

John Thomas frowned. Her anger seemed out of
place. She was the one who'd sent back a drawerful of
unopened letters. But this wasn't the time to discuss
who was to blame. There was more at stake here than
the old history between them.

He jammed the key into the keyhole and turned it
with a vicious twist. The door swung open as he
reached inside and flipped a switch, instantly shedding
all kinds of light onto the situation.

He cupped her elbow and guided her into the house,
then turned and locked the door. Wordlessly, he picked
up her bag and headed toward the back of the house,
expecting her to follow. She did.

The door to the spare bedroom swung open silently
as he flipped on another light.

"Bath's down the hall. We'll have to share."

Without waiting for a response, he walked across the room and opened the window beside her bed. Fresh air slipped surreptitiously inside.

"Got everything you need?" he asked quietly.

She nodded, feeling suddenly shy in front of the big, solemn-eyed man.

He started out the door and then stopped and turned. "Sam."

She looked up.

"I'm only going to say this once. What happened between us was a long time ago, but it was mutual. You don't need to feel threatened by me, or afraid of being here alone with me. No matter what else you may think, I wouldn't take advantage of you or the situation. I like my women willing. So go to sleep."

Her heart thumped once as he closed the door behind him, and then settled down into a regular rhythm. *Willing?* Once she hadn't been any other way. But she was too weary to bother about sorting out her mixed feelings. There would be time enough to go through those later.

She unearthed an extra large T-shirt that had faithfully served as her favorite item of sleepwear for the last five years, and quickly traded it for what she was wearing, then sat on the bed and listened to the sounds of water running in the bath at the end of the hall.

After Johnny's footsteps had silenced and he'd entered the room opposite hers, she ventured out and down the shadowy hallway, smiling to herself at the thoughtfulness of a man who would leave a light on in the bathroom for a house guest unfamiliar with the territory. It didn't take long to do what she had to do, then sluice a little water on her weary body.

As she buried her face in the towel by the sink, intent on drying what was left of her quickie cleanup, she inhaled the faint but lingering scent of his shaving cream.

Instead of drying her face, she found herself moving the towel all across her neck, and then down her arms, and across her body in a slow, thoughtful motion.

Minutes later as she crawled into bed and pulled up the sheet, she turned her face into the pillow and inhaled again. Now, not only did she catch the pine-scented air filtering through the screen of her open window, but she'd taken a bit of Johnny Knight to bed with her.

It was an intriguing notion and one on which she dwelled only a minute before exhaustion claimed her.

4

SAMANTHA WOKE SLOWLY. For a moment before she opened her eyes, she expected her mother to call out at any moment that it was time to get up, and that she was going to be late for school.

The familiar scents of bacon frying, coffee perking, and fresh air wafting through the open windows told her she was home in Cotton. She buried her face in her pillow, reluctant to move from the comfort of her bed, and smiled in half sleep as the piney woods beckoned. At the same time she thought of Johnny, she remembered where she was, and then why she was here.

She *was* in Cotton, or so close that the difference hardly counted. Later she would learn that Johnny Knight's home was barely two miles outside of Cotton's city limits. Only a few miles to the southeast was Rusk, the county seat of Cherokee County. But she hadn't come back for a visit, she'd come for her health. By anyone's standards, dying was an unhealthy state of being.

She rolled over onto her back, stretched and yawned, and then opened her eyes and gasped with surprise. She didn't know whether to glare, or just throw back the covers and invite him in. He was standing in the doorway, watching her sleep.

"Mornin', Sam," he said softly, and took a deep draw on the cup of coffee in his hands. Swallowing it slowly saved him from saying anything else that might get his face slapped. He knew that he'd intruded. He should have looked in as planned, then pulled the door shut and let her awaken alone. All he'd meant to do was check on her. He hadn't intended to stay.

But that wild, long, black hair splayed out across the sheets, the way she'd jammed her turned-up nose forcefully into the pillow, and the peaceful sprawl of her long arms and legs as she slept soundly on her stomach had mesmerized him. He hadn't been able to move.

She pulled the covers up beneath her chin and gave him what she hoped would pass for a glare. She did not know that, to John Thomas, it looked more like an invitation. Her eyelids were still heavy with sleep, and her mouth was all soft and vulnerable, just like the look in her eyes.

"When you're dressed, there's breakfast, if you're hungry."

She gulped. *He* looked good enough to eat in his low-riding Levi's and his shirt untucked and only half buttoned. From the appearance of that thick black hair framing his face, she suspected that he'd ignored propriety and used his fingers for a comb.

She managed a nod.

"Did you sleep okay?" he asked, and still didn't move, unable, or unwilling, to give her the space she obviously needed to crawl out of bed.

"Yes, thank you, I slept just fine. Now get, Johnny, so I can get up." She smiled. "Or maybe I should call you John Thomas, since you're so important and proper these days."

"You can call me anything you want. You always did."

She thought about the implications of that statement, and for the moment, decided not to pursue them. She folded her arms across her chest, cocked an eyebrow, and stared, waiting for him to move.

He grinned. "I get the message. But you better hurry before Rebel gets what's left."

Samantha's attention piqued. "Who's Rebel?"

He pointed toward the low, open window beside her bed and waited for her reaction. It wasn't what he'd expected, but he remembered later that Sam always had a way of making her point without a fight.

She squealed with surprise at the face in the window. A large, brown, lop-eared hound with the saddest face she'd ever seen was staring at them through the screen. His tongue lolled to one side of his mouth as his soulful brown eyes fixed on Samantha intently, seeming to beg for a bite of the food he smelled inside the house.

She pursed her lips and whistled softly, then called out the dog's name. Rebel seemed pleased at being noticed. Samantha grinned.

"He has your eyes," she said.

John Thomas laughed. "You win," he said, as he toasted her wit with his half-empty coffee cup, and pulled the door shut behind him, leaving her to get dressed in private.

"Well," Samantha drawled, staring pointedly at the big hound who remained at the window. "I don't suppose you have any more manners than your master."

But Rebel didn't move other than to lick his chops, then swallow as he let his tongue shift to the other side of his open, panting mouth.

"I didn't think so," she said, and laughed softly to herself as she crawled out of bed.

"Are you ready for this?" John Thomas asked, as they entered the outskirts of Cotton.

He knew that this homecoming, forced though it may be, would be emotional for Samantha. The last time she'd been here life had been simple. She'd been a young girl with a family intact.

"I think so," she said, and watched with interest as

he turned the corner of Fourth and Downey. The spurt of excitement she felt was echoed in her voice. "Oh, Johnny, it's still here!"

The joy on her face made him smile. "I know, Sam. You didn't think I'd bring you back to your old street just to give you a big letdown, did you?"

She shook her head and then refocused her gaze on the wide veranda of the small house and the trellis on the east end that hung heavy with wisteria and honeysuckle.

Besides, he had no intention of telling her how often he still drove past the old house and remembered the girl-child who'd lived inside so many years ago. He also had no intention of telling her how devastated he'd been when he came home for his father's funeral and found it empty.

Samantha shifted in the seat and pointed in excitement.

"Even the flowers are still there."

"Or some just like them. Remember, it's been a long time."

"It seems like it was only yesterday," she said softly, then pointed. "I would try to slip out the back door to meet you without Mama knowing, but the hinges always squeaked."

"I'm really sorry about your parents. I know how close you were. You must miss them a lot."

She nodded slowly, remembering the gentle way of life and the long, slow days of summer. The days when she thought she'd be a child forever and that things would never change.

Just then a small girl ran out of the old house, obviously hell-bent on escape from something or someone inside. Her head was thrown back, her wispy blond hair flying in the breeze as she ran, and a smile of delight was spread across her face.

"Look!" Samantha cried and pointed. "A family with children lives in my house."

John Thomas grinned. "Yes, I know. And you'll never guess who."

She looked at him expectantly.

"Remember Hank Carver?"

"The one who made me cry? How could I forget him? He was the first, and the last, dragon anyone ever slayed for me. That's not something a girl ever forgets, Johnny. Not even if she's only twelve years old."

John Thomas wished with all his heart that he could slay the dragons that threatened her now as easily as he'd decked Hank Carver. He looked at her out of the corner of his eye, unwilling for her to know what he was thinking.

I wish I understood how you forgot our love so easily. How could you lie down beneath me and love me so sweet, then leave me without a word?

But there was no answer for a question that couldn't be asked. And John Thomas had no intention of asking. He'd learned long ago that asking questions often got you answers you wouldn't like.

"Johnny?"

"Hmm?"

"Exactly why did you punch Hank Carver in the nose?"

His hands froze on the steering wheel as his memory somersaulted back in time to the day when he'd been forced to realize that Samantha Jean might not stay his personal property forever.

He cocked an eyebrow. "You sure you want to know?"

She frowned. "Of course, or I wouldn't have asked."

"I punched his lights out because he noticed you were wearing a bra."

A slight flush stained her cheeks, but she managed a grin. "And that made you mad?"

"No, not exactly. What made me maddest was that he'd seen you were growing up and I hadn't. You were mine, Samantha. Always had been. Always would—"

He froze in midsentence and glared at the road before him. "Hell."

His anger was unexpected, as if she were somehow to blame, and yet only she knew how certainly that was untrue.

"Come on," Samantha urged. The shadows on his face made her nervous and she wanted to erase them. "Show me some more. Let's drive by the school. Then if we have time, we could go out to the old Kellog place and see if the blackberries are ripe. Oh, Johnny, remember the berries and what fun we had?"

"It's too early for berries. And yes, we had fun,

Sam. We sure did." *Probably the most fun I ever had in my life, Samantha Jean. And it ended the day that you left me.*

"Whatever you want," she said. "Just drive, I'll look. That'll be enough to satisfy me."

He watched the play of emotions cross her face and wondered who would be sick enough to want to snuff out the life of someone like Samantha Carlyle. He couldn't fathom the world without her in it, somewhere.

Breeze came through the rolled-down window of his pickup truck and lifted the hair away from her face. The old T-shirt she had on and the blue jeans she'd rolled up to her knees somehow made her look younger—more vulnerable—and yet too damned much of a woman. Their little trip through Cotton might satisfy her, but he was in serious doubt about his own satisfaction, or his diminishing peace of mind.

It hadn't taken long for word to get around that little Samantha Carlyle was back in town, and why. Tongues were wagging on every corner.

John Thomas had figured that the simplest way to protect her was to tell everyone what had happened to her. And the quickest way to get the word around was simply to tell Angus Weaver. Angus never could keep a secret and he always got his facts straight.

People needed to know that if a stranger came to

town, the sheriff was to be informed immediately. So, he'd told Angus Weaver all about the letters and the other threats Samantha had received in L.A.—and he'd added that the police in L.A. hadn't really believed she was in danger. That was all it took.

The townspeople had taken to the intrigue of the story as if they had a mission. Suddenly every poor soul who now had the misfortune to stop for gas or a bite to eat at the local truck stop was greeted with less than the usual friendly enthusiasm. After all, Samantha was one of Cotton's own and someone had threatened her life.

Now that the telling was done, the waiting began. And that was the single most difficult thing of it all.

John Thomas stared at the clock by his bedside table and wished it to hell and back for reminding him that there were at least four more hours of darkness before he could arise with dignity.

The past four days had been some of the best and the worst that he could remember. It was wonderful to know that Samantha was here at his own home, and torture to know that when night came they would part company in the shadowy hallway to go to separate rooms . . . and separate beds. The bonds of their childhood were strong, and he often felt himself slipping back into an adult attraction that they'd barely explored.

Once in a while he got glimpses of the child that

she'd been, but most of the time, it was the woman she was now that made him crazy. The shadows in her eyes faded a little each day, and the smile on her lips grew wider each time she tried it. And the fact that she'd left home with exactly three changes of clothing didn't bother him at all. He liked the shorts and jeans that she'd stuffed into her carryall when they'd made their escape. He especially liked the soft T-shirts she wore. They cupped her body in the exact same places that he would, if he could.

He didn't know that Samantha had seen that look on his face when he thought she wasn't looking. He didn't know that she was watching his interest turn to intrigue, and intrigue to desire. If he had, he would have denied it in a heartbeat, as Samantha would have done.

In her opinion, her Johnny had been faithful and trustworthy to a fault. And she already knew that John Thomas Knight could be trusted with her life. He'd proven that by coming after her. She just wasn't certain how far to trust John Thomas, the man, with her heart.

He'd made love with her and then made tracks with her trust. After seeing him again, she realized that she'd never really forgiven him. And so they circled each other, warily and carefully, and tried to pretend nothing was wrong.

John Thomas stared at the clock again as an owl hooted in a tree outside his window. Rebel woofed softly from the porch as a reminder to whatever was out there that invading his territory was not permitted.

The bedsprings squeaked in the room across the hall and, even from here, John Thomas could hear her moan. He could tell from the sounds of her tossing and turning that she was dreaming again. He swung his long legs over the side of the bed, and then sat quietly in the darkness, listening. When the scream came, he was across the hall and into her room before Rebel even had time to react to the broken silence.

"No!" she screamed.

Samantha was running. Her legs moved, but seemed to cover no distance. The clutch of hands on her shoulder was painful and swift. The swirl of heat from his breath on the back of her neck sent her rocketing forward, fighting the tangle of bedclothes and dreams in a desperate desire to escape from the nightmare. And then she was snatched from hell into heaven as strong arms yanked her from her bed.

"Samantha, honey. Wake up! Wake up! It's me, Johnny. You're safe. I've got you."

He dropped down onto the side of her bed and pulled her across his lap, rocking his body along with hers as she threw her arms around his neck, buried her face beneath his chin, and swallowed the last of her sobs.

And when she could think past the panic, she sighed and leaned against the wall of his chest, holding her hands against her breasts in an odd, protective manner. But it was not to keep John Thomas from touching her. It was to keep her hammering heart where it belonged. Long moments passed as he held her and rocked her, allowing panic to subside and reality to return.

"Are you okay?" he finally asked.

His voice was deep. It echoed in the quiet . . . in the dark . . . and in her heart. In that moment, Samantha faced a fact she'd been trying to ignore. She knew that she had to find a way to renew her faith and trust in this man, because if she had to tell Johnny good-bye a second time, she'd never be okay again.

The summer heat drew them together, melding the softness of her skin with the muscle of his own. Another kind of heat simmered between them. An awareness that if they'd let it, more than comfort would pass between them this night.

She stirred in his lap and felt the answering response of his own body beneath her. Then she moaned softly and buried her face in her hands. She wasn't ready for this, but needn't have worried. John Thomas wasn't either. He had his own set of demons to exorcise.

He lifted her from his lap, laying her gently back onto the bed, and walked from the room without explanation. Certain that she'd angered him, she was vaguely surprised when he returned moments later.

The stark whiteness of his briefs and the long, muscular shape of his body were easy to discern through the half-light of moonglow. An old memory of how their bodies had once joined in love and passion over-whelmed her. She had the strongest urge to just lie back on the bed and hold out her arms to him. Instead, she waited for him to make the move.

He came closer. She could smell the heat of his body and the faint, but lingering scent of soap from his bath. She closed her eyes, expecting everything but the cool dampness of the cloth that he wiped across her face.

"Here, honey," he said gently. "This will cool you off and maybe you can get back to sleep."

Not in this lifetime, she thought.

"Bad night, huh?"

"It was," she said, and sighed, allowing him to min-ister to her as he would a child. "It's not so bad now. In fact, it's been a while since I had my face washed." She smiled, knowing that her expression was hidden in the darkness.

But John Thomas heard the smile in her voice and before he'd thought, leaned forward and kissed the edge of her forehead where tiny wisps of her hair, damp from the cloth, curled baby-soft against his lips.

"And even longer since I had a good night kiss," she added breathlessly.

He heard the tenor of her voice change from tease to plea. It was one he couldn't resist. He bent a bit farther, and this time when his lips touched flesh, they con-nected with purpose against the surprised pout of her mouth.

He felt her gasp as the inward rush of air slipped past his lips and then that was the last thing he remembered until he felt her hands on his shoulders and her nails digging into his arms and heard her moan softly as their bodies aligned themselves on the bed.

"Hell," he said softly, and stopped, painfully conscious of the ache in his loins that had nothing to do with nightmares and everything to do with need. Here he was, on top of her in bed, hard and aching. This shouldn't be happening.

"No, Johnny." Her soft, husky voice held him pinned to the bed and her body as firmly as if she'd tied him. "It wasn't hell at all. In fact, it felt nice, very, very nice. I just don't—"

"Don't say it, Sam." His voice was rough. "I'm sorry I let this get out of hand, and I can promise you it won't happen again. I don't intend to get burned twice."

With a groan he rolled off her body and out of bed, trying manfully to ignore the throb between his legs and the emptiness of his arms now that he was apart from her.

He walked out the door without looking back and Samantha wondered why he'd been the one with all the anger. She was the one who'd been abandoned.

She thought she'd never sleep again. But when she closed her eyes, it came quickly, and with it came the memories of a man's hands and his mouth, and the weight of his body, and the flash fire of heat that had burned between them.

And in the morning, the texture of the air seemed different as an awareness between them began to grow. The days evened out, and Samantha forgot for minutes, and eventually even hours at a time, that someone wanted her dead. But she never, quite ever, let down her guard.

John Thomas got up every morning, leaving Samantha at home to occupy herself with nothing more serious than deciding what to cook for supper. He went to work, and fumed about the red tape and paperwork that was holding up the arrival of his new deputy, and then went home each evening knowing that when he got there, Sam would be waiting.

Complacency became the norm, and guard became lax, and because of it all, when panic struck, it came fresh and fast, as if, somehow, after all they'd been through, it was still unexpected.

"Carol Ann, would you get Sam on the phone for me while I finish signing these papers?"

The dispatcher smiled as she complied. Sheriff Knight had done a complete about-face since he'd returned from California with his old friend in tow. He'd gone from practically living for his work, to living for quitting time, like most normal people.

After dialing the number Carol Ann waited, expecting to hear the husky drawl of Samantha Carlyle's voice within the first two or three rings. It didn't happen. She frowned and after at least a dozen rings, hung up and tried again, thinking that maybe she'd misdialed.

This time, she let it ring an even twenty times before she hung up. The look on her face matched the shock in his eyes when she announced, "She doesn't answer."

John Thomas frowned. "Try it again, maybe you dialed a wrong number," he ordered.

"I already did."

He yanked the phone from her hand and dialed his number himself, and this time, he lost count of the number of rings. All he could hear was the empty sound of the bell as it echoed and echoed in his ear.

Carol Ann wasn't surprised when he slammed the phone down and announced that he was going home. She would have been a fool not to have noticed how much Sheriff Knight had been affected by his house guest's presence. Depending on his moods, he was either cautious or cranky whenever her name was mentioned.

John Thomas hadn't forgotten that the reason Samantha was in Texas was because her life had been threatened. But the last few days had been so calm that she might have let her guard slip. And if her life was in danger, one slip would be all it would take.

He ignored his own truck parked behind the building in favor of the county squad car, thinking he might need more speed than his truck could manage, yet praying that he was wrong. He was out of town in seconds.

As he skidded around the corner on the road above his house, he realized they'd both become lax. He corrected the skid before increasing the squad car's speed, ignoring the draw in his belly and the band tightening around his heart. He couldn't face losing Samantha. Not now. Not when he'd just found her again. And while his conscience kept reminding him that she wasn't his to lose, he ignored it and accelerated.

He turned into his driveway, jumped out of the car before the dust had time to settle, and hit the front door of his house with the flat of his hand, yelling her name as he ran through the empty rooms. The sound of his bootheels echoed along with his voice. But only silence answered, and his worry increased.

He made two complete turns through the house before he convinced himself that nothing was out of place. Nothing was missing . . . except Sam.

He ran outside and then stopped, standing at the edge of the porch as he stared intently toward the line of trees surrounding his house. For the first time in his life, he saw them not as a shelter, but as a place in which anything —or anyone—could hide.

He cupped his hands to his mouth, intent on shouting her name, when he saw them coming through the hay meadow beyond the road and felt as if all the blood in his body had suddenly dropped to his feet. He began to shake, and more than once, tried to move. But so vast was his relief, that for the moment, it was impossible.

The slow breeze that made its way through the thick line of trees kept teasing at the ponytail she'd made of her hair, blowing wisps of it back and forth across her mouth and eyes as she absently kicked at the dust beneath her feet, and now and then tossed a stick for Rebel to fetch.

Her long legs and arms were bare beneath her well-washed, once-blue T-shirt and faded cutoff jeans. He watched her bend over in the ankle-high grass and pick up a stick, then wind up and give it a fling. Her head tilted back as she followed its arc through the air, and then clapped her hands in delight as Rebel instantly gave chase. The smile on her face as the dog bounded away made him ache. He took a deep breath and started toward her on shaky legs.

She looked up. When she saw Johnny coming across the meadow, she waved and then began to run.

"Hi!" she said, breathless from the jaunt as she came to an abrupt halt in front of him. "I didn't expect you home."

"You didn't answer the phone," he said quietly.

She looked up, surprised by the depth of emotion in those few words, and knew that he'd been afraid.

"I'm sorry," she said quickly. "I just got so fed up being inside alone. And it was so pretty out I didn't think it would matter if . . ."

He shrugged. "I overreacted. No big deal."

But she knew that it was. "We've been to the creek," she said, waving her hand to include Rebel who trotted up at that moment and dropped at her feet the stick that she'd thrown.

John Thomas was spellbound. Her eyes were a mirror image of the blue sky behind her. A bead of sweat rolled down from her hairline and headed for the neck of her shirt. He watched, fascinated by the track it took as it traveled, and knew that soon it would disappear onto . . .

He caught himself in time to stop the meandering path of lust his thoughts had taken.

"Which one of you was doing the chasing and which one of you was heading them off at the pass?" he asked.

"What do you mean?"

"You and Rebel look like you've been chasing rabbits. And you're both hot and sweaty and dragging your tails in the dirt. It's obvious as hell from the mud on your feet that you've been *in* the creek." He grinned slightly. "Simple police deduction."

Her mouth dropped open. She looked at Rebel, and then down at herself and laughed. It was a throw-your-head-back kind of laugh that made his stomach tilt. And there, in the middle of a hay meadow at high noon, John Thomas felt the earth shift.

To save face, instead of taking her in his arms and pulling her down into the grass beneath their feet, he bent over, brushed the dust from her knees, and swung his Stetson at Rebel, scooting them both toward his house and its shady front porch.

Later, they sat together on the steps, sharing sand-
wiches and lemonade with the dog who lay a few feet
away, relishing the cool shady dirt beneath the tall pine
near the porch.

It was with extreme reluctance that John Thomas
made the decision to return to Rusk.

"I guess that it's time I got back to work," he said,
and was slightly satisfied to see the disappointment in
Sam's eyes.

But her dejection was too much to ignore, and before he'd thought, he found himself cupping the back
of her head with both hands.

Their lips met suddenly. Her mouth was slightly
open in shock, his swift and determined. And when his
hard kiss exploded her emotions and rocked her world,
she groaned and submitted to his demand without
protest.

Then he turned her loose as quickly as he'd claimed
her.

"Be careful, damn it," he growled, and stalked
toward the squad car with single-minded intent. He
had to get away before he did something they both
might regret.

Samantha thought to remind herself later—when
she could think—that it was only a kiss between
friends.

Two days later, halfway across the country, another
kind of explosion rocked the early morning silence in

the pink stucco apartment complex in L.A. Walls shifted, the ground shook, and residents came screaming from the rooms in sleepy terror, thinking that an earthquake had just occurred.

It was several minutes later before someone noticed that there was little or no damage—except around the area of Apartment 214.

Within minutes of the fire department's arrival, it was determined that the explosion had not been natural. By the time they realized that the bomb that had gone off had been detonated from a different location, fear and confusion reigned. The subsequent discovery that it was Samantha Carlyle's residence changed the complexion of the incident altogether. That was when Detective Mike Pulaski of LAPD got the call.

"Pulaski here," he answered, talking around a bite of bagel and cream cheese.

The color in his ruddy complexion faded to a pasty white, and he choked twice then coughed before taking a large swallow of hot coffee to wash down the news he'd been given.

"You're certain?" he asked, writing as he listened.

Minutes later he hung up, stared down at the notes on the paper, and began to curse. It was the last thing he'd expected to hear. The call made him angry. He, Mike Pulaski, was hardly ever wrong. And he hated to be wrong, especially about something like this. The threat to Samantha Carlyle's safety had suddenly become fact, and at the same time, he had to face guilt and a guilty conscience. So she'd been telling the truth all along!

It didn't take Pulaski long to show up at the site of the explosion. And what he learned made him sick. Bits and pieces of what was left of Samantha Carlyle's home were scattered all over the three-room apartment as well as out into the courtyard.

He had all the proof he needed that her life was really in danger, because only he knew first-hand that one Miss Samantha Carlyle, late of Los Angeles, California, was now in the safe hands of a Texas sheriff. She'd been thousands of miles away when what was left of her world had gone up in smoke.

He went back to his office, leaving the gathering of evidence to the experts from the crime lab. He had a call to make, and it was not going to be an easy one. It took him several minutes to locate the card that John Thomas Knight had tossed on his desk, and once he did he had to pause to ponder what he was going to say.

Daylight came two hours earlier in Texas than it did in L.A., so he knew that the sheriff would be in his office. He took a deep breath and dialed. And while he waited for Knight to come to the phone, he realized that he hadn't planned on eating his own words for breakfast.

"When?"

The question was staccato sharp, and Pulaski winced and held the phone away from his ear.

"This morning," he answered, then looked down at

his watch. "What would have been about ten o'clock your time."

John Thomas inhaled slowly, closed his eyes, and pinched the bridge of his nose to alleviate the pressure of a headache that had suddenly appeared.

"What do you know so far?" John Thomas asked.

Pulaski sighed. "Not much."

"Well, hell, why am I not surprised?"

"Look! I had that coming. I don't deny it. But we've got a damned good bomb unit. If there's something to find, they'll find it."

"And while they're looking through what's left of Sam's life, what do you expect me to do? Do you know what this news is going to do to her? Dammit to hell, Pulaski, why didn't you believe her earlier, before it went this far?"

Pulaski sighed, remembering how casually Samantha Carlyle's own bosses at the agency had treated the threats after weeks had passed without an incident to prove her theory. The fact that he'd let their opinion of her behavior color his own judgment didn't sit any better.

"I wish I could change what's happened, but I can't. Look, Sheriff, I'm only human, you know. We all are. All I can tell you is to be on the lookout for strangers."

John Thomas snorted softly. "Well hell, Pulaski, that won't be hard. With a population of less than twenty-five hundred, around here strangers stand out like cows in a pen full of steers."

Pulaski rolled his eyes at the metaphor, assuming that what Knight just said made some sort of sense in Texas.

"Okay then," he said. "I'll call you as soon as I know more. For now, you should work under the assumption that Samantha's stalker knows she's gone and is obviously angry."

"What makes you think he knows?" John Thomas asked. The warning was unexpected, and he didn't like its implications. He didn't like it at all.

"Because the bomb was placed on her bed, that's why. And my police psychologist tells me that the location of the bomb can be read two ways. The stalker is angry that she left with you, another man. By blowing up her bed, he's telling her that leaving her bed to crawl into yours was unacceptable. It's that, or else it was leaving L.A. altogether that set him off. Either way, the stalker has to know she's gone."

"Oh hell."

"My sentiments exactly," Pulaski said, and hung up.

John Thomas frowned as the line went dead. He set the receiver carefully in place, and then covered his face with his hands.

"Horseshit."

"Bad news?" Carol Ann asked.

John Thomas smiled. It was not an expression of joy. The look on his face made the dispatcher shiver.

"Well hell, Carol Ann, in this business is there any other kind?"

The door slammed behind him as he headed for his

truck. The last thing he wanted to do was go home and tell Samantha what he'd just learned, and then watch the smile die on her face.

But while it might be the last thing he wanted, he had no choice. Before the night was over, what he'd learned would put fear back into her world.

5

REBEL BARKED ONCE at the sound of a pickup truck pulling to a stop outside, and then dropped his chin back onto his paws and refocused his attention on the woman who was standing at the kitchen sink.

Samantha looked at the soulful expression on the dog's face and laughed, using her wooden stirring spoon for a pointer as she waved him out of the kitchen.

"If that's the best you can do, then get, you worthless animal," she said, and looked up to see John Thomas standing in the kitchen doorway with an odd expression on his face.

"But I just got here," he said. "Can't I eat before you run me out?"

She grinned. "I didn't mean you," she said. "I was talking to Rebel."

"Talking to dogs now, are you?"

She heard the laughter in his voice and knew that she was being made sport of.

"At least he doesn't argue with me," Samantha said.

His smile disappeared as he turned away to hang his hat on the hook inside the door. She could tell Johnny was trying too hard to be congenial and that wasn't like him. Something was bothering him. Samantha could feel it. But she supposed if he wanted to talk about it, he'd do so in his own good time.

"I'm going to wash up and change," he said. "Be back in a minute to help you finish up supper."

As he walked away, she noted the stiff set of his shoulders, and the way he all but stomped from the room. Being the sheriff of an entire county had to have its drawbacks, as well as its rewards. Obviously, today the former had outweighed the latter.

In his room, John Thomas slammed his gun and holster up on the closet shelf and then dropped onto the edge of the bed. The springs creaked loudly under his weight.

He unbuckled his belt, yanked his shirt from the waist of his pants, and then pulled sharply at the collar. Snaps gave way to the angry insistence of his fingers. He closed his eyes and inhaled, wishing that his news wasn't going to wipe the smile from her face. And as he tried to relax, he absorbed the changes her presence had made in his solitary life.

His house was old but sturdy, with pine walls and floors. There was nothing on the floors to soften the

sound of boot-heels on wood, and nothing on the walls
but paint. It was a man's house, and he liked it that
way.

At least he had until lately. Now he caught himself
thinking about Sam's bare feet, and how they sounded
on the naked boards as she walked down the hallway
during the night. He inhaled again and caught the
good, homey smells of food cooking and the faintest
hint of soap and powder. He'd bet a month's wages that
she'd crawled out of a bath less than an hour or so ago.
His gut clenched just thinking about her naked body
and how it would look all wet and soapy.

"This is getting me nowhere," he muttered, and
grabbed the heel of one of his boots and pulled. It
wouldn't budge, and he cursed the heat of the day for
swelling his feet inside them.

"Need some help?" Samantha asked.

He straightened, a little surprised by her presence,
then told himself not to read anything into it. They met
each other look for look as they took the other's measure. Finally he nodded.

It was only then that she moved from the doorway
and into his room.

"Hike your leg," she said, grinning slightly at the
shocked expression on his face before he complied.

She swung her leg, mounting his boot as she might
a horse, giving him nothing but her backside to look at.
Then she bent slightly and gripped the boot with both
hands.

"Push," she ordered, and tried not to mind when he placed his other boot firmly on her rump and did as he was told.

She tugged fiercely, and when she felt the tight leather beginning to give, pulled even harder. She grunted with satisfaction as it finally came away in her hands.

His foot hit the floor as she dropped the boot. Blind to everything but the enticing view she'd given him, he shuddered as she straddled his other leg and said, "Next."

Next what, Samantha Jean? Wisely, he did not put the question into words, but instead did as he was told.

Samantha grasped the remaining boot, hitching his leg a bit tighter against her inner thigh while she waited patiently for his foot to center again on her backside. But this time when contact was made, it came slow and gentle, and she could feel his sock-clad foot sliding up her thigh to her hip before scooting into place.

She shivered from the contact, wishing it was his hand instead that was touching her so intimately. As a result of her frustration, her next words came out all cranky and wrong.

"What are you doing back there, homesteading? Push dammit! I'm letting supper burn."

His lips firmed and his eyes narrowed. She wanted him to push? Well hell, who was he to argue? He shoved firmly, smiling with satisfaction as his leg straightened and sent her shapely body flying, taking the boot with her as he ejected her from her perch.

She stumbled and staggered, catching herself just before she fell across a chair. Then she turned and glared, daring him to laugh or tease. He did neither.

"Thank you, Samantha."

His voice was as deep and full of meaning as those damned brown eyes of his that held secrets she'd never been able to share.

She frowned as she ran her hand across her hips, expecting to feel the heat from a sizzling brand, because the imprint of his foot was as vivid as if it was still in place.

"Don't mention it," she said shortly.

Rebel barked once.

Samantha sniffed the air. "I guess the pork chops are done," she said.

John Thomas sat on the edge of his bed and watched as she hurried away.

"Oh great! My dog talks to her, too. What's scary is that she understands him," he muttered. He just wished to hell that he understood what was happening between them as easily as that.

A lid banged against a pan in the kitchen and he heard the sound of running water.

"Johnny!" she called.

"Coming," he said. He hustled out of his work clothes and into a well-worn pair of jeans, sliding his feet into old canvas deck shoes as he bolted for the door.

He grabbed a shirt from a hanger on his way to the

bathroom. The food had given him a reprieve from having to tell her about the call from California. He'd wait until after supper before he broke the news. But it couldn't wait any longer than that. Samantha had to know that the stalker had struck again, and this time it had been with more than words.

John Thomas took the last pan from the drainer as Samantha let the dishwater run from the sink. He gave it a halfhearted swipe with a soppy dishtowel and then stacked it inside a larger one in the cabinet below.

"All done," she said.

He nodded, and tried to return her smile.

"Let's go outside a while," he said. "After all that cooking, you've got to be feeling this heat."

"It's not so bad once you get used to it. Besides, staying busy helps pass the time, and right now I have more time on my hands than I know what to do with."

The screen door squeaked in protest as he pushed it wide, waiting for her to follow. As she walked past, he reached back inside and switched off the light.

"So the bugs won't come," he explained unnecessarily. She remembered how the night moths and June bugs would dive-bomb a light source, slamming themselves without caution into whatever stood in their path.

"I guess I should have a fan or something inside the house to cool it off. But I never much liked central air-conditioning," he said. "Makes me feel all cooped up."

Samantha dropped into the porch swing, leaving him room to join her, and leaned her head against the high wooden back. The swing gave a jerk, then righted itself as he slid his arm across the back to balance their weight, giving him the excuse to get that much closer to her.

"And you need your space, don't you, Johnny? With me here, I doubt you've had one free minute to yourself. I'm sorry everything is so —"

"He blew up your apartment."

The words came like a thief in the night, suddenly and without warning. It took a moment for what he'd said to sink in and then when it did, she forgot what she'd been going to say.

A coyote yipped once beyond the trees, and somewhere behind the swing, a cricket in the grass ran its raspy but melodic scales. Bullfrogs bassooned beyond the hill, echoing profusely along the creek bank as they joined the other creatures of the night in welcoming darkness.

"Oh God."

He'd been waiting for her reaction. But that soft, helpless cry made him sick. He stared at her face, trying to perforate the darkness to gauge the depth of her fear. And then he heard it. The quiet, almost hopeless sound of a sob. The swing rocked as she buried her face in her hands.

"Dammit, Sam. Don't cry."

He turned with an almost violent motion, pulled her

across his lap as tremors of shock had their way with her sanity.

Her pain was almost more than he could bear. He held and he caressed, he whispered and he begged. But her tears continued and her body shook, in spite of everything he knew how to do.

Fury came swiftly. Like heat lightning in the middle of the night. In spite of the fact that he had sworn to uphold the law, John Thomas knew that, in that moment, had he been face-to-face with the monster who'd perpetrated Samantha's hell, he could have killed him.

"I won't let him hurt you," he whispered against her cheek. Suddenly he forgot that she'd lied to him long ago. He forgot that she'd been untrue to their love. He forgot, because he wanted to.

"I will take care of you, Sam. I promise. Cross my heart and hope to die. I will always be here. You know that."

Samantha shuddered as his hands roughly brushed away the tears lingering on her cheeks. She sighed, then rested her forehead against his shoulder and wished that she could see his face. She'd heard his words, and believed them completely. But she'd have given a lot to have been able to see the expression on his face when he'd said them.

Suddenly, selfishly, she didn't want what he'd just sworn to do to come from a sense of duty. She wanted more than that from Johnny Knight. She just wasn't certain what he was willing to give, other than empty promises. Once she would have bet her life on his love. But she'd been wrong then. She could be wrong now.

"Are you going to be all right?"

"I have no other choice, do I?" she said. "I guess I should be thankful I wasn't inside when it happened, instead of here, crying for what is gone."

He inhaled, remembering that there was more he hadn't told.

She felt the massive swell of his chest as he took the breath, and tried to quell a second wave of fear. "What?" she asked.

"Pulaski says that it happened—the bombing, I mean—out of some kind of spite. The police psychologist says that the stalker was sending you a message."

"What kind of message?" she whispered, unaware that she'd gathered a fistful of his shirt in each hand as she clung to him on the swing.

"That he knows you're gone. And probably knows that you went with me."

"I don't understand," Samantha whispered. "How can they know all that just from a bomb going off in my apartment? Did he leave some kind of message or . . ."

"In a manner of speaking," John Thomas said. He tightened his arms as he unconsciously pulled her closer to his chest. "The bomb was detonated from somewhere else, but it was on your bed when it went off."

"My bed?"

"Sort of a pissed-off, thumb-your-nose warning that you can't go from that bed to mine without retribution."

She was silent too long. And he had nothing left to say.

"I am so sick of this I could scream," she said finally.

He was surprised to hear anger in her voice.

"I don't know who the hell this wacko is, yet he's trying to tell me who I can and can't sleep with? Oh, this is great!" Her laugh was harsh as she swung her long legs out of his lap and stomped toward the screen door. "If he only knew. I've slept alone so damned long I wouldn't know how to share a bed if I had to."

The door slammed shut behind her, leaving John Thomas with nothing but the darkness for company. He sat so long on the swing that his foot fell asleep. But he didn't care. He'd been unable to move, let alone think after what she'd said. She slept alone! That meant there wasn't anyone special. Hadn't been anyone special. At least not in a long, long time.

Hours later he lay in his bed staring up at the ceiling and wondering how long this ache between them could continue before something happened. The more time he spent with her, the more intrigued he became with the woman that Samantha had become. He rolled over and punched the pillow beneath his head.

He shouldn't trust her. Once her troubles were over she'd be gone and he'd be right back where he'd been years ago, alone and hurting. But knowing and doing were two completely different things. It remained to be seen which would win out—his dignity, or his emotions.

The next morning, in front of Cotton's only garage, Pete Meuller, the mechanic in charge, witnessed another explosion. Only this one happened in front of his station, and came from beneath the hood of a dusty, burgundy Jaguar. Right after the blast came steam, hissing and pouring from every opening and crack possible. The driver did a fair job of erupting himself as he swore, in what Pete would later claim to have been three different languages.

Aaron Reuben cursed cars and engines, mechanics and motors, taxes and Texas, kicking futilely at each wheel in turn as he circled his dying car.

"Great! I'm in the middle of nowhere. How the hell am I supposed to get to Dallas if I'm in the middle of nowhere?" Reuben yelled.

Pete stuck his grease rag in his left hip pocket, and sauntered toward the man and the car, making bets with himself as he neared about which of them was doing the most hissing.

"You ain't in Nowhere, mister. You're in Cotton. Would you like me to take a look at your car?"

Reuben sneered. "Look all you want. But answer me this. Have you ever worked on a Jag?"

Pete shook his head.

Reuben rolled his eyes. "Have you ever worked on *anything* other than trucks and tractors?"

Pete stuffed his hands in his pockets and started walking away. He was of the opinion that the son of a bitch was either crazy or stupid. Why would he insult the only man in sight who'd just offered to help? Then he looked down as he started past the car and noticed the California plates. That would explain it. A dumb tourist.

"Hey!" Reuben yelled, realizing that he'd insulted his only means of escape. "See what you can do about this, will you?"

Pete turned and shrugged. "I ain't promising nothin'," he said.

"Why am I not surprised?" Reuben muttered. And then he asked louder, "Where's the nearest motel?"

Pete pointed. "Closest one—only one. Three blocks down and then to your right."

He watched the man walking away and remembered what he'd heard about Samantha Carlyle's ordeal. He made a mental note to himself to tell Sheriff Knight about the man from California who would be residing at the Texas Pig Motel for the next few days.

Reuben yanked a suitcase from the backseat and started down the street, kicking up fuss and dust with every other step. And his nature did not improve when he turned the corner and saw the larger than life-size concrete armadillo mounted on a slab of limestone. It served as the only source of decoration in the motel's tiny yard.

The minuscule, individual houses sat in a neat row of seven, while a sign over the office door proclaimed that there were vacancies at the Texas Pig Motel.

"Again, why am I not surprised?" Reuben muttered, shifted his bag to the other hand, and headed for the door.

John Thomas sat stiff-backed in his chair and tried not to frown as he watched his new deputy sign the last of the papers before him and then hand them back.

He looked again at the signature. *Montgomery Turner.* Turner wasn't the deputy he'd been expecting, and the excuse he'd gotten from the greenhorn on the other side of his desk did nothing to ease his worry.

The man couldn't be more than twenty-five. He was above average height, but if he weighed more than a hundred and fifty pounds John Thomas would have been surprised. He looked too frail for the heavy leather gun belt riding his hip. And the gun butt protruding from the holster seemed too bulky for his hand. But there was a glint in his eyes, and a jut to his chin that told John Thomas the kid had possibilities.

Age would help. A regimen of good diet and weight-lifting would give him some bulk. But only time would tell whether Montgomery Turner had what it took to be a Texas lawman.

"Okay, Montgomery, you're officially on the payroll. You've got your schedule, your badge, and as of one minute ago, your new title. You are now a duly sworn deputy of Cherokee County."

Monty grinned. This had been almost too easy. He'd feared a hellfire and brimstone fit from the famous

John Thomas Knight because he was not the deputy the sheriff had been expecting. Instead, he'd been welcomed. Not warmly, but welcomed nevertheless.

"Please, sir, call me Monty."

John Thomas nodded. "Only if you don't call me sir. I'll answer to Sheriff, or John Thomas, even boss. The sirs and the misters sort of put me off, if you know what I mean."

Monty nodded. "It's a deal, Sheriff. Now, I've got one more hurdle before I can start work. I don't have a place to stay and the only available apartments in Rusk are, at the moment, a little out of my price range. Do you have any suggestions?"

John Thomas thought for a moment. Rusk didn't have an overabundance of rental property. The few places that rented were nearly always full. Then he remembered. The old Earl place. Maybe there was a vacancy there.

"I might, if you're not all that picky," John Thomas said.

"Lead the way," Monty said.

John Thomas did.

An old two-story house, which looked as if it had been built before statehood, sat beneath a cluster of live oaks and pines that might have been there since the beginning of time.

The branches of the oaks were wide-spreading and laden with thick clumps of leaves that let only the faintest of sunbeams filter through onto the ground beneath them. The pines interspersed among the oaks were tall, ancient soldiers pointing accusing, fingerlike branches upward toward the sun.

Montgomery Turner prided himself on being able to hide his feelings. All he allowed himself was a long, deep breath as he climbed out of the squad car and followed the sheriff up the walk toward the house. He squinted his eyes against the sun's bright glare and casually pulled a pair of sunglasses from his pocket and slid them up the bridge of his nose.

"Damn hot for this time of year, don't you think?" Monty drawled, as he hitched his single piece of luggage to the other hand.

John Thomas grinned to himself. The kid had spunk. The old Earl place would obviously have never made the cover of *Better Homes and Gardens,* but he liked to think it had a certain charm.

"The rooms have air conditioners," John Thomas answered.

Thank God for small favors, Monty thought.

The wood siding had once been white, but the years had not been kind, and now it was nothing more than a soft, weathered gray. Honeysuckle and English ivy covered the entire south wall of the house. Neat rectangles had been cut in the growth to allow viewing from the two sets of double windows on both floors, but other than that, it had been allowed to grow at will.

A wide roof ran across the entire front of the house.

Had the structure been erected a few hundred miles to the east, it would have been called a veranda. But the house was in Texas, and so it was only a porch.

Yet it was a grand, imposing edifice, and the roof gave the house a stately sort of character in spite of its rather decrepit appearance. The longer you looked at the porch, the more it resembled a fine, wide-brimmed hat sitting upon the gray, aging head of an elderly lady.

"Here we are," John Thomas said. He opened the door and entered, pointing to the grand, imposing staircase a few steps in front of them. "That must lead to the two apartments upstairs. The realtor said you had—" he peered down the shadowed hall at the two numbered doors directly opposite one another, and pointed again, "number two, downstairs." He handed Monty the door key, and stepped aside to let the young man pass.

Montgomery bumped into the wall, and then flushed as he fumbled with the sunglasses that had been hiding his expression. In this dark, shaded hallway, they were a hindrance rather than a help.

"Thanks," he said, as he stuffed the glasses back in his pocket and took the key from John Thomas. "Let's take a look at 'home sweet home.' "

The door squeaked once as it opened. Montgomery stared at the upper hinge on the door and frowned.

"Needs a little oil," he said, and then looked around the rooms. Both men were rather surprised. It looked better inside than out.

Furnished in early garage sale right down to an old faded braided rug, everything—oddly enough—still matched. The curtains at the windows were clean and white. The slipcovers on the old sofa were dark green with a small burgundy stripe. Matching burgundy throw pillows littered the couch as well as the single easy chair covered in plain but coordinating greens.

Off to the right of the sitting room, Montgomery saw the edge of a table and chair, and heard the hum of an old refrigerator motor. That was obviously the kitchen.

He entered, motioning for the sheriff to follow, and walked to his left toward the only closed door. It opened a few inches and he had to shove his shoulder against it to push it the rest of the way open.

"Sticks a bit." He entered the nondescript bedroom and tossed his bag onto the bed. He gave the single bath a halfhearted glance as he walked back out of the room. "It'll do just fine, Sheriff. Thanks for the tip."

John Thomas nodded, pleased that the young man hadn't voiced a single complaint about the apartment. He certainly looked as if he'd never roughed it.

"How about a lift back to the station to pick up your car?" John Thomas asked. "You can use the rest of the day to settle in, pick up some groceries, and familiarize yourself with the streets in Rusk, as well as the surrounding area. Our work involves the rural areas outside the jurisdiction of city government, but you still need to know your way around."

Montgomery grinned and shoved his wide-brimmed hat a little firmer down upon his forehead.

"Just point me in the general direction of the nearest eating place and I'll be happy. As a single man, I'm not much of a cook."

"Places to eat are all over," John Thomas answered. "And as for being single, if you play the field too wild and fast, don't blame me if someone's daddy takes a shotgun to your behind. And if you mess around with someone's wife, I'll be right behind her husband with the tar and feathers. Do we understand each other?"

Then he was surprised by the strange, almost lost expression that crossed Monty's face.

"I have no desire to chase around, and I don't cross lines," he said. "Neither legal nor moral."

A single look passed between the men, and when it had come and gone, both seemed satisfied with what they had seen in each other.

"Good enough," John Thomas said. "After I drop you off to pick up your car, I'll see you tomorrow. I've got to get home and check on a female." He said it in jest to hide the truth of what he felt.

John Thomas started out the door with his deputy close behind. His boot was on the top step and he was about to descend the porch when Montgomery Turner's question stopped him in midmotion.

"Is she your wife, sir?"

John Thomas pivoted. Old anger surfaced at how she could have been—if she'd been true. It made his answer shorter than he would have liked. "I thought I told you to can the 'sir' business."

Monty nodded. "What's her name?"

"Her name is Sam. She's in trouble. I'm sort of babysitting."

Monty's eyes narrowed as he nodded.

"We grew up together," John Thomas added. *We made promises and we made love.* And then he thought about why he'd gone so far out of his way when her letter had arrived. If he was so angry with her, why had he bothered? The only thing he could come up with was that the promises they'd made had kept better than the love.

Montgomery watched his boss's back stiffen, and saw the way his shoulders straightened as his long legs quickly covered the distance to the squad car. He took the steps down two at a time and slid into the passenger seat just as John Thomas shoved the car into gear.

He must have said something that made the sheriff mad.

6

JOHN THOMAS PULLED into the driveway at home and parked. His heartbeat accelerated as Samantha opened the door and stepped out onto the porch with a smile on her face that made him hasten his exit from the truck.

For a second, he almost opened his arms, ready to give her a welcome of his own. But he caught himself just in time.

Damn you, Sam. Damn you for making me want you all over again.

Rebel bounded past her out of the house and came off the porch, his tail wagging and his tongue lolling out of his mouth, begging for the scratch behind his left ear and the firm thump of his master's hand along the back of his head.

"You'd better say hello," Samantha said, pointing to Rebel's antsy wiggle in front of John Thomas's legs as he walked toward the house. "He's been lying by the door for nearly an hour listening for the sound of your truck. I think he's in love."

Oh hell, darlin', John Thomas thought, looking absently down at the dog at his feet, *of course he is. Neither one of us has a lick of good sense left. Not since you came into our lives.*

"Are you sure it's me he's in love with?" he asked, relishing the blush that spread across her face.

He tugged gently on the dog's ear and then thumped the ridge of backbone on his hairy back just hard enough to make the dust poof.

Rebel flopped down into the dirt beside the porch and began scratching his belly just as John Thomas stepped over him and up onto the steps.

Unable to resist needling her a little, John Thomas cocked an eyebrow at Rebel, then back at Samantha and teased.

"Got an itch you need scratched?"

He slid his arm around Samantha's waist and aimed his lips toward the vicinity of her cheek, knowing she was going to rebuff him. He was right.

She punched him lightly in the belly, and sidestepped the invitation she saw in those warm, brown eyes.

"You are insufferable," she muttered, and pointed toward the open door. "Supper is waiting."

"So am I," he said, and stood his ground, staring down into the slightly shocked expression on her face, and the wide, nearly blank look in those clear blue eyes.

A long, silent moment passed, and finally Samantha knew that he wouldn't move until she answered.

"For what?" she asked, unable to break the spell of his look.

"For my answer, Samantha Jean. Do you?"

"Do I what?" she muttered, and started to look away when he grabbed her chin with his thumb and forefinger and gently tilted her face back toward his gaze. She sighed and stared him in the eyes, almost daring him to continue. He did.

"Do you have an itch you want scratched, or maybe you're just in need of a hug?"

The tone of his voice was teasing, but the look in his eyes was not. Samantha shivered.

"I guess I could stand a hug," she muttered, knowing full well she would get that and more if she'd give him half a chance.

"But only a hug, Johnny," she added in warning.

His smile was lopsided and promised nothing. He opened his arms and waited.

She sighed and walked into them, relishing the instant feeling of safety and warmth, and the knowledge that with this man, she would never be lonely again. And yet, knowing all of this, she couldn't forget their past and the fact that he'd loved her and left her once. It could happen just as easily again.

"Welcome home, Johnny. I missed you," she said softly, and pressed her nose and lips against his shirt, loving the feel of his heartbeat beneath her cheek and the way his arms wrapped around her, aligning her so perfectly against him that she knew moving away would hurt.

"Thank you, Sam. It's nice to know I was missed. What's for dinner?"

He let her go and walked past her into the house, unable to look at the shock on her face. He hadn't meant to be so abrupt, but when he'd felt her body against his, it had been all he could do not to lift her off her feet and carry her to his bed, strip her naked, and bury himself so far inside her that he'd lose his way out.

Samantha staggered once and grasped the porch post to steady herself as she watched him open the screen to go inside. What had gotten into him? she wondered.

And then she remembered his hug and the near-desperate manner in which he'd held her, and decided she'd be better off ignoring the answer to her own question. She had a feeling she knew.

"Chicken," she answered, as she started to follow him into the house.

At her remark, John Thomas turned short and stood stone-faced, watching the blush on her face spread even farther across her body as it slid out of sight beneath the collar of her shirt.

"I hope you're telling me what you cooked, and not calling me names, darlin', 'cause I need to remind you, just in case you forgot, that I always take dares."

"Oh God," Samantha whispered, and took a step backward. "It is—I mean, I am . . . I mean . . ."

She spluttered helplessly a few more times before she could come to her senses. When she did, she pushed past him in anger.

"Dammit, Johnny! Don't do that! Don't make me any crazier than I already am." She stomped past him on her way into the kitchen. "I fried chicken. You can either eat it or wear it."

His fingers curled into fists as he repressed the need to reach out and grab her as she moved past him. Then he had to grin at the angry sway of her backside as she disappeared into the kitchen.

"I can't wait to sink my teeth," he said just loud enough for her to hear.

He heard her stumble and then heard her curse. "I'll just go wash up," he called out, for the moment unable to face the look he knew she must be wearing.

And then he laughed aloud as she called out down the hallway, unable to resist having the last word.

"Don't forget your mouth," she said.

His suitcase was empty. Montgomery Turner hung his last pair of pants in the narrow closet of the apartment and closed the door, then stepped back, listening to the rattle and hum of the window unit air conditioner in the next room, and knew that at least he would sleep cool.

He walked into the kitchen and opened the refrigerator door, staring at the meager contents before slamming it shut again. He'd shopped. But he couldn't cook worth a damn, and wasn't in the mood for cornflakes and milk. Not tonight.

He had already checked out the assorted dining facilities in Rusk. They looked good and the choice was varied. He knew he could more or less have his pick of any sort of food he desired, but tonight he wanted something more than going into a strange establishment and eating alone. He wanted atmosphere.

Remembering that the sheriff lived just outside of Cotton, and knowing that it was a long time until sunset, he decided to scout the territory in that direction and see where it and his stomach led him.

It didn't take long to drive out of town, and it took only a few minutes more before the rooftop of an obviously busy truck stop café just outside of Cotton came into view. He knew from experience that a truck stop often produced the best food and the nearest to home cooking that a man could find.

But Montgomery had a sudden longing for more than food. He wanted to feel like he belonged. He was tired of being on the outside looking in. And the hell his life had been in over the past few months was beginning to wear his patience thin.

Without further consideration, he wheeled into the truck stop and parked between a purple and chrome eighteen-wheeler and a pickup truck pulling an empty cattle trailer.

An odor of drying cattle manure blended harshly with the faint scent of diesel. Wrinkling his nose with disgust, he made a beeline for the entrance. The smell of hot grease, cigarette smoke, and cool air met him at the door. It should have been as unappealing as what he'd left behind him, but for some strange reason it was not.

Friendly faces looked up and then back down at the plates in front of them. Truckers nodded without missing a chew and a waitress wiggled by, winking at him and ogling his uniform and wide-brimmed Stetson as she deftly balanced four steaming plates of food bound for the table by the door.

Montgomery grinned and touched the brim of his hat with a forefinger. He had a feeling this was the kind of place a man could lose himself in and still not feel one bit lonely. This was the atmosphere he'd been needing.

"Sit yourself, honey," a well-used, but shapely blond woman muttered, as she hurried by with a full pot of coffee. "I'll be with you in a minute."

Montgomery sat himself as ordered, and waited. He didn't wait long. The woman was as good as her word.

"Hey there," she said, as she came to an abrupt halt at his table, slapped a menu in front of him, a glass of water and eating utensils wrapped in a paper napkin near his left hand. "I'm Marylee. You must be the new deputy John Thomas was waiting for. Heard you were in town. Chicken fry is good, pork chops are better. You have a choice of two vegetables besides the fries. The list is on the menu. What's your name, honey, and what do you want to drink?"

"Call me Monty, and iced tea."

Marylee grinned. "Back with your tea in a jiff, Monty."

He leaned back in his seat and smiled. Now he knew where to go if he was lonesome. The food might not be so great, but the ambiance was downright welcoming. That and Marylee. Together they made a man feel good all over.

He was right in the middle of chewing his second pork chop when a commotion outside overrode the dull roar of conversation inside, even through the thick outer door of the café.

"No! No! You can't do this to me!" a woman screamed.

Monty sat spellbound, as did the other customers of Marylee's Truck Stop Café, and listened to the drama unfolding outside.

"Damn you, Tony! You promised!"

Silence answered her fervent pleas, and then a familiar sound of a big eighteen-wheeler firing up and jerking as the driver slammed it in gear drowned out the rest of the woman's tirade.

The customers sat as one and listened for the next bit of dialogue to continue. But there were no more shouts and screams, just a slender, blond woman dressed in slacks and a tank top who came through the door sobbing and sniffing, oblivious to her gaping audience. She dropped a small duffle bag just inside the entrance and began brushing at the streaks of dust on her clothes as she struggled with hysteria.

Montgomery wasn't the only customer who stopped in midchew and stared, although he felt guilty for having done so as the woman looked up and noticed the entire assembly watching her. She bit her lip, took a deep breath, and then began talking and pointing out through the window through thick, choking sobs.

"That sorry road jockey. He's gone! Just like that! And he said he loved me." She then buried her face in her hands and cried some more. Her blond curls bobbed as her slender shoulders shook from her sobs.

Montgomery stared some more and then remembered his mouthful of food and swallowed, chasing the half-chewed bite with a long drink of iced tea.

"What's your name, honey?" Marylee asked.

The woman's face was covered in tears along with long, black streaks of cheap mascara that ran in jet rivulets down her painted cheeks.

"Claudia," she mumbled, and wiped at her face with the handful of paper napkins Marylee thrust in her hands. "Tony is a pig. A dirty, lying pig. He said he loved me. We were going cross-country and when we got home to Las Vegas, we were going to get married."

With that bit of shared news, she began sobbing again and buried her face on Marylee's shoulders. Marylee was slightly shocked that the woman had all but thrust herself into her arms, but couldn't prevent the spurt of shared grief she felt at the news. She'd been on the receiving end of some male lies in her life, too.

"There, there," Marylee said, and patted Claudia roughly on the back. "It'll be all right. It always is, honey. You just have to pick up and go on like you never knew him. Don't let the sorry s.o.b. get you down, you hear?"

Several men in the café looked around nervously, as if half expecting the women in the place to suddenly turn on them and use them for punching bags in place of the missing Tony who'd just left Claudia behind.

Claudia bobbed her head against Marylee's neck and sobbed a little more before allowing herself to be pushed away. She turned a tearful face toward Marylee.

"I need help," she said.

Marylee swallowed a groan. She should have known.

"I'm not asking for charity, you understand," Claudia said, wiping furiously at her face. "But I wonder if you would have an opening. I'm a good waitress. I'll only need to work long enough to get the money for a bus ticket home. I've got family back in Nevada who'll take me in until I can get on my feet."

Marylee didn't have an opening. But she had a soft heart. Just thinking about her own past misfortunes made her even more sympathetic toward the abandoned woman.

"I suppose I could put you on the evening shift," Marylee said. "It's only minimum wage, but the tips are good. It shouldn't take you long to make enough for a ticket out of here."

"Oh, thank you! Thank you!" Claudia threw her arms around Marylee's neck, totally ignoring the fact that they were in a public place, and that she'd just unloaded her entire world of troubles for any and everyone to hear.

Marylee grinned and started to herd her new employee toward the kitchen, when Claudia's next question stopped her in her tracks. At the time, she began to wonder what she'd gotten herself into.

"I don't suppose you know of a cheap place to stay, just until I get my money?"

Marylee sighed. This was getting out of hand fast.

Montgomery saw the waitress's panic. He fidgeted in his seat for a moment, and then as his gaze met Marylee's nervous look, he heard himself telling her that there was an empty upstairs apartment at the old Earl house in Rusk. Then he felt like an idiot for involving himself in the drama.

But when Claudia turned and gave him a smile that made him drop his fork into his tea glass, he decided that maybe he'd done the proper thing after all. Besides, he *was* an officer of the law, sworn to uphold justice and protect the innocent. And this Claudia person sure looked as if she needed protection.

"Come on, girl," Marylee said. "I'll make the call. I know the realtor. Maybe he'll let you rent on a week to week basis."

"Is it far from here?" Claudia asked, as Marylee ushered her into her tiny, makeshift office off the kitchen area. "I don't mind walking a bit, but if it's too far . . ."

Marylee then heard herself offering the use of her old, black pickup—just until Claudia earned her bus money—and reminded her that it was a piece of junk.

"I haven't used it for anything more than hauling off trash for years. You can't be driving it far," Marylee warned.

Claudia's pale, green eyes shimmered through the mascara tracks on her face as she clasped her hands over her breasts and praised Marylee as a wonderful savior.

Embarrassed by the stranger's fuss, Marylee hastened her toward the kitchen of the café. In no time, Claudia found herself in possession of a new home, an old pickup truck, and ten dollars advanced on her first paycheck.

By the time Montgomery was through with blackberry cobbler, the dessert of the evening, a place had been made for Claudia on the floor, and the waitresses on duty had gladly offered to share the first night of tips with the newcomer.

On the way home later that evening, Montgomery remembered that he would probably be seeing more of Claudia than just at the café. How strange fate was, he thought, as he drove back to the outskirts of Rusk. All he'd intended was to go to supper. What he'd done was inadvertently get himself involved in a strange woman's plight. He wasn't sure whether he'd done the right thing or not, but it was too late to worry. What was done was done. Besides, he had his own set of worries, and they had nothing to do with stranded women and sorry-ass truckers.

John Thomas rolled over and sat straight up in bed, listening again for the sound that had pulled him from a deep, dreamless sleep. There! He heard it again and this time recognized it for what it was. The floorboards in his living room were squeaking, just as they always did when someone walked across them.

"Sam."

He knew the moment he said her name that this time he would follow the sounds to the woman who made them. This wasn't the first time he'd heard her walking the floor when she should have been sleeping. She didn't rest easy, even at night. With him in the same house—in the next room—it had become impossible for both of them.

He crawled out of bed and into a pair of blue jeans, leaving the top two buttons undone in his haste to get to her. He hurried down the hallway to the living room. There he stopped, staring into the shadows at the silhouette of the woman standing at his window, looking out into the night.

"What's wrong?"

His voice made Samantha gasp. She turned in fright,

and then leaned against the window with relief as she recognized the familiar figure in the doorway.

Her answer was a shrug.

A faint glow of moonlight filtered through the trees around the house, past the thin, transparent curtains at the windows. He saw the slight movement of her shoulders, and the way her head tilted downward in a weary gesture of defeat. In seconds he was across the room and pulling her into his arms.

"I couldn't sleep," she said. Then she let him hold her. There was no fight left in her tonight. She needed what he had, what he was willing to give, his strength and his protection.

"You haven't slept good in days," John Thomas whispered, splaying his hand across the back of her hair and pulling her close so that his chin rested on the top of her head.

He threaded his fingers through the silky strands and then absently combed them downward in a calm, soothing gesture. He shuddered as she stepped closer and sighed, letting herself go limp within his embrace.

"Ah God, Sam," he whispered, and wrapped both arms around her shoulders. "I wish I could make this better for you. I would give a year of my life to know that you never had to suffer anything like this."

Tears pricked at the back of Samantha's eyes, but she couldn't let herself fall apart. She was afraid if she did, even John Thomas, as strong as he was, would never be able to put her together again.

"Never barter away your life, Johnny," she whispered, and wrapped her arms around his waist, loving the feel of his bare chest against her cheek and the way his heartbeat increased as she moved against him.

"It wasn't a trade. It was a gift. And I meant it." His hands splayed across her back and then in spite of his resolve, moved down and stopped just above the place where her hips flared. It took everything he had not to move those few inches more and let his fingers cup the shape of her.

"Go back to bed, Johnny. You'll feel awful tomorrow if you don't get some sleep."

"Not without you."

His words shocked her. She wasn't certain whether he'd meant it. Without speaking, she tilted her head, peering into the darkness, trying to see past the shadows to the familiar features of the man she was learning to love all over again.

He stepped back. His right hand touched her shoulder and then slid slowly downward along her arm past her elbow, until he came to her hand hanging limply at her side.

Samantha shook as his fingers threaded through her own and he tugged once, gently but firmly, begging by action what he could not say again.

For a moment neither moved. And then without conscious thought, she found herself walking beside him through the darkness down the hallway. He stopped at the doorway to their rooms, and for a long, silent moment all that could be heard was their harsh, labored breathing.

Knowing that what he needed to do might take more strength of character than he had left, John Thomas moved in front of her and led her through the doorway to her bed.

He leaned over and carefully straightened the rumpled sheets, then gave her a gentle push toward the bed that she'd abandoned.

Samantha's head hit the pillow at the same time that he bent down and pulled the thin covering over her feet and legs and up above her waist. His hands lingered just below the curve of her breasts long enough to let her know that denial was torture to him.

She looked up into the shadowy features of her first love, and knew that from this moment on, the young boy would be forever lost to her. The man that he'd become was so much more.

"Johnny . . ."

"Go to sleep, Samantha Jean," he whispered, and ran his fingers one last time through the fan of black hair lying across her pillow before he straightened with a heavy sigh. "You have nothing to be afraid of."

When morning came, he ate breakfast in anger while the dark circles beneath her eyes haunted him. They were all it took for John Thomas to make a decision.

"Get dressed. You're coming with me," he said, and exited onto the back porch without looking back to see if she was listening. "I need to leave in about fifteen minutes so don't dawdle."

Samantha swallowed her mouthful of coffee and stared.

"Where did that come from?" she asked, but there was no one to answer.

She set her cup on the table and followed him outside. The hood was up on his pickup, and he was busy adding a quart of oil to the engine.

"What was that all about?" she asked, as she walked up behind him.

"You've been alone too long out here, that's what. I shouldn't have left you out here with only Rebel for company."

Samantha smiled and folded her arms across her chest, unaware of the tempting picture she made standing barefoot in the dirt, wearing only cutoff jeans and one of John Thomas's old T-shirts.

"Don't argue with me," he continued. "I don't have time."

"I didn't say a word," Samantha said sweetly, and turned toward the house. "I'll be ready when you are. Just honk."

"Well, fine then," he said. But in his experience, when a woman should argue and didn't, it was time to be wary.

Oil dripped on the toe of his boot. He looked down and then grimaced just as the sticky drop connected with leather. "Shoot," he muttered, and swiped at it with the rag in his hand.

Five minutes later he crawled into the pickup and shut the door, squirming and fidgeting behind the steering wheel until he knew he'd delayed all he could. The flat of his hand was on the center of the steering wheel, ready to honk, when she came out the door.

The warning hadn't been necessary after all. Samantha was as good as her word. She had hurried. She was dressed. And she was smiling. He swallowed once and then leaned across the seat and opened the door on the passenger side.

She climbed in, slammed the door shut, and began fumbling with the seat belt. She looked up, unintentionally surprising an expression on John Thomas's face he hadn't had time to hide.

"So what are you waiting for, Christmas?" she asked, and then without waiting for his answer, began tucking her T-shirt into the waistband of her jeans.

He grinned, happy to see some life back in her eyes.

"Someone made a real smart-ass out of you, didn't they, Sam?"

She returned the smile. "There was this boy I knew when I was a kid. He had an answer for everything, whether it was right or not. I guess some of it rubbed off."

"I guess it did," he said, and put the pickup in gear.

Carol Ann, the dispatcher, grinned as her boss turned three shades of red, and then ducked her head when the lady he'd just introduced as Samantha blithely kissed him on the cheek before going out the door.

"Yes, I'll call in every couple of hours," Samantha repeated, aware that the reminder was probably hanging on the tip of John Thomas's tongue. "No, I won't take candy from strangers, and I will not put my lips on the water fountains or sit down on public toilets."

"Well, Jesus Christ, Samantha Jean. Watch your language," John Thomas muttered, and frowned when he heard Carol Ann's whoop of delight echoing in the room behind him.

"Look who's talking," she said with a smile.

He shoved her out the door and then gazed after her, spellbound by the way the Texas sun bounced off her hair, making it shine like polished jet.

"You're so damned pretty," he said softly, and hated himself instantly for his weakness in admitting it to her face.

"Why, Johnny, how you do talk," Samantha murmured, and turned to walk away, trying valiantly to ignore the spurt of joy his words had evoked in her.

"Check back with me around noon," he reminded her. "If I'm not out on a call, we can eat lunch together."

She turned. The smile on her face stopped every conscious thought he had. Absently noting her nod of agreement, he watched her walk away without saying another word.

Montgomery Turner pulled up in front of the sheriff's department just in time to see the young, pretty woman wave good-bye to the boss. He froze in place as a sad expression crossed his face, but by the time he'd exited his car, it was gone.

"Morning, Sheriff," Monty said, as he stepped up onto the sidewalk.

John Thomas jumped. He hadn't even heard his new deputy drive up. He glared down at the young man, and in doing so, missed his last sight of Samantha as she turned the street corner and disappeared from view.

"I see you brought your lady to town with you today," Monty said. "Going to do a little shopping?"

"I suppose," John Thomas muttered, and started into the office. "And she's not my lady," he added angrily, then wondered why he was mad.

"Sorry. I saw you cozying up to each other. I guess I just jumped to conclusions. Should have known that no L.A. lady would have anything to do with a Texas cop."

Embarrassed, John Thomas stomped into the office, leaving the young deputy to follow. In a few minutes Monty was gone, having been sent to investigate a matter of possible poisoned animals on the Wright farm just outside of Cotton.

He'd been gone for several minutes before it occurred to John Thomas to wonder how Montgomery Turner knew that Samantha was from California. A strange fear shot through him, and then disappeared as quickly as it came. Someone in town had probably told him. It was impossible to have a private personal life in a town this small.

"I'll be shooting at shadows, if I don't get a grip," John Thomas muttered, and slammed a stack of folders into a wire basket on his desk.

"Did you say something, Sheriff?" Carol Ann called from the other room.

"Nothing worth repeating," he answered, and began going through his phone messages with one eye on the clock and the other on the door, wishing he didn't have such a suspicious nature. With Samantha loose on the streets, his imagination was going to play hell with his peace of mind today for sure.

7

NEARLY A WEEK had come and gone since John Thomas started taking Sam with him to work, with each day becoming a repeat of the last. She would prowl the streets of Rusk, making herself just as at home there as she had on the streets of Cotton as a child.

She made friends with the owners of Memories, an antique and collectibles shop on the square, and now had a standing appointment at Beaute Queste every other week, just for the pleasure of letting someone else wash and dry her long, thick hair.

She was more familiar with the stock in Marie's Unique Boutique than the sales clerks who worked there, and two days ago had discovered that she'd gone to school with one of the tellers at Southern Cherokee Federal Credit Union. She was reclaiming herself and her past, and in a small way, regaining her independence.

*   *   *

It was nearing Carol Ann's quitting time. She stood and stretched, thankful that her shift as day dispatcher in the sheriff's office was nearly over, then began gathering her belongings as her replacement came in the back door.

"Well my Lord, Delmar, it's about time," she said. "I've been ready to go since I got here this morning." Then she smiled to soften her complaint.

"Has it been that bad?" Delmar Follett asked, and then lowered his voice when Carol Ann frowned and pointed toward the doorway leading to John Thomas's office.

"More like, has *he* been that bad?" Carol Ann whispered. "I don't know how much longer his mood is going to last, but I suspect he's just about ready to crack."

The older man grinned. "I've knowed Johnny Knight since he was a baby. He's got more guts than good sense. My money's on the man, Carol Ann. Whatever's botherin' him, he can handle it."

"Nothing's *wrong* with him except the fact that he's in love. Now either he doesn't know it, or won't admit it. My money's on the latter. Other than that, he's the same old sheriff."

"Ooh Lordy! That's a whole 'nother story. Thanks for the warnin'," he said, and then grinned. "I'll mind my p's and q's stay out of his way until things get better."

The bell over the front door jangled. It was their only warning that someone had just entered the outer office. And since the secretary at the front desk had been out sick for two days, it was the dispatcher's duty to intercept.

"I'll get it," she told Delmar, "but the next one's yours."

It was Samantha.

"Is he about ready to go?" Samantha asked, lowering her own voice an octave or two, as aware as the rest of the people John Thomas worked with that his usual good nature was out to lunch, and had been for days.

"You ask him," Carol Ann said. "I'm ready to clock out. I'd hate to have to cry all the way home just because he yelled at me again for no reason."

Samantha rolled her eyes and sighed. "I'm sorry. I think I'm getting on his nerves. It must be difficult for a confirmed bachelor to share his space, especially with a woman on the run."

"I don't think sharing space is his problem, girl," Carol Ann said. "What I think is there's already too much space between you and him. If you really want to help, kiss him senseless and put him out of his misery."

"Carol Ann!" Samantha's face turned a deep shade of red. "The things you say!" Then she forgot the outrage she knew she should have felt as she contemplated doing exactly what Carol Ann had suggested.

"See you tomorrow," Carol Ann said, grinning in a conspiratorial manner as she left.

Samantha hesitated all of a minute while debating
whether to intrude on Sheriff John Thomas Knight's
inner sanctum. Then she consoled herself with the
thought: *He might be Sheriff to everyone else, but he's
still just Johnny to me.*

She took a deep breath, pasted on a smile she wasn't
feeling, and entered the office. When she realized that
he hadn't noticed her, she stopped just inside the door
and relished the chance to watch him unobserved.

He was deep in concentration as he sifted through
the stack of paperwork before him. The muscles in his
jaw clenched and unclenched in an abstract pattern as
he tapped a pen against an empty soft drink can.

*Oh, God, Johnny. Why didn't you come after me
years ago? Why did it take a killer to make you care?*

But there was no rhyme or reason to the sudden and
unexplained end of their young love.

If her stomach hadn't rumbled quietly as a reminder
to be fed, she could have admired far longer the way
his broad shoulders filled out his long-sleeved blue
shirt, and the way he kept combing a hand through his
hair, disrupting the short, thick strands into an untamed
look rather than the carefully styled manner befitting a
lawman.

When she knew that she'd watched him far too long
for her own good, she cleared her throat just enough to
get his attention. Surprised by the sound, he looked up
and frowned, and at that moment, looked more outlaw
than officer of the law.

"Sam!" How long had she been standing there?

The thought of being watched made him feel defenseless, and with this woman, he needed every defense he could maintain just to get through each day.

He glanced up at the clock and then back at her.

"Sorry. I didn't know it was so late."

But she didn't answer, and he wondered what she was up to now.

When she sauntered toward him from across the room and circled his desk like a she-wolf circling her kill, his heart jumped into his throat.

What the hell is she playing at?

Watching the way her body moved beneath slim-legged jeans and a loose-fitting cowboy shirt made him restless. She leaned toward him, spilling long dark hair across her shoulder and down toward his desk. *Jesus!*

All he had to do was reach up, grab a fistful of hair and pull her—

Samantha smiled, took the pen from his hand, laid the papers he was holding back on top of the stack in front of him, and pretended to ignore his wary expression.

"Were there any hostage situations today?" she asked.

He shook his head, too surprised to speak.

"Did any banks get robbed, or anyone get murdered while I was buying makeup?"

"No," he said, wondering where the hell this was leading.

"Then don't you think it's time you took me home

and fed me? I'm starving." She leaned forward until she could see herself reflected in the warm brown pupils of his eyes and took heart in the fact that they kept widening by the second. "Please," she added, and sighed just enough that her breath fanned his cheeks in a whisper.

He shuddered, muttered a curse she couldn't interpret, and stood so quickly that his chair hit the wall behind him. The pen rolled off the desk and onto the floor as he took her by the hand. Then he yanked his hat off the hook and shoved it onto his head and made for the door without a word.

Samantha seated herself in the pickup with a small but satisfied expression on her mouth, then looked out the window as if the scenery had suddenly become all-important.

"I need to stop in Cotton on the way home and pick up some wire and fence posts," John Thomas said, as he backed out of the parking space.

"Okay. You know me. I can always find something to do."

He stared long and hard at the innocent expression on her face and then sighed, telling himself that he'd just read more into her actions than he should have, warning himself not to fall back into the same old trap. But he was so damned miserable remembering what they'd had, and trying to figure out why it hadn't mattered to her as much as it had to him, that he was making himself crazy.

They drove out of town in silence.

*   *   *

"Got everything you need?" the clerk from the hardware store asked as he tossed the last roll of wire into the back of John Thomas's pickup truck.

"Everything but my passenger," John Thomas said and then looked down Cotton's main street, expecting to see Samantha lingering along the storefronts.

"I saw her heading toward the park," the clerk answered.

John Thomas bolted across the street to the park on the other side. A spurt of adrenaline shot through his belly as he started across the grass. He had a sudden suspicion that he knew where Sam had gone. The path to their old, childhood hideaway lay in this direction.

She saw him coming. His long legs made short work of the distance between them as she watched from her vantage point behind the thicket. But when he stopped and shouted her name, she couldn't ignore his call now, any more than she'd been able to ignore him when they were children.

"I'm here," she said, and stepped out of the line of trees just long enough to let him see where she was.

He started toward her, unable to calm the rapid thump of his heartbeat as she smiled and waved.

"I should have known," he said, as he stepped beneath the shade and pulled teasingly at the long dark braid hanging down her back.

"Come look, Johnny. It's just like it was when we

were kids. Even the mimosa looks the same, only bigger." She grasped his hand and pulled him even deeper into the woods surrounding the park.

He followed. It wouldn't have mattered where she was leading him, he would have gone. Refusing her wasn't in his vocabulary and never had been.

"Look!" She pointed to the ground beneath the old mimosa tree where they'd taken blood oaths and pledged to be friends forever. "Remember, Johnny? Remember the night we—"

He turned her in his arms, his hands cupping her face and stopping the last of her words in midsentence as his brown eyes bored into her soul.

"I remember the last time we were here. It was the best and worst night of my life. You gave me something special, Sam. But why? Why didn't you care enough to make it last?"

His words hurt. The joy she'd been experiencing moments ago disappeared beneath his accusations.

"Me? Why didn't *I* care? You were the one who made the hit and run. I was the victim, not you. Remember?"

Her anger ate into his good sense. What he should have done, had he considered it, was simply walk away. But it was impossible in the face of what they'd just dug up.

"Me? Remember? Damn you, Sam, this is what I remember."

Before she could think, he was holding her. The world tilted as his mouth swept across her face in an unerring move toward her lips. And then he was there, and she felt the breath leave her body as they connected with firm resolve.

John Thomas groaned and slipped the edge of his tongue just inside her lips, tracing her teeth and feeling her body shaking so fiercely against him that he thought she was crying.

Even that knowledge couldn't stop what they'd begun. He lifted her feet off the ground and pulled her between his legs as he staggered toward the trunk of the mimosa. If he didn't anchor soon, they'd both be on the ground, and he remembered all too damn well what had happened before beneath this tree.

Samantha groaned and took everything that he was willing to give, knowing full well that if he turned her loose now, she might die. And then she remembered where this had led before . . . and the fact that she'd barely survived then. She wouldn't— she couldn't— let it happen again.

Far off in the distance thunder rumbled, reminding whoever cared to listen that rain was imminent.

John Thomas's body ached, and his heart kept forgetting to beat as she wrapped herself around him. Each wanted more than what was, for the moment, possible to take.

"Ah damn," he mumbled, and removed his mouth from her lips with reluctance. It was probably going to kill him, but he definitely needed to let her go.

Samantha sighed and then bit her lower lip when he

lifted his head, shuddering as she tasted Johnny on her tongue. She slid down his body as he turned her loose, but was unable to move other than to rest her forehead against the front of his shirt. Neither of them seemed willing to make the break.

"It's getting dark," she whispered, as John Thomas trailed kisses across her cheek, his mouth lingering at the lobe of her ear in a way that sent shivers of longing running down her spine.

"I think it's going to rain," he murmured, when her hands slid around his waist and then into the back pockets of his pants, cupping his hips through the fabric and then urging him on to more than he was giving.

He shuddered, closing his eyes and swallowing harshly at the want that followed her actions. She was puling him closer and still it wasn't enough to assuage each other's needs.

"What was it we were about to do?" she asked, as his hands dug through the tangle he'd made of her hair, and then fisted around the braid down her back as she moved against his lower body in a helpless dance of unfulfilled passion.

"What we were about to do earlier was eat," John Thomas groaned, as his body swelled against the restrictions of his clothing. "What we're about to do now is something else altogether unless we get the hell out of these trees."

"Oh Johnny." She went limp in his arms, leaning her forehead helplessly against the hammerlike rhythm his heart was making behind the wall of his chest. "What happened to us? It was so perfect. What in heaven's name went wrong?"

"I don't know, darlin'. God help me, I don't." With a reluctant groan and one last kiss, he stepped back, looking at the dazed expression in her eyes.

Her lips were slightly red and more than a little swollen. He'd been rougher than he'd meant to be and smiled gently in an apology as the ball of his thumb traced the path his mouth had taken earlier.

"I hurt you," he said. "I'm sorry."

"I hurt," she answered. "But only because you stopped."

"Damn you," he mumbled, then grabbed her wrist and started out of the trees, moving at a fast pace toward the place where he'd parked his truck.

"What's the hurry?" she gasped, as she tried to keep up.

He stopped. As darkness enveloped him, all she could hear was the shocked surprise in his voice as he answered.

"You have to ask?"

He couldn't see her smile, but he felt it just the same.

"Let's go. Suddenly I'm starving to death," Samantha said, and before he knew it, she was leading the way.

Marylee's Truck Stop Café was nearly empty, but it could have been full and overflowing and they still wouldn't have noticed. John Thomas had ordered, but for the life of him, he couldn't remember what. He guessed when it came he would be surprised.

Samantha couldn't quit watching the way his lips curved around the rim of the glass as he took a long, thirsty drink of his iced tea. Or the small drop of moisture that hung at the corner of his mouth when he set it down.

She closed her eyes and thought about the way that same mouth had felt on hers and the way those same hands had stirred fires within her that she'd almost forgotten existed.

"Are you all right, Sam?"

He'd seen her look away. He'd watched her lips tremble. His voice was anxious, his touch tender, as his hand slid across the table and grasped her fingers.

"I'm fine," she said, then looked up and tried to smile. She traced his knuckles with the tip of her forefinger and then covered his hand with her own as she looked up. "I was just . . . remembering."

He took a deep breath and hoped to hell he made it through this meal without making a fool of himself.

"I know, Sam. Between us, there's a lot to remember."

She nodded, then looked down at the table, struck dumb by the memories that suddenly assaulted her. The one night of joy that he'd given her. She wanted it back, and all of the years in between.

Don't be a fool, she told herself. *You're forgetting the years of regret he left behind.*

John Thomas ached in so many places he was afraid
to move. And yet as much as he wanted her now, he
couldn't forget how crazy he'd been before. He would
have died for her, and it hadn't been enough to keep her.

Old, nearly forgotten misery was resurrected as they
tried not to look, tried not to touch, and tried to forget
that once upon a time in Cotton, their world had re-
volved around their love.

Marylee grinned as she watched the couple from
behind the counter. "Oowwee, the sheriff is long gone
on this one," she said softly, wiggling her eyebrows as
she gazed toward their booth.

Claudia turned and stared. Her red mouth pursed as
she squinted for a better look.

"So that's the famous Sheriff Knight. I've been
hearing all about him," she said.

"Whatever you heard still doesn't cover what that
man is about," Marylee said. "Now that's the kind of
man you need to be fallin' for. Not a no'count trucker
with a woman in every town and a lie on his lips just
waitin' to be heard."

Claudia sniffed. "It's not my fault my man is gone.
I did all I knew how to keep him."

"Order up," the cook called, and Marylee turned to
get the plates he shoved out the pass-through from the
kitchen.

"I'll get them," Claudia said to Marylee. "You go
ahead and take your break. You've been on your feet all
day. I just got here."

"Thanks, honey," Marylee said. "I appreciate it."

Claudia shrugged. "I owe you more than a few favors," she said, as she balanced the steaming plates in both hands between a bottle of catsup and another of hot sauce.

"Here you are," Claudia said with a smile, as she set their plates in front of them.

Samantha looked up at their waitress. She had an instant impression of Shirley Temple curls and a Dolly Parton mouth, and wondered what had possessed the woman to put that combination together, and then wondered why she cared.

"Be needing anything else?" Claudia asked.

"Not right now," Samantha said. "If we do, we'll let you know."

Claudia gave Samantha a single, cool stare, and then bustled off.

"What's wrong with her?" John Thomas asked.

"I don't think she likes my looks half as much as she likes yours, that's what I think," Samantha muttered.

He grinned and shook the catsup bottle several times before unscrewing the lid and dumping a generous river of thick red sauce all over his fries.

"Yuk. That's disgusting," she said, eyeing his plate, and then calmly picking the onion off of her hamburger.

He picked up a french fry, dipped it in the catsup, and then held it toward her mouth.

"Open your mouth and close your eyes, I'll give you something to make you wise."

Samantha laughed aloud. It had been years since she'd heard that silly childhood rhyme. Suddenly everything that had been happening over the past few months fell so far back in her memory that it could very well never have happened. It was good to be home with Johnny Knight.

"I'll taste it," she said. "But I'm going to do so with both eyes open. I never do anything blindfolded"

"Not even making love?" he asked, as he poked the french fry into her mouth. "You should try it sometime. It's a hell of a high."

Samantha gasped.

"What you do is," he continued, as if he hadn't purposely dropped a sexual time bomb in the middle of their meal, "you concentrate on touching, and feeling. You'd be surprised how many little spots on your body can be explosive."

Samantha forgot to chew. The french fry hung from her gaping lips like a limp cigarette.

"Don't play with your food, Sam. I know your mother taught you better manners than that." He took a healthy bite of his burger, ignoring the look of shock that came and went on her face.

"I will make you pay," she muttered, as she stuffed the fry the rest of the way into her mouth and chewed with vicious intent, taking out all her frustrations on her food rather than on the man opposite her.

"It won't be necessary, darlin'," he said calmly, as he took a long drink of iced tea and then winked. "For you, it's free."

She stared and then glared. There was nothing left
to say.

"We're not going to beat the rain," Samantha said, as
lightning flashed across the sky in front of the windshield of the truck. "You took too long over dessert."

"I ate it because I didn't think you were quite ready
to come home," he said calmly, as he negotiated the
dark, single-lane road leading to his house with only
the narrow beams of his headlights to guide him.

"Why ever not?" she asked.

"Because every time I looked at you, you kept looking away, that's why," he said. "I decided to put some
time between what happened in the park and bedtime,
just in case I misread the situation."

"Oh."

Her quiet answer did nothing to assure him that he
was wrong. A weary feeling settled around the region
of his heart. *Oh God, Sam. I need you, girl. Please
don't let me be wrong about this.*

"We're here," he said, as he pulled into the yard then
angled the truck as close to the graveled walk as possible, using the headlights for a beacon to shine her way
to the porch. "You're going to have to make a run for it."

"Give me the keys," she said.

He shook his head. "When you get there, wait for
me. I don't want you going into a dark house alone."

"Don't be silly," she said, as her hand touched the
door handle. "It's just your house."

His fingers wrapped around her arm. "Yes, I know, Sam," he said quietly. "And it was your house, too, back in L.A., wasn't it? Bad things still happen at home, no matter where home is located."

From the glow of the dashboard lights, he saw the fear on her face. It softened the tone of his voice, but not his words.

"I don't mean to frighten you, darlin'. But you can't assume anything, ever, until he's caught. Not even here, okay?"

She swallowed, then nodded. Squeezing her eyes against the near-blinding rain, she jumped out of the truck, landing with both feet square in an inches-deep puddle that splashed muddy water above her knees.

He grinned at her squeal of dismay, and then watched, transfixed by the sight of her long legs and shapely body suddenly illuminated by the headlights of his truck like a young doe caught in a poacher's spotlight. She leaped up onto the porch then turned and waved, wiping rain from her face, and shivering from adrenaline as well as a chill as she waited for him to follow.

"Here goes nothing," he said, switched off the lights, and opened the door. In seconds he'd made the dash across the distance between the truck and the house with only one flash of lightning to guide the way.

"Damn! For a summer thunderstorm, that rain's plenty cold," he muttered, as he bounded up onto the porch, clearing the steps in one long leap. He glanced back at his pickup and the rain hammering down upon it. "Hope it doesn't hail."

"Hurry," Samantha said, her teeth chattering and her body shivering as he nudged against him in an effort to stay warm. "I'm freezing."

"I am hurrying," he grumbled, fumbling with the keys in his wet hand. "Don't push me or you'll make me drop them. I don't know why you're always in such a hog-killing rush to be alone with me inside a dark house."

Samantha mumbled something beneath her breath and thumped him on the shoulder with a fist.

"My daddy told me about fast women like you," John Thomas said, his voice light and teasing as the door finally swung open. He yanked her inside, then locked the door and turned on the lights.

A bright-white glow instantly illuminated the single room, momentarily blinding them. But when he could see, John Thomas knew he should never have hit that switch.

She was soaked. Her wet clothes clung to every indentation and curve of her body with tenacious persistence, outlining what he yearned to explore; the ripeness of her breasts, the slender, wandlike breadth of her rib cage, the way her hips flared at just the right point as a reminder of what lay hidden between.

"You take the bathroom first," he muttered, and looked away, tossing the keys on the table by the door before stomping past her toward the kitchen. "I'll make some coffee."

Samantha's mouth drooped as she started down the darkened hallway toward her room. This was a disappointing and unexpected ending to the way this evening began. Despite what they were each obviously feeling, neither had enough trust in the other to explore.

Aching in spirit as well as in bones, she had her hand on the doorknob when his footsteps echoed on the bare floor at the end of the hall. She turned.

He was watching her.

Silhouetted by the light behind him, he stood with legs braced for a blow he might not be able to take, hands curved into fists ready to do battle, shoulders thrust back, as if ready to argue his right to be here.

"Don't, Sam," he said quietly.

"Don't what?" Puzzled by his actions, she couldn't ignore the spark of hope that filtered through her system.

"Don't shut me out. I need you. I need you to need me . . . for more than a bodyguard."

His words knocked the breath from her body. She leaned against the door of her room, unable to stand without a brace. Her knees were going weak, and she couldn't even see his face. And yet she knew she wouldn't have to see him to know that he could see her, all too well. Her hands fluttered up the front of her shirt. When she found where it was fastened, she started to pull.

He tensed, bracing himself as the first snap on her shirt came undone with a small but distinct pop.

She never even saw him move, but suddenly he was in front of her. Words froze in her throat as he caught her hands.

"Let me," he begged. And when she did not deny him, felt himself shaking from the relief.

He tugged gently, pulling the tail of her shirt from the waistband of her jeans, and then with a single, sharp motion, suddenly yanked at the neck of the shirt, as if waiting had become an impossible task. All six of the remaining snaps came undone in one long, continuous pop until her shirt was open and hanging. She shivered.

"I'm sorry, darlin'. You must be cold." He slid his arms around her, pulling her gently until they were touching, chest to breast, unmoving, yet close enough to feel each other's heartbeat.

"It's not from cold, it's from nerves," she said, and then jumped at the sound of her own voice as it echoed in the house.

Lightning flashed, faintly lighting the end of the hallway where the bathroom door stood open, framing the small, narrow window above the sink that looked out into the wet, rainy night.

In that moment, John Thomas had a fleeting glimpse of the expression on her face and imagined that she looked sad, but as swiftly as it came, it was gone. His hand slid around the back of her head and cradled her against him as he rocked them quietly together in the hallway.

"Please God, tell me you're not afraid of me, Sam. I don't think I could take that. You've got to know that I'll walk away now without a word if that's what you want."

His lips grazed the top of her hair, pressing against the damp texture, wishing he could take all of her fears and toss them out into the night with the storm.

"No, Johnny, you misunderstood."

He felt her hands slide up his belly and come to rest on the region over his heart.

"I'm not afraid of you. I'm afraid I won't measure up. I told you, it's been a long time since I've—"

She didn't have time to finish as his soft chuckle broke her concentration.

"Honey, I arrest the experts. Besides, you don't have to know all the tricks, because I do." His voice was thick with joy as he bent down.

"Oh my God," she gasped, half laughing, half crying, as he lifted her off her feet and kicked open the door to his bedroom.

"Now, Samantha Jean, if you're going to start praying, I'm just going to have to carry you back across the hall and leave you to sleep alone. I can't compete with the Good Lord. Not at a time like this."

"Just shut up, Johnny, and teach me." Her hands brushed across his belt buckle as he deposited her at the foot of his bed. "Teach me how to love you right. Teach me everything." *And maybe this time you won't leave me.* But she never voiced the last thought.

When her hands brushed across the hard bulge behind his zipper, he groaned and slid the shirt from her body. She tilted toward him, pressing the flat of her hands against his chest to brace herself as his arms encircled her body. Slowly, he unfastened the hooks on her bra. She sighed as she spilled loose from the silken confinement.

"Now, pay close attention, darlin'," John Thomas said, as he began removing the rest of her clothing.

"I am," she whispered, as she returned the favor and began unbuckling his belt buckle and unzipping his jeans. "But if I miss something, maybe we can do it again until I get the hang of it."

"It would be my pleasure," he said. "But first . . . it's going to be yours."

8

SAMANTHA WAS MESMERIZED by the man standing at the foot of her bed, and by his slow, methodical striptease. She didn't even stop to wonder why only moments ago her body had been chilled and shaking, and now the air around her was thick and too close to breathe.

Her hands moved in a shaky path across her skin, lifting hair from her face and neck where it clung, hot and damp; a complete opposite to the cool sheet beneath her.

Lightning cracked so close that, for a moment, the flash blinded her to what Johnny was doing. She blinked rapidly, unwilling to lose sight of the man who had become her entire universe. As her vision cleared, she saw that he had crossed the narrow space between the wall and the bed, and was in the act of opening a window.

And when a swift draft of cool, fresh, rainwashed air followed him to her bed, she inhaled and stretched;

a sensual appreciation of the brisk air that blew across her heated skin.

John Thomas slid onto the bed and then stretched full length beside her, laying his hand across the flat of her stomach in a possessive yet undemanding gesture. She shivered and turned toward him, letting her fingers stray downward until she'd encircled him, relishing the power he'd given her by putting himself in her hands.

"I wish that my stalker were here, right now," Samantha whispered, as she moved even closer.

"Why?" John Thomas asked, shocked by her words.

"So that I could thank him in person for bringing me back to you. When I lost you before, my life and my world were so empty."

You lie.

The thought came so quickly that he almost didn't remember pushing her hands from his body, or rolling up and away. He sat up on the edge of the bed, bringing their lovemaking to a sudden halt.

"Johnny?"

The room was so dark that she had to imagine his facial expression, and then another flash of lightning sent a short burst of light into the room. It only lasted a second, but it was long enough for Samantha to see the pain on his face.

"You didn't lose me, Samantha Jean. You threw me away."

He got up from the bed, grabbing his jeans as he

passed, and walked out of the room, unable to stay and listen to more lies. He was also unable to admit to himself that regardless of what she'd done, he didn't want her any less.

Samantha threw back the covers, grabbed her shirt, and followed him into the kitchen.

"*I* threw *you* away? I don't think so!" she shouted.

Her indignation surprised him. Speechless, he could only stand and listen to her continue.

"I'm the one who believed you when you said you loved me. I'm the one who waited and waited and waited—" Her voice broke, but she refused to give in to the tears hovering behind her eyes. "You're the one who didn't write. After we moved, I had no way of contacting you other than to wait for your letter with the address of your boot camp. The letter I was so certain would come."

Samantha hated herself for wanting to cry. And at that moment, she hated Johnny for making her feel this old misery all over again.

"Damn you, Johnny, for giving up on me and what we had!" She picked up the nearest thing she could get her hands on.

The coffee cup sailed past his head and shattered on the wall behind him as she stomped from the room.

John Thomas stared in shock at her violent reaction. It was the first time that it had ever occurred to him that maybe, just maybe, someone else was to blame. Her reaction was too full of hurt to be faked. Maybe

Samantha never did see his letters. Maybe it was her
parents who'd been responsible for sending them back.

He stepped over the broken cup and went to get a
broom. An odd smile was sitting just off-center on his
face as he carefully swept up what she'd done. When
he had finished, he turned out the light and started back
to his room, only this time alone.

Just outside her door he paused and listened. From
the repetitive squeak of bedsprings, it sounded as if she
was doing some serious tossing and turning.

"Sam."

The squeaks ceased instantly. But she didn't answer.
It didn't matter. He had her attention, and that was all
he'd wanted.

"I did write."

He walked into his room and closed the door. *Let
her sleep on that for a while,* he thought. He damned
sure had.

The smell of fresh-brewed coffee tickled her nose.
Samantha opened her eyes and stared up into John
Thomas's face as he stood beside her bed.

"Mornin'," he said.

She grunted a reply that needed no translation, and
then hated herself for wanting him now as badly as she
had last night, before he'd torn a hole in her heart and
set a whole series of thoughts in motion.

He looked magnificent. Still damp from his shower,
his hair glistened seal-black. Wearing nothing but

boots, jeans, and a guarded expression, he handed her a cup of coffee and then stepped away.

Samantha set the coffee on the table beside her and stared at the half-dressed man standing at the foot of the bed, trying to read his solemn eyes. There was no hint as to how he felt about what had happened between them last night.

Those damnable three words he'd said before disappearing into his room had left her wide awake and aching for more than half the night. When she finally did fall asleep, she'd dreamt of a young man with tears on his face who kept shouting the same thing at her over and over. *I did write. I did write.*

She felt even more miserable now. What if he'd told her the truth? And if he had, why didn't she get the letters that he'd written?

The same answer kept coming back, and it was one she didn't want to face. If he was telling her the truth, then that could only mean that one or both of her parents had been responsible for keeping them apart. The fact that they were dead now and couldn't answer for themselves was even worse. Samantha didn't know how to be mad at ghosts.

"Where are you going?" she asked.

"To work. I just wanted to tell you to get dressed or we're going to be late."

She stared at him.

And then he lost his composure. "What the hell do you want from me?" he asked.

Only the truth.

But she didn't say it. It would have done nothing but revive the same vicious cycle of accusations that had nowhere to go but back to the start.

"That's what I thought," he muttered. "Hurry up, Sam. I've got a meeting at eight."

Two days had come and gone since their fight. During that time, the feelings between them grew deeper and deeper, while the time they spent together became increasingly strained. Samantha was beginning to object to being dragged to work each day like a puppy who wouldn't stay tied. And she was running out of things to do in Rusk to occupy her time. John Thomas had his work. All she did was wait for five o'clock to roll around. It was the slow, tedious days of heat and boredom that made her balk on the third day after the storm.

"But I'll be fine," she argued, as they stood in the early morning shade beside his truck. "I'm not depressed or suicidal, for God's sake. But I swear, Johnny, if I have to watch that woman change the window display one more time at Monique's I'm going to scream. There's only so much fun a woman can stand and still remain sane."

He sighed. He knew their current routine had to be trying her patience. And not once since they left L.A. had anything resembling a threat occurred. Maybe Detective Pulaski was a little off base. Granted the stalker knew Samantha Carlyle was gone, but that didn't mean he knew where to.

"I don't know," he said, watching the desperate expression on her face growing more intense with each passing minute. Something nudged his leg. He glanced down, then instantly started trying to sidestep the wet muddy dog who'd just ambled in from the field across the road.

Rebel snuffed along the ground and then across John Thomas's boot tops, leaving a wet muddy trail from his huge black nose. He looked up with dark, pleading eyes, as if to make certain that he wasn't in trouble, and that the tone of their voices had nothing to do with him.

"Rebel can be my watchdog," Samantha said, pointing to the flop-eared hound that was now sitting between his master's legs.

"Rebel isn't a watchdog, Sam. He's a tracker. There's a world of difference."

"So . . . if I get lost he can find me. Please, let me stay home. Just for today. Please."

It was the please that did it. That and the gentle way her smile nudged his achy, needy body.

"Oh damn, Samantha Jean. Women like you should be against the law." His mouth swooped in a fierce, hard kiss that sucked the air from her lungs and the sense from her mind.

Samantha staggered slightly as he pushed her away and pointed toward the doorway.

"Take Killer here," he pointed toward Rebel who was now snapping halfheartedly at a fly, "go inside, lock the door, and don't come out this evening until you hear the sound of my voice. Okay?"

"Thank you, Johnny."

She whistled once. Rebel came to instant attention and trotted into the house ahead of her as if he'd just graduated first in his class from obedience school.

John Thomas shook his head and frowned as she closed the door between them. Reluctantly, he got into his truck and drove away. The sooner he got to work, the sooner it would be done. Then he could go home and sort through the emotions he and Sam were trying to ignore.

"So you left the pretty lady at home all by herself today," Monty said, as he sidled in the door and shifted the bulky gun belt on his hip to a less binding position.

John Thomas looked long and hard at the innocent expression on his new deputy's face before he answered, and when he did, it sounded more like a grunt than a yes.

"Monty, sometimes I think you're about as smart as a rock," Carol Ann said, as she watched the sunny disposition the sheriff had come to work with turning slightly sour.

"What did I say?" he asked, and then grinned and winked as she tossed up her hands and sauntered past the still-absent secretary's desk to her own little cubicle in the back.

"We've got trouble," John Thomas said. "I was waiting for you to get here. Willis and Lawler have gone to check out a three-car wreck on the county line road. That leaves just you and me to investigate the cattle theft on the Watkins ranch."

"I'm your man," he said. "You want me to drive?"

Before John Thomas could answer, they both heard the phone ringing back in the dispatcher's office. He paused. The way this morning had gone, it was bound to be more bad news.

"Wait!" Carol Ann shouted, as she ran into the front office with a slip of paper in her hand. "Glad I caught you. You'll need to get right on this, Sheriff. Lizzy Marshall just called in hysterics. She said her ex just called and is on his way out to the house with a gun— again!"

"Oh hell," John Thomas said, as he snatched the paper with the details of the call. "Monty, you're on your own. Carol Ann, give him directions to the Watkins ranch. Deputy, take down all the necessary information before you leave. Take a camera with you, and take—"

"Sheriff, I passed all my tests. I know what I need for an on-site investigation. This won't be my first, you know."

John Thomas frowned, but he had no choice. He wasn't sending a green deputy like Montgomery Turner out to Lizzy Marshall's to face that crazy ex-husband of hers. Last time they'd gone out there on a call, it had taken two deputies and Lizzy's brother in addition to himself to subdue Lem Marshall.

John Thomas looked long and hard at his new deputy's eager face. Every man came to a place in his life when it was time to fish or cut bait. It looked like this was Monty's day.

"Check in periodically with Carol Ann. If I need you, she'll let you know," John Thomas ordered.

"Yes sir," Monty said, already out the door as he spoke.

John Thomas sighed. "Call home for me from time to time and check on Samantha, would you, Carol Ann?"

She nodded as the sheriff stepped out the door and yelled at Monty who was about to get inside his squad car.

"Hey, Deputy! Don't you want to know where you're supposed to go?" John Thomas asked.

Monty's face turned three shades of red, but then of course he'd bolted from the office without chewing the information he needed to take with him.

"It might help at that," he said, then grinned and followed the dispatcher back inside.

John Thomas got into his own car and left, lights flashing, siren squalling for all in his path to move aside. He had to beat Lem Marshall to the house before the man did something rash, like taking Lizzy and all seven children hostage for the hell of it.

*   *   *

Noon had come and gone. And as the sun began its descent west, the heat came. The slow, sweltering kind that made bones weak and temperatures rise. Even Rebel had succumbed, and was on his third nap of the day, in the hallway, the only place in the house that still boasted a breeze as well as shade.

The heat and Samantha's lack of choice in clothing had sent her digging through John Thomas's closets, hoping to find something to wear that was looser and cooler than what she had. The top shelf of his closet looked promising.

Sam dragged over a chair and then climbed up on it, using the extra height to reach the oversize T-shirts that she'd seen.

In her haste, she pulled too fast and sent the whole stack tumbling toward her, bringing boxes with it as it fell. Muttering in frustration, she climbed down and began to pick up the shirts.

It was when she lifted the last shirt that she saw them, spilling out of an old shoe box that had fallen along with the clothes. Samantha stared, unable to believe her eyes. Letters. Addressed to her, in Johnny's handwriting. There were so many, and every one of them was unopened and stamped, *Return to sender.*

In that instant, fifteen years of disappointment disappeared.

"Oh, Johnny. I thought you hadn't cared."

With shaking hands, she gathered them into a pile in the middle of her lap, sorting them one by one according to the date of the postmark. And when she had them all in order, she opened the first. They were, after all, hers to read.

It didn't take long for the first tears to fall. By the time she'd opened the last letter and read of Johnny's pain and uncertainty, she felt sick with regret. He had cared. He had written. And in spite of the fact that she'd never answered, he'd still come home to Cotton, expecting her to be there.

She closed her eyes, imagining him at eighteen, in pain and shame. Seeing him alone at his father's funeral, standing ramrod stiff and unyielding in his uniform as they lowered his father into the grave, and thinking that she'd abandoned him without a care.

"Johnny . . . Johnny, I didn't know. I didn't know."

She rolled over onto her side, clutching the letters against her chest, and cried. Finally, it took Rebel's cold nose against her neck to bring her out of her shock.

She put back everything the way she'd found it on the closet shelf, except the letters. They were hers. Just fifteen years late in being delivered. Samantha hiccuped on a sob. If only they hadn't come too late. How could she make him understand?

She stepped over the dog, and began shedding her clothes as she made her way to the bathroom. She couldn't go outside to have a swim, but she'd settle for the next best thing. She was going to run Johnny's old-fashioned, chin-deep, claw-footed bathtub full to the top with tepid water, crawl in, and pretend she was at some secluded California beach.

And for the next two hours, she did exactly that. She soaked until her fingers and toes looked like white prunes, and her body felt both relaxed and rejuvenated.

Rebel whuffed once as she climbed out of the tub. Her heartbeat accelerated as she hurriedly began to dry. Maybe it was Johnny coming home early! That would be wonderful. They could pack a picnic and she could lie on the creek bank beneath that big willow above the spring while he fished and she would find a way to tell him what she'd found. There had to be a way to make him believe she hadn't known. Afterward they would eat, and then maybe they would . . .

Her meandering thoughts took a sharp nosedive as Rebel jumped to his feet and started baying loudly. Her nerves skittered as she tried to yank a pair of cutoff shorts up still-damp legs. *What's gotten into that dog? Why would he be barking like that at Johnny?*

Then she realized that, of course, he wouldn't. It had to be someone else! She ran down the hallway, her T-shirt clinging to her damp body, her bare feet padding softly against the pine flooring

Rebel was at the door in what she could only call a stance of defense. When she tried to get around him to look out the window, he growled low in his throat, refusing to let her pass.

"Rebel. What on earth?"

Samantha bent down and patted him on the head.

He acknowledged her touch, yet refused to let her by. A sound on the other side of the door startled her. It sounded like something—or someone—scooting their feet across the wood floor of the porch.

Rebel growled again, and this time added an ear-shattering howl that made Samantha want to cry along with him. And then she heard it, the sound of rapid footsteps moving across the front porch, and then the thump as whoever it was landed on the dirt. She gasped. He was running around the house!

"Oh my God! The back door!"

Samantha was about to stake her life on the fact that she had forgotten to lock it after tossing out the tomato peelings from her lunch. She bolted toward the kitchen, and in her haste, knocked over two dining room chairs. She fell, scraping her knee on the floor. She never even noticed that she left skin behind as she pulled herself up on all fours, half running, half crawling, until finally she staggered upright and reached the kitchen.

Running neck and neck, with only the walls of a house to separate them, Samantha hit the back door at the same time that the sound of footsteps outside hit the back porch.

With shaking hands, she grabbed for the dead bolt and tried to slide it in place. The door was just enough off plumb that the lock wouldn't catch. Using all her weight in a last-ditch effort, she threw herself against the door just as the bolt slid home.

With breaths coming in hard, aching gulps interspersed with tears of hysteria, Samantha leaned forward, resting her forehead against the solid wood, and heard a similar sound of heavy breathing on the other side of the door . . . and knew that it was not her own.

She gasped and jumped back, then stared in horror at the doorknob as it turned first one way and then the other. There was no other sound, no other movement, except the knob slowly turning in place.

Then a low, ugly chuckle emanated from the other side of the wall while Sam's heart forgot to beat.

Behind her, Rebel growled fiercely as her hand dropped to her side, blindly searching for the meager comfort the dog might provide.

She inhaled slowly, then listened while the footsteps moved across the porch. Only after she heard the sound of a soft, muted thump as he landed in the dirt did she exhale, and then she waited as the sounds faded away.

The sudden need to see his face sent her bolting to the window over the sink. With shaking hands, she parted the curtains and peered out between the panels, hoping to catch a glimpse of the intruder. There was nothing in sight but a blackbird flying across the yard on its way to the stand of trees beyond the back fence.

"Oh God! Oh God!"

She buried her face in her hands and dropped to her knees. This couldn't be happening. She thought she'd left this horror and this hell behind her in L.A. But he must have found her.

"Johnny! I've got to tell Johnny. He'll know what to do."

Ignoring the tremble in her fingers, she made the call to John Thomas's office, and then pressed the receiver to her ear while she leaned again, peering through the slit in the curtains just to make sure he hadn't come back.

But the phone didn't ring.

"Darn," she mumbled, and took a deep breath, convinced that in her panic, she must have misdialed. Just as she started to repeat the procedure, she realized that there was no dial tone.

"No! Not that! Please not that! I can't be cut off from Johnny."

With Rebel at her heels, she ran to the living room phone. When she lifted the receiver, the only sound she could hear was the swift rush of her own blood pulsing through her body. The line was dead. Just as she would be if she couldn't get help.

Leaving the house on foot was impossible. The worst thing that could happen would be to go outside and then be unable to elude or outrun him. She pivoted and scanned the room for an answer. There was none. Only the sound of her heartbeat and harsh, ugly gasps for air as she tried to breathe past sobs. Long moments passed while she stood in terror and wondered if this was the day she was going to die.

But something happened as she stood there. She remembered the letters she'd just found, and the wasted years, and got angry all over again at the loss they had suffered.

Her tears dried. The tremble in her lip disappeared as her mouth firmed in anger. If he came again, she would be ready.

With Rebel at her heels, she began moving furniture across the doorway. When she was convinced that it would take an army to get inside, she repeated the process in the kitchen, shoving the table and bracing the chairs by tilting them on two legs. Her barricades were in place.

After satisfying herself that all the windows were locked and the curtains drawn, she began searching the house for weapons. Johnny was a lawman. Surely he had other weapons somewhere in the house besides the one he carried.

She found one on the shelf in the closet with the cleaning supplies: a double-barreled shotgun of blue steel with a smooth, well-polished wood stock. When she lifted it to her shoulder and tried to aim it, she staggered from the size and weight.

But her elation died when she realized that it was empty. And no amount of searching provided a single shell. She slid to the floor, resting her head on her knees. A sob thickened low in her throat, but she refused to let it have its way.

"Johnny, help me. I can't find the damned ammunition!" And then she beat her fist against her leg in frustration.

But there was no one but Rebel to hear her dismay, and she refused to give up. Dodging windows as she crawled toward the kitchen, she settled into the corner opposite the door with a knife in her hand and the empty gun across her lap, then tried to find a comfortable spot upon the floor.

Moments later, Rebel came and flopped down beside her, resting his head on her knee, whining every now and then as if to tell her she wasn't alone, that he understood.

With tears in her eyes and a knot in her stomach, Samantha prepared herself to wait. Someone would come. Either it would be Johnny . . . or it would be the intruder. Whichever, whenever, this time she would be ready.

It was closer to seven than he liked to consider when John Thomas walked back into the office with Lem Marshall in tow, handcuffed and cursing with every step. It was hard to say which of the men looked the worse for wear. Delmar, the evening dispatcher, stared in amazement.

"Damn, Sheriff! I can't believe you took him alone!"

"Me neither," he said wearily. "Help me lock him up."

Delmar ambled out from behind the cubicle wall and then circled the old, grizzled fellow who looked more beast than man. "Exactly where do I get ahold, John Thomas?"

"You just unlock the cell, I'll do the rest," John Thomas said shortly, and yanked at Lem's cuffed hands as he half dragged, half walked his prisoner into the holding cell.

"Delmar, did Carol Ann think to call Samantha and tell her I'd be late?" John Thomas asked, as he unlocked the cuffs and shoved Lem to the back of the cell at the same time that Delmar slammed the cell door shut and locked it.

"Funny thing about that," Delmar muttered. "She said she never could get through. Said it rang and rang but no one answered. I think she said she called at least five or six times this afternoon."

John Thomas felt queasy. For a moment, the room shifted and he felt as if he were turning inside out.

"What do you mean, no one answered?"

Delmar frowned. "Just what I said. Shoot, I even stood and watched her make the last call. That was just after I come on duty. Must have been around five, five-fifteen. Something like that. Carol Ann seemed real worried. She said she never could raise you on the radio to tell you."

"I was otherwise occupied," John Thomas said, glaring at the man in the cell who just may have cost him more than a good shirt. It was then that he made the decision. "I'm going home, Delmar. I'll do the paperwork on Lem's arrest tomorrow."

"I'll start it for you," Delmar offered. "You can fill in the blanks in the morning when you get here. Shoot, by now I know old Lem's statistics almost as well as my own."

But John Thomas wasn't listening. His mind was stuck on the sound of a ringing phone in an empty house and wondering where the hell his lady had gone. Taking the squad car in place of his pickup on the off chance that he might need to use the radio to call for help, he made the run from Rusk to his farm in little under eight minutes and was thankful that he was on the good side of the law. In his youth, he could easily have wound up in jail for pulling a stunt like this.

It was close to dusk as he turned down the driveway. Even from here he could tell that the house was too dark. There was no door opening in welcome, or Samantha's smile to pull him inside. No dog came bounding out to meet him. There was nothing to prove anyone was inside.

He parked in a skid of flying dirt and gravel and jumped out on the run, praying with every step that she would be there, and then praying that she wouldn't. At least if she was gone, she might still be alive.

He knocked on the door and then yelled her name but got no answer. With fear lending speed to his steps, he leaped off the porch and began running around the house toward the back door. If he had to, he would break it down.

9

SAMANTHA'S LEFT FOOT was asleep and her back ached from the cramped position in which she was sitting. Slumped in the corner of the kitchen, she watched while the afternoon sun fell toward the horizon and then long after the evening shadows had nearly covered the entire floor space.

Her eyes burned and the intense fear with which she'd begun her standoff had turned into steel-lipped determination. The months of living in fear that had nearly destroyed her were gone. Being in Johnny's company for the past few weeks had given her a whole new perspective on being stalked. She might not be able to stop her killer, but she had spent her last day feeling helpless.

More than once her eyes had strayed to the kitchen clock over the sink as she prayed for five o'clock to come. But when it had come and gone with no sign of Johnny, it had taken some of her bravado with it.

A sudden fear surfaced. What if the stalker had decided to take out part of his anger on the man who'd stolen her away? What if Johnny's life was also in danger and they hadn't suspected?

"Johnny, come home," she whispered. He needed to know that she'd found the letters. She needed to tell him how much he still meant to her.

Shocked by the panic in her own voice, she took a deep breath and squeezed her eyes shut, only to feel tears trailing down the inside of her cheek past her nose.

Rebel sighed and shifted position beside her, but he did not move other than to scoot his head a little higher along her thigh, nosing toward the hand that rested along the wooden stock of the double-barreled shotgun.

Lost in a half-doze, she didn't hear the sound of the car driving up. But the footsteps that hit the wooden planks on the front porch and the sharp and sudden pounding that began at the other end of the house brought her upright and shaking in seconds.

She head shouts, but before she could hear what was being said, Rebel began to bark and then all she could hear was his wild, frantic baying echoing in what had, moments ago, been deathly silence.

"Oh my God," Samantha moaned. "He's back!"

She struggled to her feet and set the butcher knife on the sill beside her, needing both hands to steady the gun she'd shifted to hip level. If he broke in, maybe she could bluff him into thinking it was loaded. If not, the knife was near at hand. It was all she could do except run, and that time was past. As she waited in fear, a small and unexpected surge of relief came with it. At least the waiting was over.

Everything was a replay of before. The sound of running footsteps along the outside of the house, and then the distinct thud they made when they hit the back porch at a dead run.

Samantha's hands shook as she stared at the inside of the kitchen door, trying to imagine her stalker on the other side, trying to picture what his intentions must be. But the voice she heard was unexpected and so very, very welcome. Her prayers had been answered.

"Sam! *Samantha Jean!* Are you in there? Dammit, honey, open the door!"

It was Johnny! And from the way he was shouting and knocking, if she didn't hurry, he would be coming through the door, rather than waiting for her to open it. Rebel danced at her feet as she dropped the gun and staggered over the furniture she'd barricaded at the door.

"Johnny, is that you?"

John Thomas went weak at the sound of her voice.

"Cross my heart and hope to die," he said, startled to hear the tremble in his own voice, and then leaned his forehead against the rough outer surface of the door and waited to see her face.

He heard the sounds of furniture being moved, his

dog's crazy welcome bark that wouldn't stop, and the metallic slide of the dead bolt being moved. The door opened, and without giving him time to come inside, Samantha flew into his arms.

"My God, Sam, what's wrong? What the hell happened to you? You didn't answer the phone. I was afraid—"

He stopped talking as he began to absorb the terrible shudders of her body and the state of the kitchen behind her. With a firm push, he walked them both inside the house, then closed the door and grabbed her by the shoulders.

"Talk to me."

She looked up and then started to cry. As the tears fell, the story spilled out of her in achy gulps.

"Someone tried to break in. Rebel kept barking and growling at the front door and then I heard whoever it was come around to the back of the house."

She took a deep breath and pointed toward the overturned chairs in the room behind her.

"That was when I realized the back door wasn't locked. I outran him to the kitchen and . . . almost didn't make it."

When he looked down at her skinned knees and the lingering terror in her eyes, he realized how close her call had been.

"Jesus Christ!" The anger in is voice wasn't directed at her and she knew it, and still Samantha couldn't stop herself from flinching.

"Oh, honey, that wasn't meant for you," he said, angry with himself at the fear he'd put on her face. He opened his arms. She walked into them without hesitation.

"I know, Johnny. But for lack of a better explanation, I've just had a really bad day." She tried to smile and wound up crying harder when he cupped her face and kissed each corner of her mouth with gentle anguish.

John Thomas felt sick. "Why didn't you call me, sweetheart? Carol Ann said she tried all afternoon to contact you and each time, all it did was ring."

His hands traced and retraced the contour of her body as he held her. When he thought of how fragile life was and how close he'd come to losing her, he shook.

"The phones are dead, Johnny. I tried both of them. When I knew I couldn't get you, I just hid and waited for you to come get me."

"My God."

It was then he noticed the shotgun lying on the table and caught a glimpse of the butcher knife resting on the windowsill just beneath the curtain. What hell had she gone through waiting for him to come home?

"Sam, that gun is empty."

"I know."

Guilt hit him in the belly like a fist. He couldn't bear to think of how helpless she must have felt sitting alone in the house with a dog, a knife, and an empty gun for protection.

"Wait here, honey. I'm going outside to look around." After one last hug, he headed out the door with Rebel at his heels.

It didn't take him long to find the smaller set of footprints beside his own, or notice the way they had circled the house. It took even less time to see that the phone wire had been cut and was lying half covered by the loose dirt. He picked it up and looked at the neat, clean incision that had severed Samantha's connection with the outside world.

"Son of a bitch." There was nothing else he could say. While John Thomas had been out playing sheriff and arresting a man who needed to be locked up for life in the nearest rehab center, the stalker had come and played havoc with Samantha's sanity.

And he had no doubt that the bastard had been playing with her. From the isolation of his house and the fact that Sam had no way of leaving, it was obvious that he could have done with her as he chose, even burned down the place with her inside had he wanted. Evidently he had more torment in mind for her before it came to that.

John Thomas shuddered, remembering the hate mail and the phone threats she'd received, as well as the stalker's promises that death would cleanse, death would heal. Just who the hell needed healing was no secret to John Thomas, but next time it would be a race to the death if he couldn't beat the stalker to Samantha.

He cursed helplessly as he headed for his squad car

to call for help, unable to believe that his own home was now the scene of a crime.

Deputy Lawler came with Monty. The squall of their siren and the whirling lights atop the county squad car as they pulled into the yard set Rebel off into another round of howling.

"They're here," Samantha said, glimpsing the flashing lights through the living room curtains as she slid off of John Thomas's lap.

It was dusk, but John Thomas had a need to follow up on one more idea before nightfall, and he'd had to wait until help arrived before he could implement his plan.

After giving Samantha a quick hug, he bolted from the couch and out the door.

"Leave your lights on," he ordered as his deputies parked, "and don't walk in the area I've roped off. That's where he ran."

"What happened?" Monty asked. "All we were told was someone tried to break in. Is Samantha all right?"

"She's fine. Scared to death. But unhurt, except for skinned knees. Right now, I want you two to go over the crime scene. Maybe you'll find something I missed. I've got another plan in mind, and I couldn't leave until you got here to stay with Sam."

"We ain't budgin'," Mike Lawler said.

"I'll be back before too long," John Thomas said. "Whatever you do, just don't leave her here alone."

"You can count on us, boss," Monty said, and got his flashlight out from beneath the seat.

Samantha walked out onto the porch and tried not to let it show, but the tremble in her voice gave her away. She was still scared to death.

"Where are you going?" she asked.

John Thomas walked back up the steps and took her in his arms. He smoothed the hair away from her face and traced the tilt of her upturned nose with his fore-finger.

"I'm going to take Rebel and see if he can track him. If I can find a starting and stopping point, it'll go a long way toward finding out who it might have been."

"We'll be right here with you," Mike Lawler assured her.

She nodded, satisfied with his explanation and the fact that she wouldn't be alone. "I'm going to make supper. You guys will stay and eat, won't you?"

"Yes, ma'am," they answered in unison.

When she'd walked out onto the porch, both men had seen the remnants of stark terror and lingering tears. At this point, they would have refused her nothing.

Monty looked away. He couldn't bear to watch the way the sheriff was holding Samantha. It reminded him too much of his own personal loss. Anger filled him, and then he cursed beneath his breath and stuffed his emotions back where they belonged. He began his

own investigation, leaving Lawler to whatever he chose
to do.

When Samantha went back into the house, she purposely left the door ajar. Somehow, just hearing the
men's voices so close by, and knowing that she was no
longer trapped within the four walls of the house, made
it easier to bear.

"Damn!"

John Thomas kicked at a rock on the side road
where Rebel's trail had ended. He knelt, lightly tracing
his fingers across the faint tracks of the vehicle that
had been parked there earlier.

Whoever it was had been driving an oil burner with
a narrow wheel base. From the size of the big, greasy
stain on the ground, it leaked like a sieve.

Rebel whined and circled the area, his nose to the
dirt in a constant snuffle as he tried to pick up the lost
scent.

"It's no use, boy," he said, and whistled him home.
"Your prey got tricky. This one didn't climb a tree on
you. He crawled into a vehicle and just drove the hell
away."

Minutes later John Thomas came out of the woods
at a jog with Rebel off the leash, yards ahead of him
and chasing shadows. The lights of home welcomed
him from across the meadow. It looked and sounded
like any other warm, summer night.

Crickets were singing. A tree frog had turned up on

the creek, and at least half a dozen bullfrogs were in full chorus competition. But it wasn't like any other night. Today someone had invaded his privacy and threatened his woman, and he was mad as hell.

Then he paused, *My woman? When did I start thinking of her as mine?*

But there was no answer other than the one inside John Thomas's heart. Right where it had been all along.

It was after ten o'clock before John Thomas sent the deputies home. After dinner they had pooled information they'd gleaned from their separate investigations.

All Samantha knew was that the telephone would be fixed tomorrow. Past that, they'd told her nothing. She suspected it was because there was nothing to tell.

She, better than anyone, knew how tricky her stalker could be. He'd fooled the entire LAPD, and depending on which side you took, had made her look either like a fanatic with a vivid imagination, or a nutcase with a persecution complex.

John Thomas watched the men leave, then left Rebel standing guard on the front porch as he came inside, shut the door, then locked it behind him.

"You think that's going to keep him out?" Samantha asked quietly.

The resignation on her face and the weary slump of her shoulders worried him. She couldn't give up now.

"Why don't you go take a bath, darlin'? I'll clean up the kitchen."

She shook her head. "When he came . . . I was taking a bath. I don't want to go in there by myself again."

He held out his hand. "Then come on, Sam. You don't have to do anything by yourself, ever. Remember? That's why you have me."

She reached up for him, and as she did, her fingers gently traced the path of the old, faint scar on his wrist.

He smiled.

Their hands clasped and then intertwined just as his words had wrapped around her heart and gave her legs the strength to stand.

"Will you wash my back?" she asked, trying to lighten the moment.

"If you will wash my hair," he said with a grin. "You haven't heard the story of me and Lem Marshall fighting in the barnyard, and how I fell headfirst into the cow lot before he tripped on the milk bucket and knocked himself out."

"You're kidding!" Samantha had to chuckle at the far-fetched image.

"I wish I was, but I'm not. And what I told you is a secret. No one besides Lem knows what really happened, and he was so drunk he won't remember all the facts. At least I hope to hell he doesn't. I'll never live it down if he starts telling everyone that I was face-first in dry cow manure when he captured himself."

Samantha's face broke into a wide grin. "It seems I wasn't the only one who had a bad hair day."

Their shared laughter was enough to get them to the

bathroom. And it lasted until the water started running. But when it came time for their clothes to come off, neither could find the words to say that would make this work.

"Why don't you go first," he offered. "You can leave the door open. I'll be right outside. When you're through, we'll just trade places."

She nodded.

John Thomas walked out of the bathroom. His heart ached for her. And he was sick and tired of this stalemate between them.

Dammit! She had been his best friend before she was his lover. He wanted that back now . . and more.

He knew he needed to find a way to tell her he didn't care that she hadn't answered his damn letters. That was years ago. What was past, was past. What mattered was here and now, and as far as he was concerned, he was as lost in love as he'd been fifteen years ago.

Minutes passed. He heard water splashing, and bubbles popping, and soon after, the swift sucking sound of water flowing down the drain. He leaned against the wall and closed his eyes, trying to ignore the fact that only three or so feet away, Samantha was as bare as the day she was born, because he was only three or so feet away, as hard and aching as he'd ever been in his life.

"Johnny."

"What?"

"I found my letters."

Without thinking, shock pulled him through the door. She was standing by the tub with the towel clutched in front of her, a nervous expression in her eyes, and a tremble on her lips.

He took a deep breath and stuffed his hands in his jeans to keep from yanking the towel out of her arms.

"And?" he prodded.

"I read them." She started to cry.

Speech was impossible. And as he crossed the distance between them and took her in his arms, the towel slipped unheeded to the floor between them.

"I should have believed you. I should have known better than to doubt you," she whispered, as she wrapped her arms around him and buried her face against his chest. "Can you ever forgive me? I swear I didn't know."

"I'd already figured that much out, darlin'," he said softly.

"When?" she asked, startled by his revelation.

"The other night when you threw the coffee cup at me. I never knew anyone to have that much righteous indignation and still be lying."

She smiled through tears. "Where do we go from here?" she asked.

He leaned down, picked up the towel, and handed it to her with a weak grin.

"I wash Lem Marshall's manure off of me and you crawl in bed. After that, we'll see."

To Samantha, it sounded like too good a deal to pass

up. But her day had been too traumatic. In spite of anxious anticipation, she fell asleep holding his pillow.

And when John Thomas came into the room a few minutes later, he didn't have the heart to wake her. He simply unwound her from his pillow, slipped his arms around her, and pulled her as close against him as he could get her. It was the only way he could face closing his eyes. He'd come too close to losing her today.

It was 3 A.M. when Samantha rolled over in bed and sat up with a scream on her lips that never made it to life. John Thomas was awake instantly, telling her over and over in his deep, husky voice that she was safe, and the rough texture of his hands on her body added the final note of assurance.

She turned and fell into his arms. "Love me, Johnny. Please."

Her plea shook his soul. With a harsh, muttered oath, he rolled over on top of her and slid between her legs before she had time to think. And when he could think, he remembered the protection he'd forgotten to use and started to withdraw.

"Don't," Samantha pleaded. "Don't leave me."

"I'm not going anywhere. I just wasn't . . . dressed . . . for the occasion."

He dug in the bedside table and then held up the small, foil packet to emphasize his point. Moments later he was back.

He shook as he held her. The memory of their first time together kept getting tangled in the need of the moment. Then he'd been clumsy and so crazy for her that he'd nearly lost his head before he'd ever claimed her. But somehow she hadn't noticed, or hadn't cared.

To this day, he could still remember her shudder and then her sigh when he'd taken her virginity. After that, most of it was a blur of white-hot emotion and a blinding rush toward a climax he couldn't stop. This time, he'd be damn sure that Samantha got the best of the bargain.

Her breath caught in the back of her throat as his lips moved from her arm to her breast and back again. A low growl of satisfaction came up his throat, tingling the surface of her skin.

"Hurry, Johnny."

"No, baby," he whispered. "Not this time. This time, you come first."

She shivered as his tongue traced the darker center of her breasts. He laughed softly, and the sound scattered against her skin as his hands did a search and seizure of their own. She dug her fingers into his hair and held on, because she knew that if she didn't, she would fall off of this ride.

"So small," he whispered, circling her waist with his hands. "Ah, God, so soft. So ready," he said, as his fingers dipped between her legs and tested the territory for future invasion.

Samantha moaned. He was playing with her and she

didn't care. Every touch of his mouth made her ache. Every stroke of his hands made her want. Every pressure point on her body had been marked by a kiss, and it was not enough.

He moved. And when the weight of his body settled upon her, Samantha sighed. The feeling was like coming home. It was familiar, and at the same time, so different. The boy that had loved her had become a man. So much a man.

"Please, Johnny. Make love to me," she whispered. "You could always make everything right." Her voice broke as she hugged him to her. His hair felt thick and springy beneath her hands as she cradled his head against her breast. "I need you to do that for me again, Johnny. I need you to make me forget everything but you."

"Then make room for me," he said.

Within a heartbeat, her legs had shifted, giving way to the stronger, more urgent thrust of his manhood. At the moment of entry, he paused.

"This time, Sam, it won't hurt," he whispered. "I'll never hurt you again."

He moved. And when he did, bit his lower lip and closed his eyes to keep from losing control. But it was hopeless. After the second stroke he knew he could very well be in danger of dying of joy. He tried to slow down the inevitable. He wanted this pleasure, this closeness, never to end. But it was an impossible thing to hope for. He'd waited too long for this feeling, and it was too good to stop.

Samantha moved. She wrapped her legs around his waist, and pulled him closer, deeper, tighter. And when she did, everything spiraled as sensation overcame sanity. Pleasure splintered thought, and became a means to an end as Samantha began to burn.

John Thomas groaned as her legs tightened around him. And when she cried aloud from joy, and her honey poured over him, the pleasure became more than he could bear.

He felt it coming. The loss of control. The sensation of losing oneself within another human being. And in that moment when there was nothing left in the world but the fireburst, it happened. Colors splintered behind his eyelids as a warm weakness flooded throughout his body.

"Johnny . . ."

"Don't talk, love," he whispered, as he rained kisses across her face and mouth "And don't move. I'll be right back."

Samantha sighed as he rolled out of bed and walked out of the room. And moments later, when he came back, he scooped her into his arms, and began kissing her all over again.

"Just so I don't forget the good spots," he said softly.

She laughed and then she began to cry. Only this time, it was from joy.

"I don't think 1 deserve you, Johnny," she said through tears.

"Probably not," he whispered, and then grinned. "But we all make sacrifices in the line of duty."

John Thomas never knew whether it was from joy or from fear, but when she finally quit crying, she slept. Only then could he give in to his own desperate fears when, for a space of time today, he thought he'd lost her.

He closed his eyes, moved her closer so that her head rested against his chest, and wrapped his arms around her shoulders to hold her in place.

All of his life Johnny Knight had fought for the right to be, and only Sam had understood and accepted him the way he was. He sighed as his fingers traced the tracks of drying tears on her cheeks.

He couldn't remember the last time he'd cried, but he knew for a fact that it was before he ever started school. After that, he hadn't had time to. He'd been too busy trying to survive.

Samantha sighed, and he shifted slightly beneath her, allowing her to settle back before he brushed the stray lock of her hair away from his face.

It was then that he felt the tears on his own cheeks and realized he had been crying and didn't know why, and told himself that it was too late and too dark to care. God willing, there would be other days and other nights to figure out why a woman had done what a lifetime of fighting had been unable to do.

"Is this entirely necessary?" Samantha asked, as she stuffed the last of her meager belongings into a suitcase and added it to the stash of stuff by the door.

"You can't stay out here by yourself again. And I'm not willing to lock you up in jail just to keep you safe. We're going to rent a place in Rusk until that son of a bitch is caught, and that's that."

"I wasn't arguing, I was just asking," she said.

"And I just answered," he said shortly. "I love you too damned much to risk another fright like we both had yesterday. Hell, lady. I nearly died of a heat attack and I'm only thirty-three years old."

She smiled at the thought. Johnny loved her.

"Who will take care of Rebel?" she asked.

"Mike Lawler's brother rents the farmland from me. He's out every day to check on his cattle. He said he'd feed and water my dog until we came back."

She nodded. It seemed that he'd thought of everything.

"Do you have a place in mind?" she asked, aware that Rusk wasn't actually overflowing with rental property on a day-to-day basis.

"There's an empty upstairs apartment in the house where Monty lives. It's right in the heart of the old part of town. The house isn't much, but there are neighbors on all sides and it's only a couple of blocks from the office."

"I'm ready when you are," Samantha said.

"Then let's go, darlin'. I've got one madman on the loose, and another in jail that I've got to transfer out, not to mention a band of rustlers and one unhappy rancher who's shy fifty head of prime beef."

"But at least you're starting out with clean hair," she said with a grin.

"I may regret ever telling you that," he said, rolling his eyes as he began carrying bags and suitcases to the squad car.

"No you won't," Samantha said, suddenly serious after such a lighthearted remark. "I always kept your secrets, Johnny. Remember?"

He turned and then stared at the look on her face. Suddenly, without warning, he dropped the bags and started toward her with an expression she was coming to recognize.

"You'll be late for work," she said, as she started to back up.

"At this point, do you think I care?"

Daringly, she reached out and gently cupped the hard bulge behind his zipper then shook her head.

"Darlin,' you just read my mind."

"I always knew your brain was in your pants," she said, teasing him a little as he picked her up and started down the hall toward the bedroom.

"I have no brains where you're concerned. Only love, Sam. A deep, abiding, overwhelming love."

The thick trees surrounding the old, gray lady of a house spread welcome shade beneath which John Thomas parked.

"So, what do you think?" he asked nervously, fear-

ing that its decrepit look might be the last thing it took
to push Samantha over the edge.

"I like it," she said, smiling and pointing at the same
time toward the upstairs windows. "It has air-
conditioning."

He laughed. He should have known it would take
more than an aging house to put her off, especially
after what she'd been through.

He looked in the rear-view mirror at the car pulling
up, and then smiled. "Your ride has arrived."

Samantha looked out the widow. Deputy Turner had
driven up in the pickup John Thomas had left at the department last night.

As he helped her out of the squad car, Sam craned
her head for a better look at the deputy and Johnny's
truck.

"What do you mean, my ride? Is Monty taking me
somewhere?"

"No, darlin'. I'm leaving my pickup for you. You don't
think I'm going to leave you here afoot, do you? Until this
sucker's caught, I'll drive the squad car and you get the
truck. I don't want you to ever feel trapped again."

Monty rounded the end of the car with the truck
keys in his hand just as she stepped into John Thomas's
arms.

"Oh, Johnny, I'm already trapped . . . by you." She
traced the outline of his belt buckle with her fingernail,
delighting in the way his eyes widened with shock as

it scratched lightly against the metal. "If I could bottle and sell what you have, we'd both be millionaires."

She laughed aloud at the faint blush spreading across his cheeks but didn't regret a word that she'd said. It did him good to get nervous once in a while.

Monty stopped in midstep and did an about-face. He'd seen the way they were looking at each other, as well as the flush that swept across his boss's face. He'd heard her soft, gentle laugh, and the way she'd stepped into his arms as if she were coming home. His heart ached, thinking of what they had and what he'd lost.

"Hey, Turner," John Thomas said, as he saw his newest deputy turn away. "Now's no time to get bashful. Besides, if I know Sam, it'll only make her worse. Come make yourself useful. We've got to empty this squad car before we can go back to work."

Monty ducked his head, and handed Samantha the keys before loading up with bags and heading up the steps with the sheriff and his lady right behind him.

"Whose truck is that?" John Thomas asked, pointing to the old black pickup parked at the end of the yard beneath a tall pine.

"A waitress from Marylee's Café outside of Cotton drives it. Marylee gave her a job and loaned her the truck until she can make enough money to get home. She got dumped by some trucker. Real shame how some women get treated. Her name's Claudia something or other. She won't bother you any. She works nights, sleeps days."

John Thomas laughed. "I think I know who you mean, but did you happen to get her age, make, and serial number, buddy? You seem to know everything else about her."

Monty blushed and grinned but refused to admit to anything other than what he'd already revealed.

"I got the key just like you asked," Monty said, as they reached the door to their apartment. "Let me set this stuff down and I'll unlock it for you."

The door swung open with a slight squeak. "Just needs a little WD-40," he explained, and then looked away, unwilling to see the joy on Samantha's face.

Samantha wondered as she entered why the deputy stared at her when he thought she wasn't looking, and then looked away when she was. She couldn't quite put her finger on it, but felt that there was something very sad about him.

"Wow!" She walked around the rooms, staring and poking at everything in sight. "No one would believe this."

"I know it's a little rough," John Thomas said. "But remember, it's only temporary."

"No," she said. "You don't understand. This stuff would bring a fortune back in L.A. Vintage thirties and forties furnishings are in vogue, you know."

Monty tried not to grin, but John Thomas's chuckle was too infectious to ignore. "Are you kidding me?" John Thomas asked, staring at the aging furniture and accessories.

"No way! You know how people with money are. They want what they can't or don't have."

"Well, that sounds sort of stupid," Monty said before he thought. "I'm physically unable to have babies and have yet to have a heart attack, and honestly folks, I'm not losing any sleep over either loss."

Samantha collapsed onto the wing-back sofa, buried her face in her hands, and laughed. Every time she looked back up at the young deputy and the sheepish grin on his face, she laughed even harder.

John Thomas rolled his eyes and went after the rest of their belongings. He didn't care why or at whose expense it came, but he was damned glad to hear her happy.

Sometime later, when everything had been moved indoors, and Samantha was in possession of all the necessary keys and money for groceries, she found herself alone. And this time, for some strange reason, she wasn't afraid.

Maybe it was because she knew she was only blocks away from the sheriff's office. Or maybe it was because she'd lived so long in a city that being able to look out a window and see other people and into other homes gave her a false sense of security.

Regardless of the reason, Samantha knew that from now on, whatever happened, she would be ready.

10

IN THE DAYS THAT FOLLOWED, it became evident that neither Samantha nor John Thomas was good at waiting. Sometimes she believed that they'd outmaneuvered the stalker by moving into town, but other times she felt as if she'd traded one jail for another. She was still hiding behind four walls.

And John Thomas watched with a nervous eye as Samantha's nerves deteriorated. Day by day she became edgier and he saw her mask frustration behind smiles. When he tried to get her to talk, she turned and walked out of the room. The only part of their relationship that wasn't suffering from the prolonged waiting was the long nights of making love.

On this day, as every day since this nightmare had started, he sat at his desk with a formidable stack of paperwork yet to be done and tried unsuccessfully to concentrate. His mind kept wandering to the inhabitants of the house where he and Sam were staying. Even though the four apartment units in the old Earl house were now all rented, they were rarely occupied at the same time.

Claudia the waitress worked from 3 P.M. to 11 P.M. and didn't actually count in the scheme of things. She was a transient in the act of moving on as soon as she accumulated enough money for a bus ticket home.

And his deputy, he was the most surprising element of all. John Thomas knew for a fact that the man rarely, if ever, slept there. When he was off duty, his car was never in the parking lot and the lights in his apartment were never on.

When he heard Monty's voice in the back of the office and then heard Carol Ann's high-pitched giggle, he smiled. It shouldn't surprise him that Montgomery Turner didn't sleep alone. He was young and, he supposed, unattached.

But John Thomas wondered, if Monty was keeping such footloose hours with his free time, why he wasn't also coming to work with a bleary-eyed but smiling face. Why the sad, haunted expression instead?

So he sleeps in another woman's bed. That's on big deal, John Thomas told himself, and picked up another file on his desk. But curiosity about the inhabitants of the old house kept niggling at his lawman's soul.

As for the young couple across the hall from his deputy, their life was pretty much an open book. They hadn't been hitched long enough for the *Just Married* letters painted across their back windshield in white shoe polish to have washed away. And from the look of the young girl's swollen belly, they'd barely made it to the altar before their first child was to enter into this world.

He tossed down his pen, kicked his heels up on the desk, and locked his hands behind his head as he stared absently at the ceiling.

If Samantha's family had never left Cotton, she would have been here when I came home on leave. Maybe then her father would have seen I could be trusted. Maybe he would have . . .

He closed his eyes and cursed softly to himself. Just thinking about Samantha and marriage and babies made him ache. He'd never dreamed of having a home because, after Samantha, he'd never found a woman he wanted to spend more than a night with. But that was before her letter. Before she came back into his life. Now he couldn't imagine his world without her.

What-ifs weren't in John Thomas's vocabulary. He was partial to the facts and the facts were that he was head over heels in love with a woman who was being stalked, and that he couldn't keep her safe. Here he was, an officer of the law, with all the latest crime-fighting tools at his disposal and he still couldn't catch one sick son of a bitch who got off by scaring women.

As for the waitress across the hall, she was the least ⸍ their worries. She left for work before he came ⸍ne. Rarely did he get more than a glimpse of her.

She seemed friendly, but always in a hurry. And he had to admit that it was nice to have the entire top floor of the house to themselves when they went to bed. Having a witness within hearing distance of their love-making might have been intimidating.

And as he thought about making love to Samantha, his boots came off the desk with a thump. He was out of the office before Carol Ann knew he was gone.

The front door slammed. Carol Ann looked up in time to see an odd, resigned expression slide over Deputy Turner's face.

"There he goes again," Monty said. "I didn't know he had a call."

"The only call he hears these days is a call of the wild." She laughed at her own wit.

Monty nodded. "I didn't hear any bells ring, but I'll lay money the boss did. Hell, maybe he's hearing wedding bells and just doesn't know it."

Carol Ann started to laugh again, and then she saw the sad expression on Monty's face.

"I think I'll take a drive out toward the Watkins ranch and circle the section a time or two. Maybe our cattle rustlers will be stupid enough to try for a repeat. If they do, we'll be ready," he said.

He tipped his hat at her and winked, but the shadows were still in place. Carol Ann made a note of where he was going, and winced as the back door slammed behind him.

Now why would a young fellow like Monty Turn

resent John Thomas? Carol Ann wondered. There was no earthly reason he should care what his boss did.

Samantha heard his footsteps on the stairs, closed her eyes, and counted the number of thumps that he made then smiled. He was running. She shivered in anticipation of what was coming.

Maybe she should get undressed. Then she changed her mind within the same breath. There was no reason to make his life any easier than it already was.

In spite of her determination to ignore the fact that he was forty-five minutes early, Samantha met him at the door. He took one look at the grin on her face and lifted her off of her feet.

"I suppose you think you're psychic," he growled, planting separate kisses beneath each earlobe before walking them into the room and kicking the door shut behind him.

"Why, Sheriff, whatever do you mean? And pray tell, sir, why exactly *are* you here? Am I under arrest? If so, I suppose you'll be wanting to frisk me. Should I assume the position or do you want to . . ."

His hands splayed across her rear and pulled her close within the cradle of his hips, rocking her gently against a growing ache as he tried hard to glare. "You, my woman, can assume any position you choose, and you should know that I hate a smart-mouthed criminal. Why can't I just find one who'll take her punishment quietly?"

Samantha's heart tugged. *His woman.* A long time ago she would have crawled at his feet to hear those words. Now, she wasn't exactly sure what she wanted to do, but she knew that it involved getting closer—much closer—to the man who held her fast within his arms.

"So, if I'm in trouble, exactly what did I do?" she asked, and began pulling his shirt from his pants and unbuckling his holster.

He shrugged and tried to smile when he wanted to cry. "You stole my heart, darlin'. You just walked in and took it without a word. What's a man to do when something like that happens?"

"Make the punishment fit the crime, I always say," she answered, and he beat her to the punch by taking off the rest of his clothes, boots and all, leaving them in a pile beside the front door.

The proof of his desire was there. All she had to do was look. And she did. Her breath caught as she shuddered uncontrollably, partly from anticipation, partly from need. And then his hands were on her body.

"In case you don't already know, this procedure is called a strip search." Laughter was rich in his voice as his hands teased the clothes from her body.

"All I ask is that you don't hurt me," she said, still lost in the game that they'd begun, and then gasped when his hands lingered too long in a tantalizing spot

"Darlin', what I have in mind doesn't hurt at all. fact, it's guaranteed to make the worst sinner beg mercy and plead for more."

"Then I'm all yours, Sheriff."

"I knew that, love, or I wouldn't be here," he whispered.

At that moment the game was over. When he lifted her in his arms and carried her to the bed, she clung to him in sudden desperation.

He felt the mood changing between them as she began to tremble. He cuddled her gently, stroking a finger across each dark, winged brow, marveling at the way each of her features fit together to form the woman called Samantha that he knew and loved.

"What's wrong, sweetheart?"

"I just had a premonition. What if he wins? Oh, Johnny, what if he wins?" She buried her face in her hands.

The fact that she had some of his same fears made him angry, but not at her, only at himself for being unable to make her world perfect. He pulled her hands away from her face and kissed each feature with slow deliberation.

"No, Sam, he won't! Now don't think. Don't talk. Just feel. Remember when I asked you if you'd ever made love blindfolded?"

She swallowed and then shuddered as his hands cupped her firm breasts and then traced a path down to her rib cage.

She nodded. "I remember. And you don't need to blindfold me, Johnny, I'll just close my eyes, and I promise I won't peek. Cross my heart and—"

He silenced the last of her vow as his fingers moved across her face and gently closed her eyelids.

"Remember, love. Don't move. Don't think. Just feel."

And so she did.

Claudia stood in the hallway between the two apartments with tears streaming down her face. It was an accident that she'd heard any of their conversation. Actually she'd only heard sounds, not words, but it was enough to know that on the other side of that door a man and woman were sharing something she'd lost. Love.

Once her life had been that simple. Once her life had been that happy. Then she remembered how she'd gotten here, and remembered her job and what it was going to take to get her home. She swiped angrily at her tears, and then ran down the stairs as quickly as the sheriff had run up.

It was 6 A.M. when Montgomery Turner drove into the yard of the Earl house and parked. Headlights of a vehicle pulling in behind momentarily blinded him. When his vision had cleared, he had a swift impression of long legs and blond hair. Claudia, the waitress, was getting home. It was long past her quitting time and he wondered if she'd found herself a new man. He frowned. Everyone had someone but him.

He waited until she was inside before he got out of

his car and entered his own apartment. It looked and smelled the same, and yet tonight something was very different. He was no longer the same man he'd been when he left. After what had occurred tonight, he would never be the same.

He dropped into the chair closest to the window and watched the arrival of dawn through the sheer, white curtains. The sun rose above the horizon with the promise of a new day ahead. And with that thought came a rush of gut-wrenching, heart-stopping tears.

With a loud groan of defeat, he buried his face in his hands and gave way to the pain eating away inside him. Later, when he could think, and when he could feel, he would know that everything that had happened this night was ultimately for the best. But for now, he was too lost in the pain of remembering, of thinking of how things used to be, before the nightmare began, before his world came crashing to an end.

"Hey there, Sheriff," Pete Meuller yelled, and started across the street at a jog.

About to get into his squad car and go out on a call, John Thomas looked up in surprise to see the mechanic from Cotton coming across the street toward him at a fast pace.

"What's up, Pete? I haven't seen you move like that since someone stole your best set of wrenches."

Pete puffed and grinned, holding on to his chest in an effort to stop his racing heart. "I'm gonna have to quit smoking one of these days," he muttered, and then turned away and coughed.

John Thomas waited. Knowing Pete, eventually he'd get around to telling him why he'd come calling.

"You remember asking us to all be on the lookout for strangers coming to Cotton?" Pete said.

John Thomas's pulse suddenly kicked into high gear. Just the thought of a break in the case made him anxious.

Pete waited for the sheriff to nod. When he did, then he felt ready to continue.

"Well, a short time back, a man pulled into the station in a foreign job. One of them Jaguars."

John Thomas grinned at Pete's pronunciation of the automobile. It came out sounding like *Jag-you-war*.

"Anyway, it was damn near blowed up and the driver was mad as hell, especially after I told him yesterday that it will be another week before the rest of the parts get in." He ducked his head and spit before continuing. "Just between you and me, I'll be lucky if I can get that blasted thing running again at all. He was driving it without engine oil. How come all the people who can afford nice rides don't have the faintest idea of what it takes to run 'em?"

"I don't know," John Thomas said. "Let's get back to this stranger. What did you say his name was, and where is he staying? I think I'd like to check out his reasons for being in Cotton."

Pete nodded importantly. "That's just what I thought

you'd say. His name is Aaron Reuben, and he's staying at the Texas Pig Motel."

"Thanks for the information, Pete," John Thomas said.

"Don't mention it," he said, as he started to walk away. And then he slapped his leg and stopped. "Dang! I plumb near forgot. That Reuben fellow . . ."

John Thomas waited.

"He's from California."

Pete walked away and missed seeing the blood drain from the sheriff's face. And even if he had, he probably would have chalked it up to the intense noonday heat rather than shock.

"Damn," John Thomas said, and ran back into the headquarters.

"Carol Ann, where's Lawler?"

"He's out on a call. And Willis just called in. He's on the west side of the county with a flat tire and no jack. Someone from the garage forgot to put it back when they did the overhaul. He's mad as a wet hen."

"Who's not busy?" he asked, wanting someone with him when he went on this call, just in case he got lucky. If this was really the stalker and he saw a lawman at the door, he might run. And John Thomas didn't want to risk losing him. He needed backup, just in case.

"Deputy Turner comes on duty in a few—"

"I'm right here," Monty said, as he walked up behind them.

John Thomas turned, then forgot what he'd been
going to say. The devastation on the young man's face
was too painful to miss. A long silence passed as the
two men stared at each other. Somehow, during the
time since he'd last seen Montgomery Turner, a deep,
abiding sorrow had taken root in the younger man. But
the warning in his eyes was as unmistakable as the
pain. Whatever had happened, the deputy wasn't ready
to talk about it. Not yet.

"You up to going with me to interrogate a man who
just might be our stalker?"

Monty's eyes lit up. Not much, but enough to tell
the sheriff that his deputy was ready to do his job.

"Lead the way," he said. "Right now, there's nothing
I'd like better."

"Carol Ann, if you need me, I'll be in Cotton at the
Texas Pig Motel."

"Yes sir," she said, and made a note of the time
they'd departed the office on her log sheet before reading the bulletin coming in over the fax. As the sheriff
and his deputy left town, she was posting the report on
an armed robbery suspect who'd escaped out of Dallas.

Aaron Reuben couldn't believe his ears. Someone was
actually knocking on the door to his motel room. He
punched the mute button on the TV remote so that the
Beverly Hillbillies rerun would continue without
sound.

When he opened the door, the last thing he expected

to see was two policemen, and armed with regulation pistols strapped to their hips. In an area like this, he would have expected horses and six-guns.

"Well I'll be damned," he said. "I didn't hear you ride up." Then he laughed at the insult he'd just dealt.

Being stuck in this backwater part of Texas had long since used up his allotment of social manners. As far as he was concerned, propriety belonged back in L.A., along with nouvelle cuisine, designer water, and beautiful blondes.

John Thomas held his tongue. He'd been insulted by bigger, badder men than this little fellow. He had a job to do, and if this man had any connection to the hell Sam had been going through, he was going to regret it for the rest of his life.

He lowered his voice to somewhere near the decibel level of a clap of thunder "Are you Aaron Reuben?"

The laugh died on Reuben's face. The rough, angry tone of the big lawman's voice made him nervous. He didn't think he liked the look in the lawman's eyes and was pretty sure that the big lawman didn't like him either.

"So I'm Aaron Reuben. Who might you be? Wyatt Earp?"

Monty took instant offense and John Thomas knew it. But he'd seen this man's kind before, and knew that the best way to deal with it was to ignore it.

"I'm John Thomas Knight, sheriff of Cherokee County, and this is my deputy, Montgomery Turner. We have a few questions we'd like you to answer."

Reuben's ulcer kicked into gear as he absorbed the tone of the big man's voice.

"You have questions, I have questions. The whole world wants answers. Hell of a deal, isn't it, Sheriff."

John Thomas ignored the smart-mouthed remark and continued, noting that Monty had taken out a pad and pencil and was ready to take notes.

"How long have you been in Cotton, Mr. Reuben?"

"Too damned long for my peace of mind. My car blows up and the only foreign thing this damned mechanic in Cotton had ever seen are his tools. They're all made in Japan."

Then he stomped outside toward the concrete armadillo and pointed. "And that is what is supposed to pass for art. Can you beat it? A goddamned, cement . . . whatayamacallit."

"Armadillo. It's called an armadillo," Monty said quietly.

"What's your business here, Mr. Reuben?" John Thomas continued.

"What the hell's yours?" he countered, suddenly feeling overwhelmed by this inquisition. In his opinion, it was adding insult to injury.

"Someone tried to harm a woman outside of town a few nights ago. Someone who was most likely a stranger. We are simply checking out everyone in town we don't know, that's all."

"Now that just cuts it," Aaron yelled. "Why would you assume that it has to be a stranger? Are you trying to make me believe that everyone who lives in this godforsaken, hillbilly town is a saint? It was probably just some drunk teenager out to get himself a piece, and got lost before he got off."

"No, it has to be a stranger," John Thomas said. "Because the problem didn't start here in Texas. It started in California—Los Angeles to be exact." His voice got louder and his words shorter as he stepped closer to Aaron Reuben's shocked and sweating face. "And now I find that the son of a bitch who 'got off,' as you call it, on frightening innocent women, has followed her here. That's why I'm asking. And that's why I'm waiting for you to give me an answer that I like, Mr. Reuben. Do we understand each other?"

All he could do was nod.

Monty knew it was time to intervene. He saw murder in his boss's eyes, and knew if John Thomas lost control, he would be difficult to stop. "Mr. Reuben, if you'd be so kind as to give me your driver's license?"

John Thomas recognized his deputy's quiet warning and appreciated it. For a moment, he'd lost focus on the job at hand.

Aaron Reuben quickly obeyed.

"Here." He handed Monty his license. "And just for the record, I work for a small film studio in Hollywood. I was sent to scout out locations for a low-budget movie. East Texas was on my list. When and if I ever get home, make no mistake, I will cross it off."

John Thomas handed Reuben his card. "Just so we understand each other, if you plan on leaving town anytime soon, give me a call first."

Reuben rolled his eyes. "If I could, I would already be gone. I stranded myself in a town with no access to an airport. No taxis. No rental cars. I'm lost in the god-damned twilight zone. That's what."

Having said all he felt brave enough to say, he walked back into his motel room and quietly closed the door.

"Well now," Monty said, smiling for the first time today. "I thought I heard a little dissatisfaction in his voice, what do you think, boss?"

John Thomas grinned. "When we get back to the office, have Carol Ann run the s.o.b.'s information through NCIC. Also have her check and see if there are any outstanding wants or warrants."

"Want me to drive?" Monty asked.

"Yeah, I think I do," John Thomas said, and handed the deputy his keys.

Fifteen minutes later they were the cruising main street when John Thomas turned and looked at the pickup truck that just passed them.

"There went Sam," he said, more to himself than to Monty. It was only later, when they drove up to the department and pulled into the parking lot, that John Thomas realized Monty hadn't said a word since leaving Cotton.

"You okay, Turner?" he asked.

Monty shrugged. "I'll get by." He got out of the car, tossing the car keys to the sheriff as they entered the department.

"If you need to talk . . ."

The offer was left unfinished.

"I'll just get this info to Carol Ann so she can get it on the wire," Monty said. "Do you want me to write up the report?"

"You'd better. I think I might be too personally involved in this whole damned mess for my own good."

"Yeah," Monty drawled, as he walked to his desk and stuffed a piece of typing paper in his typewriter. "That can happen to a man."

Once again Montgomery Turner made an odd comment without elaborating on it to John Thomas's satisfaction. He certainly was a man full of secrets.

A short time later, as he stood in the doorway to his office, looking out at Monty who sat typing the report, a thought occurred to John Thomas. And when it did, he realized that it wasn't the first time he'd had it.

Aaron Reuben wasn't the only stranger to come to town recently. Montgomery Turner had arrived on the heels of his return with Samantha, and what bothered John Thomas more than anything was the fact that Turner wasn't the deputy he'd been expecting. Most disturbing of all, John Thomas hadn't even questioned the switch.

Pivoting, he closed the door behind him. He had a sudden urge to make some phone calls, and maybe when he was through, he would have some answers as

to why Montgomery Turner was here and not somewhere else.

It had taken all evening, and a dozen or more phone
calls, to learn that Montgomery Turner was who he
claimed to be.

According to state headquarters, Turner had graduated near the head of the class. To John Thomas's surprise, Turner had asked to be assigned to him. It
seemed that the rookie had a case of hero-worship
where the Cherokee County sheriff was concerned.

John Thomas slumped forward in his chair, resting
his face in his hands, and then rubbed his eyes wearily
in near defeat. He had a feeling that the stalker was
close by and laughing his head off.

The phone rang.

He grabbed it before the second ring and yelled into
the receiver before he thought to mask his frustration.

"Sheriff's office!"

Mike Pulaski winced, holding the receiver away
from his ear, fearing he was about to get more of the
same. Then he tilted his chair until it hit the wall, hiked
his feet up on the desk, and let the back legs of the
chair balance him and his excess weight.

"Sheriff Knight, Mike Pulaski here."

John Thomas sighed. "Sorry. The call startled me. I
was lost in thought."

"Is that anywhere close to Cotton?" Pulaski asked.
"Get it? Lost in Thought. Lost in Cotton? Lost in L.A.?

Oh hell, never mind," he said with a sigh. "I never could tell a joke."

John Thomas grinned. "I get it," he said. "And for a California cop, it's not half bad."

"Sorry I'm so late in returning your call, but I was out of town. So what's on your mind?" Pulaski asked.

For a moment, John Thomas couldn't figure out what he meant, and then he remembered. Right after they'd moved to town, he'd called Pulaski to let him know what had happened. He'd almost forgotten that Pulaski hadn't called back.

"Oh, I just thought you might like to know that the stalker is here."

Pulaski sat straight up in his chair. "What the hell do you mean, here? Do you have him in custody?"

"Oh hell, no," John Thomas said wearily. "But he has us on pins and needles. He made an attempt to get to Samantha a short time back. She was alone at my house. Luckily my dog was inside with her and, I think, helped scare him off."

"Damn!" Pulaski said. "I'm real sorry about all this. Is she all right?"

"She's fine. And to tell the truth, I think the stalker was just playing with her. He cut the phone lines. She was in an isolated location with no way of escape, and he did nothing but terrorize her."

"Did she see him?"

"No, just heard his footsteps."

"You see what I mean," Pulaski said. "Never enough

to prove a damned thing. And always just her word for corroboration."

John Thomas instantly got mad.

"You still don't get it, do you, Pulaski? Her word has always been enough for me. Besides, I saw footprints, and they were too big for Sam's foot and not big enough for mine. Just in case you try to tell me she put on a pair of my boots and ran around outside for the hell of it."

"You misunderstand me," Pulaski said. "I know she's telling the truth. I've still got a bombed-out apartment as proof. What I meant was the stalker is damned smart. That's all."

John Thomas sighed, then relaxed. "I know. And I understand your side of it a little better myself. I feel like one of those sitting ducks in a carnival sideshow waiting for some stranger to come up and shoot my damned head off."

"Keep me posted," Pulaski said. "And if I get any news, you'll be the first to know."

John Thomas disconnected, glanced up at the clock, and realized that it was past quitting time. With a weary step, he shoved his hat on his head and walked out the door. It was time to go home to Sam.

11

SAMANTHA BURST INTO the sheriff's office and then stopped short and tried not to stare. Two elderly men sat on opposite sides of the room staring glumly at each other. Their bib overalls were covered in mud, and their shirts were spattered with blood. One had a puffy eye, the other a fat lip. Without knowing what had happened, she realized that what she'd come intending to ask was probably out of the question.

She'd just walked to the post office to pick up the mail only to be told that it had accidentally gone out on the route with the rural mail carrier. She wasn't expecting anything since no one in Los Angeles knew where she'd gone, but the thought of driving out to get it was still appealing. Convincing Johnny that it would be safe for her to do so was another matter altogether. And from the looks of the waiting room, talking to him might prove impossible.

Carol Ann walked in with a handful of papers. A wide grin spread across her face when she saw Samantha looking apprehensively at the two old men.

"I don't suppose you'd like to apply for a job?" she asked. "The secretary who's been out sick called in this morning and quit. Her husband's job transferred him to Waco. Meanwhile, because of a bull, Wiley Smith and Pete Hardy here have suddenly decided to dispute a fence line that's stood between their property for the last fifty-five years."

The disgust in her drawl was impossible to miss. Both old men ducked their heads and reminded Samantha of kids waiting to be called into the principal's office. She stared at them, wondering which was Wiley and which was Pete.

"Why does it suddenly matter where the fence is?" she asked them, and then wished she'd kept quiet as both men started talking at once.

"I thought I told you two to shut up!" John Thomas bellowed from the other room.

Samantha grinned as the two old men instantly hushed.

Carol Ann's eyebrows arched and she shrugged, a silent show of sympathy to Samantha. It was all she dared before she left the room. The sheriff was in rare form.

But John Thomas's bad mood seemed to disappear when he came out of his office and saw Samantha waiting with Pete and Wiley.

"Sam! I didn't know you were here. What's up?" he asked, relishing the spurt of pleasure he got from the smile on her face.

"I can see you're busy." She grinned when he rolled his eyes at the understatement. "I just came from the post office. Dan said he forgot to pull your mail for pickup and accidentally let it go out on the route today. One of us will have to go get it."

John Thomas frowned as he considered their options. "I guess we could go this evening after I get off work. At least it'll give us a chance to check on Rebel. He's probably lonesome and thinks I've abandoned him."

"I could go now," Samantha offered, and then could tell from the frown on Johnny's forehead that the idea didn't appeal to him.

"You could not!" he said sharply.

Both old men sat up from their slump and gave the arguing couple their undivided attention, obviously pleased that someone else besides them was in trouble. But Samantha refused to take the first no as gospel.

"I could drive one of the squad cars. It has a radio in it. I wouldn't even get out. I'd just drive up to the mailbox, get the mail, and come straight back to town. Please."

Instinct told him to refuse, but the wistfulness on her face was hard to ignore. His mind raced as he considered the wisdom of letting her have her way.

"I'd be happy to ride escort with the little lady," one of the elderly men offered.

John Thomas snorted softly and tried not to smile. It wouldn't do to let them know that they weren't in nearly as much trouble as they thought.

"You're not going anywhere, Wiley," he said. "You punched your best friend in the nose this morning and have yet to tell me why. I don't intend to let either of you leave this room until you start talking. If this isn't settled now, the next call I get concerning you two might be over a shooting, and I don't think either of you want that to happen, do you?"

They both looked down, seeming unwilling to look at the other, and finally nodded their heads in agreement.

Then the door opened. A small, gray-haired woman came into the room, accompanied by another rounded, taller version of the same sex.

"Well now," John Thomas said with a grin. "It looks like the cavalry has arrived."

Samantha tried not to smile. From the nervous expression on the old men's faces, she could tell all hell was about to break loose.

John Thomas stepped between them as the two elderly women came scurrying into the room. "Mrs. Smith, Mrs. Hardy, I'm glad you could come in and help me out," he said.

"Wiley Smith, I never! What will the preacher say in church Sunday when he finds out you've been fighting? And at your age!"

Wiley looked sick as the smaller woman pushed the sheriff aside and stomped toward him with a gleam in her eye. He didn't even notice when the other woman laid into Pete.

"So, Pete Hardy. This is a fine mess you've gotten yourself into. I don't know what's wrong, but I suggest you start talking and do it now or I won't be responsible for what I do to you later," she said.

Pete looked as if someone had just offered to hand him his head on a plate.

Suddenly the room was alive with the sounds of four separate voices all shouting at once to be heard. John Thomas raked his fingers through his hair in frustration, and looked as if he would like to throttle them all. Samantha knew it was now or never. She entered her last plea.

"Johnny? Please let me go. I hate hiding like a rat in a hole. "I'll be careful, and I'll be right back."

He saw the wanting on her face, and nodded. But before she could bolt, he grabbed her arm, dug in his pocket, and handed her the keys to the extra squad car. "If you have to, don't hesitate to use the radio for contact. And come right back, okay?"

She nodded and grabbed the keys from his hand before he could change his mind. As she darted out the door she blew him a kiss. She had one last glimpse of John Thomas trying to interrupt the shouts of the elderly quartet. At least he could never complain that his job was boring.

On her way out of Rusk, she stopped at the apartment and picked up a foil-wrapped package of bones she'd been saving for Rebel. She'd promised Johnny she wouldn't get out of the car, but knowing Rebel, he would come to greet her when she stopped at the mailbox at the edge of the yard. The least she could do was scratch that itchy spot behind his left ear and tell him how much she loved him.

"Poor baby," she said to herself as she took the turn toward Cotton, imagining the hound's lonesome expression.

Then she laughed aloud. Thanks to his drooping jaw and huge, soulful eyes, that dog's expression was always lonesome.

Happy to be on her own, she accelerated and the miles sped by. Before she knew it, the driveway leading to the farm came into view. She took the turn carefully, pulling to a stop beside the mailbox.

The mail carrier had already come and gone. She could tell that from the fresh set of tracks. His four-wheel drive tires had funny little knobs on them that left perfect, doughnut-hole shapes in the loose sand, and there was a clear set beside the post.

Rebel bayed a welcome as he recognized the engine's familiar sound. Samantha quickly glanced around before opening the door, checking to make sure that the only witness to her arrival bore four legs.

"Hey, boy," she said, crooning in a low-pitched voice as she leaned out and patted and scratched on all of the dog's necessary places. When she began u wrapping the bones he all but crawled into the seat with her.

She laughed, pushing him back out the door. "I brought you a surprise. This is for being a good dog," she said, as she put one bone in his mouth and tossed the others toward the shade tree beside the porch. "Now, scoot. I've got to get back before your master comes after me."

Rebel sauntered off with his treasure. Samantha watched as he flopped down beneath the shade tree, eyed the assortment of other bones tossed on the grass, and then began gnawing indelicately on the long, T-bone.

Samantha brushed her hands on her jeans, then leaned out, scooped the handful of mail from the box, and shut and locked the car door just as she'd promised.

Humming absently, she sorted through the stack of papers and letters, and then stopped short at a large brown envelope addressed to her.

The hair on the back of her neck began to crawl.

She turned the envelope over and over in her hands, noticing that it did not have a postmark or a stamp; only her name printed in red block letters. Someone had to have driven out and personally placed it in the box. This was too much like the stalker's style to ignore.

With a pounding heart, she scanned the road in front of her, but there were so many tracks and footprints, it was impossible to say who'd put them there, or even when.

Sweat popped out across her upper lip as she turned the envelope over and realized that it wasn't sealed.

Her hands shook as she reached in and pulled out the contents, then her eyes widened and the blood drained from her face.

What should have been fear turned to instant rage. How dare he? How dare the bastard taunt her? Shaking with fury, she dropped the envelope and its contents onto the seat beside her and made a wild U-turn in the road.

In seconds she was back on the highway. And if someone had seen her flying past, they would have imagined that the sheriff was in hot pursuit of some criminal. What they didn't know was that it was only the sheriff's lady, and she was in pursuit of a stalker who wouldn't let go.

Montgomery Turner opened the door to the sheriff's department just far enough to poke his head in and shout, "Sheriff! You better come quick! It's Samantha!"

John Thomas was out of his office and on the street in seconds, looking around in panic. From the tone of his deputy's voice, it had to be bad news, but he didn't see her or the squad car anywhere. For a moment he even lost sight of Monty, until he looked past the trees on the other side of the street and saw him running toward the town square.

"What the hell," he muttered, and bolted across the street.

The patrol car she'd been driving was parked at the wrong angle against the curb. A crowd had gathered just beyond it.

But where was Sam?

His own question was answered as the crowd parted for his arrival.

Unaware of the tears running down her face, Samantha alternated between screaming with rage, or shouting in uncontrollable fury as she waved a handful of papers in the air. Every now and then she would pick one from her hand and toss it onto the ground.

"You sorry son of a bitch!" she sobbed, and threw a paper onto the ground beneath her feet.

John Thomas reached for her, but she pulled away, continuing to vent her rage.

"You're a coward! A miserable, sneaking coward!" she shouted, and waved the handful of papers in the air over her head.

"Sam, darlin', what's wrong?" he said, but she yanked away again in a vicious jerk. Her shouts rang in his ears as she refused to acknowledge his existence.

"You pervert! I'm sick and tired of playing this game with you!" She ripped a picture from the handful she was holding and waved it in the air before throwing it to the ground along with the others.

Several people in the crowd stepped back in shock,

as if by their mere presence, they were guilty of causing her pain.

"There! That's what I think about you and your
stupid methods of intimidation," she cried. "You're
the one who's afraid. Do you hear me, you snake?
You hide behind letters sent through the mail. You
make secret little phone calls because you don't have
the guts to say what you want to my face. And now
this!"

John Thomas caught the next picture before it hit
the ground. Seconds later he remembered to breathe
again and inhaled sharply, trying to maintain his equi-
librium in the face of shock.

The stalker had struck again!

"Look at this!" Samantha ran toward a man at the
edge of the crowd. "This is what cowards do. This kind
of man can't even look at himself in the mirror."

The man's face twisted in sympathy.

"Damn," Monty said, and handed the pictures she'd
thrown on the ground to the sheriff, then swiped his
hand across his face. "She's going make herself sick,
boss, that's what. Someone's got to stop her."

John Thomas looked down at the pictures. They,
like the one he'd caught, were equally threatening. The
pictures were of Samantha as she walked about the
streets of Rusk, while some of them had been taken in
Cotton.

There was one of her coming out of the grocery
store with a bag of groceries on her hip. Another of her

visiting with friends on the street, even one of her holding someone's baby. Each and every picture had a big red circle drawn right over her heart. And in the center of each circle was a big X, like the cross hairs on the scope of a rifle pointing directly at her.

John Thomas shuddered. How could he stop her hysteria when he felt like succumbing to the same reaction himself? Just as he started toward her, instinct delayed his actions, and he suddenly knew that stopping her was the worst thing he could do.

"She's already sick, Monty. Let her get it out of her system now," he said. "If she doesn't, it'll eat her alive."

Monty nodded, and then turned away from the square. His eyes narrowed as he looked down at the ground to a picture that bore a promise that seemed bound to come true.

You will die!

His mouth twisted as he read, and then he muttered beneath his breath as he bent down to pick it up. "I guess everyone has to go sometime."

And then suddenly Samantha was silent. John Thomas spun just in time to see her take a deep breath and toss the rest of the pictures onto the ground. She started walking as if hypnotized, staring straight ahead without meeting anyone's gaze. The crowd silently parted to let her pass.

"Monty, get the rest of those pictures as evidence and take everything down to the office, including the car. I'll be there later." John Thomas started after her.

"Yes sir," he said, and began picking up the scattered black-and-white 8 × 10s that she'd tossed away.

Samantha hurt. Everywhere there was a place to ache throbbed as if she'd been beaten. When she breathed she felt as if someone were poking her with hot needles. Taking a step was even worse, and yet she kept moving, one foot after the other, as she followed the yellow line down the middle of the street. It was her last act of anger—daring the stalker to strike.

All the buildings of downtown Rusk that lined the street were occupied, but at this moment, they felt vacant and Samantha felt exposed. It was impossible to see beyond the hundreds of windows or beyond the doorways. He could be anywhere right now with the rifle aimed. She should have been afraid. But she was tired, sick and tired. One way or the other she was ready for it to be over.

Her step faltered in fear as she heard someone running up behind her, but anger stayed her momentum. If it was the stalker, then so be it. She was sick—*so sick!*—of being afraid. Refusing to look back, she continued to walk. And then she heard his voice.

"Sam, darlin', wait for me."

His plea threaded through her pain.

Johnny! I should have known!

And when his fingers slipped through hers, a fresh set of tears clouded her vision. This time, without his support she would have fallen.

John Thomas grabbed her and then held her fast as

she staggered and fell into his arms. When she buried her face against his chest he wanted to cry along with her.

"Ah, Johnny, what in the world am I going to do?"

"For now, just come with me, darlin'. We'll worry about the rest later."

He had no answers, and he had no plan. But as long as they had each other, he figured they might just get through this. With his arm around her shoulders, he guided her toward the department. There was no need to worry about the next step that needed to be taken. She'd publicly thrown down the gauntlet. The rest would be up to the stalker. Samantha Carlyle had stopped running.

Days later, Montgomery Turner leaned his forehead against the hot glass of the phone booth at the corner and closed his eyes as he listened to the man at the other end of the line. Bile rolled up the back of his throat as the words kept pounding in his ear. In a fit of angry frustration, he doubled up his fist and hit the glass, unaware of the startled glance of the woman in the street who was walking past.

"I don't care how many times you say it, it doesn't change a thing!" Monty yelled. "Yes, I know I came here for a reason! And yes, it's not been easy trying to do my job and that too, but I am doing it, dammit. The last thing I need from you is advice, okay?"

He sighed as his legs went weak. He hadn't meant

to shout. It never accomplished anything with this man. He was as hardheaded as they came.

"Look. It won't be long and then it'll all be over. That much is obvious. I'm not stupid, just in love . . . and denial. Remember, don't call me at work. It'll only arouse suspicion and ruin my credibility. That's the last thing I need. Sheriff Knight is just starting to trust me. I've worked too long and too hard to get here just to have you mess things up. Please, for once, let me do things my way!"

Samantha stepped back and gasped. Everything the deputy was saying sounded suspicious, and yet she knew there had to be another explanation for what he'd said besides the one that sprang to mind.

Lost in thought, she didn't realize that he'd disconnected, or that he was about to exit the booth until she looked up. Their gazes locked, and it was hard to say who was more surprised.

Monty could tell from the shocked expression on her face that she'd heard everything he'd said. The uncertainty lay in what she intended to do with the information.

He tried to glare at her, but another face kept superimposing itself over hers. The long, black hair was the same. Even the clear blue of their eyes. He shook his head and wiped a hand across his face to clear his vision.

"Sorry," he said. "I didn't know anyone was waiting for the phone."

Without further explanation, he jumped into his car

and drove away, leaving Samantha to do as she chose with what she'd heard.

When she tried to walk, she staggered. Monty had looked as if he hated her when he came out of the phone booth. But that made no sense. She'd never seen him before he came to work for John Thomas. Or had she? All of a sudden she lost complete trust in her own judgment and panicked.

Fright came without warning, and she found herself running all the way back to the apartment. When she turned the last block and saw the old Earl place come into view, she increased her speed. With one long leap, she was up the step and into the house. Taking the stairs two at a time, she found herself stumbling on the next-to-the-last stair from the top, and began scrambling for a hold to keep from tumbling back down the steep stairwell. It didn't happen, and she realized that she couldn't stop her backward momentum. She was really going to fall!

She screamed as her arms windmilled through the air, and then suddenly a hand grabbed her wrist.

"Hold tight," Claudia said, then tightened her grip and pulled Samantha to safety. "Wow, that was close! You must have been in a real hurry, girl. What's wrong? You look like you saw a ghost."

Samantha shuddered, more than grateful for the waitress's opportune arrival. She sank down on the top step and buried her face in her hands as her heartbeat slowly regained a normal rhythm.

"Good lord," she finally managed to say. "Boy, do I owe you one."

Claudia's eyes narrowed thoughtfully before she smiled. "You don't owe me anything," she said. "I was just being neighborly." And then she giggled. "I hate to catch and run, but I'm going to be late for work."

With that, she sidestepped Samantha and hurried down the stairs, laughing at her own wit as she went out the door.

Samantha crawled to her feet, ashamed of the stupid, uncalled-for panic that had nearly caused her to break her neck.

"I overreacted, that's all," she muttered as she quickly unlocked their apartment and then locked the door behind her. "I'm starting to imagine things. If I don't get myself in gear, next I'll be blaming Johnny."

She walked past a mirror, stuck her tongue out at herself, and headed for the bathroom. For some reason she felt dirty and had a sudden need to wash herself, all over.

Dusk was settling around the Earl house when John Thomas drove up and parked. He jammed his hat on his head and walked toward the door, hating to go up and face Samantha with his news.

The pictures she'd been sent had gone straight to state headquarters for examination by the best forensic experts Texas had to offer, and they'd learned exactly nothing.

They'd been shot with a normal 35mm camera. The film had been dropped off at one place, and developed at another in New Summerfield, a town to their north.

Because of the large bulk of work the developers did daily, there was no way to put the two incidents together to remember who dropped off and picked up what. Once again, the stalker had outsmarted them.

Reluctantly, he walked up the stairs, hoping that between here and the door he'd be struck by a revelation that would help him explain it to her. But nothing happened. No hand of God came down and blessed him with an answer. He had no alternative but to go inside and face Samantha with the truth. She deserved that much.

And then he opened the door.

She was sitting by the window in the darkening room, staring blankly past the curtains into the shadows of the yard below. She didn't even say hello.

"How well do you know Montgomery Turner?"

Her question shocked the hell out of him.

He shut the door, then tossed his hat on the table, his mind racing as he considered what he would say. How could he tell her he'd suspected him enough to have him checked out? And why did she want to know?

Needing to put some momentary distance between himself and her question, he walked into the kitchen and drew a cool drink from the faucet at the sink.

Samantha watched as he tilted the glass and drained it. The long, thick column of his throat worked up and down as he swallowed gulp after gulp. She sensed his shock. But she had to know. What she'd overheard Monty say had been eating at her all evening. The least she deserved was an answer.

The glass hit the counter with a thump. He stared down at the empty sink, trying to find the best way to start.

"Why, Sam? What makes you ask that question?"

She balled her hands into fists, remembering Monty's face and his anger, and what she'd overheard. But she refused to give in to the fear.

"Because something happened today that made me wonder."

He frowned, waiting for her to continue.

Suddenly she shot out of the chair and began pacing back and forth.

"I didn't mean to eavesdrop," she began. "I was just passing by when I heard the thump."

"Thump?"

"Let me tell this my way," Samantha said.

He nodded, leaned against the kitchen counter, and crossed his arms across his chest, unaware of the judgmental appearance of his stance.

It only served to make her more nervous, and as a result, the story came out in jerks and stops. When she was through, the frown on John Thomas's face grew deeper, and his expression even darker.

Her story ended with a shaky sigh. He couldn't stand it any longer.

"Come here, Sam. I think you need a hug."

He was right about that. She willingly walked into his arms, and relaxed when they wrapped around her. Within his embrace was where she felt the safest, and the most loved. And yet as he began to talk, Samantha imagined she could feel his hesitation.

"It sounds strange, I'll admit," he said, unwilling to tell her how much her words had affected him. "But in all fairness to him, honey, it could mean a whole lot of things."

"But what about him saying that you were just beginning to trust him? What about that?"

"It's true. I am beginning to trust him. That's a thing that each new employee has to earn, right down to the dispatchers. I'll admit I thought something was wrong with him for some time now, but I never associated it with what's been happening to you."

He ignored the thrust of guilt that pricked his conscience. That was a lie. He *had* suspected Monty. But hell, he suspected everyone new, including that stranded motorist at the Texas Pig Motel.

"I'll tell you what," he said. "First thing tomorrow morning I'll call him into my office. He won't leave til I'm completely satisfied that whatever he tells me the truth."

Samantha sighed and thumped a fist lightly upon his before relaxing into his open arms.

"Okay, Johnny. I trust your judgment." She looked up, trying to smile past her fears. "Besides, I'd be silly not to when I've trusted you with my life."

"My God," he said softly, cupping her face in his hands.

She inhaled and opened her lips slightly, expecting, wanting, waiting impatiently for what she knew he could give her.

She tasted warm. And then beneath his touch, she turned hot with the need he felt coming. He obliged.

Night came without fanfare, sliding longer and darker shadows across the land until there was nothing to see but what was visible beneath the feeble streetlights hidden by the thick, tall trees surrounding the Earl house.

The windows on the second floor were dark, like glasses on the eyes of the blind. No one outside could see in, and no one inside could see out. But life was being lived to the fullest behind the apartment door on the second floor.

Lost in the moment, wrapped in each other's arms, John Thomas was making slow, deliberate love to his lady. Fear had taken a backseat to passion.

The bedsprings squeaked intermittently as Samantha moved beneath him, certain that if she tried, thi' moment and this feeling would go on forever. But li' all delusions, it suddenly disappeared in a burst of l and a blinding flash.

Through the shadows she had a momentary image of the muscles in his arms bulging and straining as he struggled to keep from collapsing upon her, and the way his upper body arched away as his lower body imprinted upon her forever.

She moaned as the feeling came fast, then went to meet him. Moments later, they lay silent and shaking in each other's arms. Samantha locked her hands around his neck and closed her eyes. But when she did, all she could see was the look on Monty's face. It was hard—and full of pain.

Just before daylight the phone rang. John Thomas groaned and rolled over, grabbing for the receiver before the second ring could waken Samantha.

"Hello." His speech was thick from sleep. And then he sat up in bed, fully alert as he continued to listen. "The hell you say. When?"

Samantha came awake to the sound of his voice. Rolling over, she listened intently to his side of the conversation, trying to guess what it might mean. She didn't have long to wonder.

"I'll be right there," he said. "Call Lawler. Willis is already on duty, right? Okay. Have them meet me there."

He hung up, switched on the lamp, and jumped out of bed in one smooth motion. "Damn, darlin'." He was grinning from ear to ear. "I think those rustlers at the Watkins ranch just outsmarted themselves."

"How so?" she asked, and then watched with delight as he raced around the room, trying to dress and talk at the same time.

"They thought they'd be sneaky and strike twice at the same location. But I've had one of my men patrolling the area around the vicinity of the Watkins ranch ever since the first fifty head disappeared. The rustlers must have seen the lights on the squad car, because they tried to take a different route out of the pasture and got themselves stuck in a bog. Willis just called in. He's got them locked inside their own trailer with fourteen more head of Watkins's prime beef, waiting for us to come help him haul them in."

The look on his face was priceless as he buckled his belt. Samantha couldn't resist a chuckle.

"You mean to tell me they're inside the trailer *with* the stolen cattle?"

"Yep," he said, as he stomped on his last boot. "They're gonna smell real bad, too. At least when I fell headfirst into Lizzie Marshall's cow lot the manure was dry. This stuff is going to be fresh and hot. You know how cattle react when you try loading them. They don't do anything but run, bawl, and poop."

She grinned. "Which one of you guys is going to haul them to jail?" She was imagining the condition of the squad cars after the rustlers rode in them.

"Not me," he said. "Hell, honey. We might just haul them trailer, cows, and all into jail. After all, thos cows are evidence, right?"

"You haven't changed a bit, Johnny Knight. You're still a devil, aren't you?"

It was good to hear laughter in her voice instead of the despair and panic that had been typical during the past few weeks.

"Oh, I can be real good when I have to, Sam," he said softly, then bent down and gave her a good-bye kiss. "Remember last night?"

Even after the echo of his footsteps on the stairs had long since disappeared, she was still smiling . . . and remembering.

12

A FEW HOURS LATER, a knock on the door startled her. Samantha stuffed the last of her biscuit in her mouth as she raced to answer it. When she opened it, shock nearly choked her as she tried to swallow the bite she'd been chewing.

Monty stood on the threshold with hat in hand and a self-conscious look on his face. "The boss sent me to get him a change of clothes."

Samantha stepped aside, motioning for him to come in. As he did, he began to look around in appreciation.

"You've made this place real homey." He smiled. "I guess it just takes a woman's touch. I've been in my apartment a lot longer than you two and it still looks like I haven't unpacked."

She'd known that sooner or later she'd have to face Monty again. Oddly enough, the meeting wasn't as trained as she'd expected.

"Why does he need clean clothes?" she asked.

Monty grinned, which made him look even younger than he was.

"It got real messy trying to get those four rustlers out of that trailer full of steers. One of them even fell down in the middle of 'em, and we had the devil's own time getting him up before he got a hoof in his mouth."

She laughed aloud. "Let me guess. John Thomas was in the thick of it all, right?"

Monty nodded. "Yes, ma'am. And he got green cowsh—" He caught himself just in time and blushed as he rephrased his explanation so that it would be proper for a lady's ears. "What I meant to say was, he has some fresh manure on his jeans and shirt."

"He shouldn't have made you come after the clothes. He could have done it himself," she said.

"Oh, no, ma'am. *He* only needed a change of clothes. They sent me home to take a bath. I was the one who had to get the damned, I mean, darned rustler up from the floor of the trailer. I even had it in my hair."

That explanation was all it took. Samantha looked at him, picturing the stampede it must have been, and started to laugh. She laughed until tears ran. And when she thought she couldn't laugh anymore, all she had to do was look at the sheepish expression on his face and it started all over again.

It would seem that in this part of Texas, cow manure and officers of the law had a magnetic attraction to one another.

"Oh Lord," she gasped, holding her side. "I'll go get his clothes, and I guess I should thank you for coming here after you bathed, and not before."

Monty grinned. "Yes, ma'am. You might be right."

She started out of the room then turned. He looked so ill at ease and out of place, her conscience dug at her.

"Monty . . ."

"Yes, ma'am." He had a guilty expression on his face.

Samantha guessed that he expected her to question him about what she'd overheard. Instead, she surprised herself as well as him.

"I started to say, since John Thomas isn't coming back to eat them, you'd better see what you can do toward finishing off the rest of the biscuits. There's fresh coffee. Clean cups are in the drainer. I just put the butter and jelly in the refrigerator. Help yourself. It'll take me a while to get his clothes together. I'll have to iron a shirt."

"Yes, ma'am," Monty said. "Thank you."

"You're welcome, Monty," she said. "And stop calling me ma'am. Call me Samantha or Sam, or Hey You. Anything but ma'am."

"You've got it," Monty said, and headed for the kitchen.

When she came out a few minutes later, Monty had ished off what was left, washed the dirty dishes, and laced the butter and jelly.

"Here you are," she said, handing him a pair of jeans

and a clean shirt to take to John Thomas, then noticed how neatly he'd cleaned up after himself. "You're real handy to have around. If you're anywhere close by at supper time, you might think about coming home with the sheriff to eat with us. I'll cook if you'll wash."

He grinned. "Sounds good, but I'll have to see," he said. "I never know what's going to happen around here. Thanks for the food and the clothes."

She saw him to the door, watched until he'd disappeared down the stairs, and then found herself staring straight into Claudia's face as the door to the other apartment opened.

"Hi there," Claudia said. "Suffering any lasting effects from your near-miss yesterday?" she asked.

It took Samantha a moment to remember that she must be referring to the fact that she'd nearly broken her neck on the stairs.

"Thanks to you, no," she said.

Claudia nodded. A silent moment passed and then she grinned as if she'd just had the greatest idea.

"Say, what are you doing this morning?" Claudia asked.

Samantha shrugged. "As usual, probably nothing, why?"

"This is my day off," Claudia said. "I'm on my way to New Summerfield to buy myself a new outfit. I fi nally got enough money saved to get my bus tick home, and I have no intention of showing up ba there with my tail between my legs. Figurati speaking of course." She wiggled her eyebrows and traced the red outline of her lipstick with her little finger as she continued. "So would you like to come with me? I know you don't get out much."

Samantha didn't answer. She was shocked by the invitation, and then wondered why Claudia knew so much about her. The moment she thought it, she got her answer without asking.

"I'm a light sleeper," Claudia said. "Sometimes I hear you moving around in here. It doesn't bother me. I just hear it, you know. I always go right back to sleep."

Samantha sighed. It would seem that everyone knew her predicament.

"I'm not sure about the shopping," Samantha said. "If you don't know it already, it's only fair to tell you that being seen with me might get you into trouble. In case you haven't heard, someone wants me dead."

"Lordy!" Claudia's eyes widened and her big red mouth formed a perfect "O." And then she shrugged. "Honey, I've been in a lot worse messes than that and I'm still here to tell the tale. If you want to go with me, then come on. I've got a black belt in karate."

Samantha laughed. She couldn't help it as she tried to superimpose the image of all those blond curls, that giggle, and the ditsy attitude over a ninja outfit.

"It's true, I do!" Claudia said, and put her hands on her hips. "So, are we on, or what?"

A small spurt of defiance surfaced. Samantha was

sick and tired of the stalker calling the shots. And although she knew John Thomas would throw a fit and tell her not to go if she asked, she knew there was nothing he could do if it was after the fact.

"Just let me change clothes," Samantha said.

Claudia closed her own door and followed Samantha into her apartment. "You don't need to change," she said, eyeing the tennis shoes, blue jeans, and the pale yellow blouse Samantha was wearing. "You look just fine."

Samantha looked down at herself, and then shrugged. "If you say so, but I need to leave Johnny a note."

Claudia nodded. While Samantha was busy composing her note, she set her purse on the table beside her, and began walking around the apartment, staring curiously, but careful not to touch.

"The rooms in this place all look the same, don't they," she said.

Samantha mumbled in agreement. she was still trying to find a way to tell John Thomas what she was about to do and make it sound like a good idea.

Claudia shrugged and continued her casual snooping. But when she came to the open bedroom door, an empty expression swept across her face as she looked inside at the bed.

In that moment, if Samantha had been watching, she might have changed her mind about accompanying Claudia to New Summerfield. But she wasn't, and when she finished John Thomas's note, Claudia had collected herself and her thoughts and was all smiles.

"Okay," Samantha said. "I'm ready. We won't be long, will we?"

"Oh no. I've got packing to do and a bus to catch. I'm going home, remember?"

They started out the door when Claudia made a quick pivot. "My purse!" she shouted, and flew back to the table where she'd left it. She grabbed for the strap, and as she did the flap opened, spilling the contents over table and floor alike.

"Shoot," she muttered, as Samantha waited by the door. "It's a good thing I don't drop things like this at Marylee's or I'd have been out of a job."

"Need any help?" Samantha asked.

"I'll get it," she said, and grabbed everything in handfuls, hastily stuffing them inside to be sorted out later.

Samantha stared absently down the stairwell and missed seeing Claudia grab her note to John Thomas and stuff it into her purse along with the rest of her things.

"Let's go," Claudia said, pulling the door shut behind her. "Better lock up. Can't be too careful these days."

Samantha locked the door, then moments later they were outside. Once there, she dubiously eyed the old black pickup Claudia had been driving. It didn't look as if it would make it across the street, let alone out of town on a shopping spree.

"Want me to drive mine?"

"No way," Claudia said, and started toward her borrowed truck. "It's my trip. We'll use my gas. Come on, time's wasting."

Samantha shrugged and followed. As she crawled into the dusty seat, she suddenly wished she had a good excuse for backing out. But other than the fact that she was having second thoughts about what John Thomas would say, she couldn't think of a plausible reason. And she did need to buy some things that were unavailable in Rusk.

They drove off in a cloud of dust.

"Boy oh boy, Sheriff. You've had a real busy week," the lawman said, as he packed the last of the rustlers into the state vehicle for transportation to a larger holding facility. "Your dispatcher tells me y'all have shipped off a crazy man, had yourselves the makin's of another Johnson County War, senior-citizen style, and now you've caught yourself some rustlers. But, oowwee," he backed up and wrinkled his nose in protest as he slammed the back door of the van shut and locked it, "the least you could have done was hose 'em down before you locked 'em up."

John Thomas grinned. "We did. You should have seen and smelled them beforehand."

The lawman laughed and shook his head. "Have a good one," he said, and waved as he drove away.

John Thomas watched until the taillights were no

longer visible, and then started toward his car. He wanted to go check on Sam.

"Sheriff! Telephone," Carol Ann yelled.

He spun in midstep and headed back into his office to pick up the phone.

"Sheriff Knight."

"Hey, there, cowboy, how are you doing?" Mike Pulaski asked.

"Pulaski?"

"Yeah, it's me," he said, unable to hide the lilt in his voice. "I've got a little bit of news for you. It's not much, but it's a definite lead."

John Thomas stood up. He could use some good news. "Let's have it."

"It seems that the last person to be seen outside Miss Carlyle's apartment before it blew up was a cleaning woman."

John Thomas sighed. This wasn't going to help him a damned bit.

Pulaski grinned. He'd heard the sigh.

"Now, don't quit on me before I'm through," he warned. "Just let me finish. The thing is, this is a mid- to low-income apartment complex. We questioned everyone, and I mean everyone. No one had that day, or for that matter any other day, ever hired a cleaning woman. The only person we didn't ask was Samantha Carlyle. Now, I've been thinking, why would a woman who was afraid of her own shadow hire some stranger to come inside her home and clean?"

John Thomas's expression darkened. "Are you telling me that there's a possibility that our stalker might be a woman?"

"You tell me."

"Damn!"

Pulaski grinned. "That's exactly what I thought."

"Thanks for the information," John Thomas said. "I've got something I need to do, and it can't wait. If you learn anything else, let me know. And Pulaski . . . thanks."

Pulaski grinned again. "No thanks needed. Besides, I owed her. I hope it helps."

"So do I, man. So do I," John Thomas said and hung up the phone.

Then he picked it back up again and dialed his apartment. It rang several times with no answer.

"Well, damn," he muttered, and checked the time.

It was nearly noon. Samantha was probably out in Rusk doing some shopping or getting a bite to eat. She hated to eat alone and obviously assumed he would be busy today. Just to make sure, he would drive by and check before he went to the farm. He had a sudden need to look at the hate mail again that Samantha had received.

It didn't take him long to cruise by the apartment. His pickup truck was right where it was this morning when he'd left for work. Either she was still in town on foot, or upstairs taking a nap, and waking her up would just deter his mission. The urgency of the entire situation changed his mind about stopping. There wasn't any more time to waste.

But when he got to the farm, the empty silence of the old house made him nervous, and unearthing the letters and tapes from the stalker made it even worse. He began rereading them from a different perspective and realized that they could as easily have been written by a woman. In fact, he wondered why he hadn't thought of it sooner. Not one of the letters made any sort of sexual reference to Samantha Carlyle. But every one of them was full of venom and hate, just the kind of reaction a vindictive woman might make, even down to the part about dying to cleanse her soul.

At the thought of Sam dying, he headed for the phone. Once again, there was no answer at the apartment and it was getting late. Where could she be?

As he listened to the unanswered rings, to his dismay, he realized that not one of the people they'd checked out in Cotton or Rusk had been a woman. In fact, he wasn't even sure how many new females had come to town.

When he couldn't stand the ringing anymore, he slammed the phone down in disgust.

"Damn it, where the hell are you, Sam?" He bolted out the door, leaving the letters where they lay. This new information spelled big trouble for Samantha. She needed to know and she needed to know now.

When he pulled back in at the apartment, his truck was still in place. But when he got inside, she was nowhere to be found. A niggle of anger settled along-side the nervousness that had drawn him back to town.

"Damn it all to hell! Where on earth can she be?" he muttered, then bolted back down the stairs as fast as he'd run up.

When he got to the car, he was on the radio before he started the engine. And when he found out that Samantha had not called in to let him know where she was, deeper worry began to surface. Before he could make another decision, Monty pulled into the yard and parked.

"Get in!" John Thomas yelled. "We need to find Samantha, and . . . we need to talk."

Monty tried not to frown as he got in the sheriff's car. He'd been expecting this ever since Samantha overheard his conversation. He took a deep breath and waited.

"Have you seen her this afternoon?"

Monty looked startled. This wasn't what he'd expected to be asked. "No sir," he said. "Not since I came after your clothes. I've been at the office all day doing the paperwork on this morning's arrest."

John Thomas felt sick. "Damn it, I need to find her. Pulaski called. He says there's a good possibility that the stalker might be a woman."

"The hell you say! Then that means everyone we've been—"

"Right! We've been barking up the wrong tree. Now, Deputy, you help me look for Samantha, and in the meantime, start talking. I know you've got troubles. And while I recognize the fact that a man needs to tend his own fires, sometimes it's not a good idea. Sometimes the fire can get out of hand and burn everyone and everything up along with it."

Monty leaned back in the seat, took off his hat, and absently traced the circle of the brim with his fingers. It was time to explain.

"I came here under false pretenses." At the startled expression on the sheriff's face, he sighed. He'd known this wouldn't be easy. "I'm sorry," he muttered. "My grandfather got me the spot because I needed to work close to Louisiana."

This was not what John Thomas expected to hear. "What are you trying to tell me? Why Louisiana, and who the hell is your grandfather?"

"Wheeler Joe Turner," Monty said, waiting for the inevitable explosion. It came.

"Cog-wheel Turner? That old Texas Ranger is your grandfather?"

Monty nodded. "I didn't want your evaluation of me to hinge on the fact that I was related to such a, well, he's—"

"He's a legend," John Thomas said. "A damned institution, that's what. But that's neither here nor there. I never judge a man on who his family is, because I'd hate like hell to be judged by mine. My father died in prison."

Monty tried not to show his shock. From the expression on the sheriff's face, he had failed miserably.

John Thomas shrugged. "Nearly everyone around

here knows it, but it's not something I'm proud of. He was a sorry s.o.b., and I've spent most of my life trying to live it down. Now, tell me what's bothering you. I can't believe that it was just worrying that I'd find out about your relationship to Cog-wheel Turner."

Monty swallowed past the lump in his throat and closed his eyes. Even now it hurt to say the words aloud. He pulled a picture out of his wallet, tracing the face of it gently to wipe before handing it over.

The car swerved beneath his control as John Thomas glanced down at the picture and then whistled softly, unable to hide his surprise.

"You know what? She looks like Sam. All that long dark hair." He glanced quickly back up at the road in front of him before taking another closer look. "She even has blue eyes." He handed it back to Monty. "What's her name?"

"Melissa, but everyone called her Lissa. She's my fiancée."

"Congratulations, man! But why haven't you said anything about her before now?"

Monty put the picture back in his wallet, his gaze lingering on the image one last time before he folded it shut and put it back in his pocket.

"Eighteen months ago she was the victim of a hit and run. She's been in Louisiana in a critical care hospice ever since, in a coma, and with no chance of recovery."

"My God," John Thomas said softly, and pul`

over on a side street and parked. He couldn't imagine any worse horror than to watch someone you loved waste away. And then he realized. "So that's where you spend your off-duty time."

"Yes sir. And the other day, when I was so, uh . . . the reason I've been . . ."

He swiped a hand across his face and felt tears on his cheeks. But for some reason it no longer mattered. Somehow telling had made the hurt a little bit less.

"When I got to the hospice that day, her folks met me at the door and told me that they'd made the decision to take her off of life support." It took another long silent minute before he could finish the story, and then when he did, he slumped into the seat, as if the telling took all of the starch out of his soul. "They don't expect her to last much longer."

John Thomas quietly ignored the harsh sob and the tears streaming down the young man's face. Giving him that much space and privacy was all that he could do, and he knew well that it was not enough. Other than a rough thump on the shoulder in understanding, words would be of little comfort to the young man. He was, however, highly relieved that his distrust of Montgomery Turner had been unfounded.

"So what are you going to do?" he finally asked.

"I guess wait for her to die," Monty said, and then turned away and stared out the window until he regained control of his emotions.

John Thomas was silent. There was nothing to say

that would make Monty's cross any easier to bear. He started the car.

"Let's go find Sam," he said.

They drove along the streets of Rusk for more than an hour, searching in every shop, each time asking the same questions while worry added up. No one knew a thing, and by the time they got back to the apartment, even Monty was beginning to worry.

"Did she leave you a note?" he asked.

"I didn't see one," John Thomas said. His expression brightened. "But I didn't look all that close. Maybe she did. Let's go see."

"Say," Monty said, as they got out of the car. "I guess Claudia must be working days instead of nights now."

John Thomas looked at the empty parking space at the end of the lot, surprised that he hadn't noticed the fact himself. The old black pickup she'd been driving was missing. There was nothing to indicate where it had been except a wide; oily stain in the dirt.

He stared at it a moment, trying to figure out why the image of that stain suddenly mattered. But Samantha's whereabouts took precedence, and he ignored the nudge of memory as he headed for the house.

His hopes fell as they entered the apartment. A complete search of the apartment failed to yield any kind of note.

"Nothing here but a tube of lipstick," Monty said, as

he picked it up from beneath the edge of the living room couch.

John Thomas stared at it as Monty dropped it in his hands. The case was a brilliant red enamel trimmed in silver, and unlike anything he'd seen Samantha use. He pulled off the top and rolled up the tube, trying to make sense of why fire-engine red lipstick would be on the floor of his apartment when it hadn't been there this morning. And Samantha was usually so neat.

"Is it hers?" Monty asked.

The sheriff shook his head. "She doesn't wear this color. It's too . . ." He shrugged for lack of a word.

Monty looked closer. "You know, this looks like the stuff that Claudia wears. Her mouth usually looks like someone just punched it. You know, all red and puffy and pouting."

Just then John Thomas's subconscious kicked in, and the memory of tracking the stalker through the woods surfaced. He remembered most of all his frustration when he found nothing but a wide, oily stain in the road where the vehicle had been parked.

"Oh hell!" He bolted across the hall and started eating on Claudia's door.

"Boss, have you lost your mind? What are you ng?"

efore John Thomas could tell him, the door swung beneath the blows.

oks like she moved," Monty said.

"I don't think so," John Thomas said. "But, oh God, I hope you're right."

Without further explanation, he ran down the stairs with Monty close at his heels. He came to a sudden stop by the curb, staring intently at the place where Claudia's black pickup was normally parked. A dark, oily stain marked the spot.

"Sucker sure leaks, doesn't it," Monty said, and then an odd expression crossed his face. "Say, boss, the day you tracked that intruder out at your place, didn't you say that his truck leaked oil like—"

He didn't finish. The look on John Thomas's face said it all. "Oh man," Monty said. "You don't suppose—?"

"Get in the car. We're going to Marylee's. I've got a sudden hunger, and it has nothing to do with food. I want to talk to Claudia. And she better have a real good explanation for where she's been the last few months of her life."

Several minutes later they wheeled into Marylee's Café. Monty breathed a huge sigh of relief. The old black pickup was parked behind the café, right in its usual parking space.

"Hey, boss. There it is. Maybe we jumped to conclusions. Lots of old cars and trucks leak oil. Maybe I was right the first time. Maybe she just got her hour changed."

"Maybe," John Thomas said. "But I want to hear from her."

The place was crowded. Marylee sailed by w

frown on her face, and her hands full of dirty dishes. The other waitress scurried to stay out of her way.

"Marylee, when you have a minute, I'd like to talk to you," John Thomas said.

She dumped the plates in the kitchen and stomped toward them with a wet cloth in her hand.

"If you want to talk, you're gonna have to follow me to do it. I'm shorthanded today. Two of my day girls called in sick. I intended to ask Claudia to cover and now I find out that she's gone."

Fear snaked through John Thomas's belly. "What do you mean, *gone?*"

"I mean, left, skipped, snuck out! That's what I mean! You just see if I do any more down-on-their-luck females another favor. I gave her a job when I didn't need help. I loaned her a truck when she didn't have wheels. And do I get a 'thank you, Marylee' when she leaves? No!" She brushed the crumbs from the table onto the floor and then turned and sighed as she swiped her hair from her eyes. "I suppose I should be happy she didn't run off with my truck, although to be honest, I suspect she didn't think it would get far."

"Where did she say she was going?" Monty asked.

"I didn't talk to her," Marylee said. "I'd been trying to all her all morning to come help and just happened to e the truck out back and figured it out. The Greyhound had already come and gone. I guess she caught it out t when it stopped to pick up passengers. You think ast she could have done was say good-bye."

"Would you mind if we took a look at the truck, Marylee?"

She shrugged as a new wave of customers came through the door. "Look all you want," she said. "Why don't you wash it while you're at it. I don't know where she drove it, but it's a mess."

John Thomas still couldn't rule out the possibility that he was jumping the gun. He had no actual proof that Samantha was really missing. She could be anywhere, doing anything. Or she could be dead. It was that thought that nearly sent him to his knees. But hope that he was wrong made him keep moving.

"Wow. Marylee was right," Monty said, as he began to circle the truck. "It's not only dirty, it's got some new-looking scratches on the fenders. And look here. Wherever she drove it, it must have been on high center at least once, because she's got a wad of weeds and grasses wound around the crankshaft."

John Thomas dropped to his knees. Monty was right. He reached beneath the truck and began pulling until he had all of the debris unwound and lying on the ground in front of him.

The grasses were tall. Wherever she'd been, it hadn't been mowed—probably some out-of-the-way farmland or pasture. The dirt around their roots, still soft and clumped, told John Thomas that the weeds were freshly uprooted.

As he began to separate the plants, something sharp pierced his hand. He yanked it back with a soft c as a length of berry vine with several hard green berries still attached separated itself from the grasses.

"Well, look here," Monty said, as the sheriff began picking thorns from his hands. "Berry vines. I had blackberry cobbler just the other day at Marylee's. She said the berries were from last year's crop, but it was still real good."

"They grow all over the place out here," John Thomas said, and carefully pulled them from the debris and tossed them aside. He sorted the rest of the grasses into separate piles, hoping to find a clue that would tell him where the truck had been.

And yet his need to know was based on the assumption that Samantha had been in this truck. Before he went any further, he had to have proof of that fact. Only then would he know that Claudia might have had something to do with Samantha's disappearance.

"I'm going to the farm," John Thomas said, as he piled the brush and grasses into the back of his car. No matter how useless they might prove to be, for the moment they were one of the few clues he had. "Wait here. I'll be right back."

Monty didn't have time to ask why. He went back inside and ordered dessert. And before he'd finished his pie and iced tea, the sheriff was back. By then, he dn't have to ask. When he saw the sheriff unloading hound dog from the squad car, he figured it out for self.

thought Rebel might be able to track her scent,"

John Thomas said, and held up a pair of shoes that she'd left at the farm. "It's a long shot, but right now, I'm willing to take it. If I look like a fool later, I'll be the first to laugh."

"You might not be so wrong after all, boss," Monty said. "I just had Lawler go by the apartment and check again to make sure that Samantha hadn't come back. The little newlywed who lives across the hall from me said she heard two women come downstairs this morning right after I left with your clothes. Said she heard them talking and laughing as they went out the door. She didn't look out to see who it was, but she heard them drive off."

"My God," John Thomas said. "Why would Sam leave with her? What on earth would make her walk off with a near-stranger without leaving me a note?"

Monty shrugged. "Maybe old Rebel there can tell us what we don't already know."

The sheriff nodded and unhooked the lead from the dog's collar. He held Samantha's shoes beneath Rebel's nose so that he got the scent and then ordered, "Search, boy! Search! Find Sam, Rebel, boy. Find Sam!"

The dog whined and tossed his big head back as he sniffed the air, and then his nose instinctively went to the earth. While they watched, Rebel made two circles in the yard, narrowing it each time until he came to the open door of the old black truck. The moment h jumped into the seat he began to bay.

"Dear God," John Thomas said, and tossed shoes back in his car.

"Does that mean what I think it means?" Monty asked.

"Sam was in that truck. I don't doubt my dog's ability to know that much. The problem is, where did Claudia leave her before she left town? And where the hell is Claudia now?"

He made a quick decision. "Monty, go inside and get all the information Marylee had on Claudia. Hell, I don't even know her last name."

He wiped a shaky hand across his face, remembering last night and the way Samantha cuddled against him as she slept. Dear God he couldn't lose that. Not when he'd just found the love of his life again.

Monty went into the café while John Thomas put Rebel in the backseat of his car along with Samantha's shoes. But his deputy came back too soon to be bringing good news.

"She said her name was Smith. Claudia Smith. And Marylee didn't get any other information because she wasn't going to withhold wages or anything like that. This was just a temporary setup. The woman was more or less a charity case. What we have on her is exactly nothing, boss. Not a damned thing."

"Somehow I'm not surprised," John Thomas said. "Let's get back to the department. I want an APB put out on Claudia Smith."

"What about Samantha?" Monty asked.

John Thomas couldn't even look his deputy in the eyes as he answered. "We've got to find her, that's all.

I promised her, dammit. I promised her I'd take care of her. I even crossed my heart and . . ."

Monty looked away as the sheriff's voice broke. He knew what that pain felt like. And he also knew that, right now, talking was impossible. That would come later, when sadness was repressed and anger took the forefront. That was how a man survived devastation.

John Thomas forced back the fear that threatened to overwhelm him. He didn't have time to panic. He had to find Samantha Carlyle and he had to do it now.

Somehow, somewhere, he knew she was still alive. If she wasn't, he would have felt it. Of that he was certain.

13

THE MILES BETWEEN Rusk and New Summerfield short-
ened as Claudia pushed the old black pickup to its limit.
The farther they drove, the better Samantha felt about it.
It almost seemed that by leaving the small town behind,
she left her troubles with it. She couldn't remember the
last time she'd felt this lighthearted and carefree.

And, in spite of her misgivings about the old
pickup's capabilities, and considering a lack of a muf-
fler or an air conditioner, it was performing valiantly.
The noisy exhaust was muted by the wind whistling
through the open windows. The gusts blew dust in their
eyes and persistently pulled at the braid in Samantha's
hair, but it was a small price to pay for freedom.

When they passed through the city limits of Cotton,
Claudia was forced to slow down. As she did, Saman-
leaned forward and pointed out the driver's side of
window.

"Look, Claudia! Do you see the third house from the left down that street?"

Claudia glanced in the direction that her passenger was pointing as Samantha explained.

"I grew up in that house." She smiled in memory. "I used to sneak out the back door when I went to meet Johnny. He was my best friend."

Claudia's grin was wide, her eyes glittering with subdued excitement. "He's sure more than that now, isn't he?"

Samantha blushed, but denying the obvious would have been silly. Out on the street, she recognized a familiar face and started to wave when the pickup swerved sharply and threw her into the floor instead.

"Sorry," Claudia said, as she increased pressure on the gas. "I almost ran over a dog." She sliced a cool glance across her shoulder out the window behind them before returning full attention to the road ahead. From the corner of her eye she could see her passenger struggling to get herself off of the floor. "Are you okay?"

Samantha laughed uneasily as her heartbeat settled back into a regular rhythm. The shock of hitting the dash, then sliding onto the floor was still too vivid to forget. For a moment, she'd imagined them about to crash.

"I think so," Samantha said, and brushed at th knees of her jeans. "But there really should be se belts in here."

Claudia laughed and patted the steering wheel. "This baby was built long before safety features came into play. That was back when you got in, sat back, and held on for dear life."

Samantha sighed and tried to smile. "I *was* trying to hold on."

"For dear life?"

Samantha shuddered. The question had come out of nowhere, but when she glanced over at the woman behind the wheel, she told herself she was imagining the threat behind it.

And so they rode.

Claudia talked nonstop and that was fine with Samantha. She had realized early on that participating in the conversation took little more than an occasional nod or smile. Most of her attention was focused on the rich green countryside and the abundance of trees lining the road. But her daydreaming quickly ended when she realized Claudia was slowing down. When she noticed her searching the roadside with a keen gaze, she couldn't help but worry.

"What's wrong?" Samantha asked.

Claudia grinned. "I've got to go," she said, and wiggled her backside in the seat to indicate her predicament. Her pink shorts and shirt were limp and dust-stained, and stuck to her body from the heat, but she didn't seem to mind. "I guess I should have stopped at that station back in Cotton, but I thought I could make it to New Summerfield first."

"You mean you need to—"

"I gotta wee," Claudia said bluntly. "And I'm not pulling over and baring my backside for just anyone to see." She laughed and arched her eyebrows. "I'm particular about who I share myself with, if you know what I mean."

Her laughter was infectious, and whatever comment Samantha might have made was sucked out the window with the air and Claudia's giggles.

"Oh look! There's a road." Claudia pointed toward a small turnoff just ahead. "I'll drive far enough up into the pasture to be out of view. Then I can do my business, and we'll be on our way to the mall in no time."

Samantha shrugged. "Okay. But you'd better be careful where you drive. You don't want to get stuck up in there. We're a long way from nowhere."

"Don't I know it," Claudia said, and made the turn with nothing more than a neat twist of her wrist without slowing down.

The tires hit the old, unused road with a bounce, instantly tossing the truck out of the overgrown ruts. At that moment, Claudia hit the gas. The tires spun out on the thick, green grass, and then suddenly fell back into the track with a sharp bump.

Samantha grabbed onto the seat with one hand, and with the other pressed up on the roof of the pickup to keep from hitting her head on it.

"Hold on!" Claudia shouted, then giggled as a jackrabbit made a mad dash to get out of their way, its long donkey ears bobbing madly like fuzzy antennae. She laughed at the look on Samantha's face when the rabbit narrowly missed being crushed beneath the wheels of the truck.

The highway quickly disappeared as the road wound over a small, knoblike hill, and then snaked toward what had once been a homestead. There was little left but a wide clearing in a scattering of trees, bounded by traces of a fence row and a dilapidated gate that was hanging only by habit. Grass was anywhere from ankle- to knee-high. A once-proud tree stood leafless and blackened beside a crumbling chimney, its skeletal branches having long since given up an attempt to provide shelter or shade.

Samantha grabbed onto the frame of the open window for support just as the underside of the pickup skinned an overgrown berry patch. She heard the hard, unripened berries whipping and thumping beneath the frame of the old truck as it came to a stop beneath the dead tree's empty branches.

"This will do," Claudia said.

Samantha rolled her eyes, thankful that they were still in one piece. She began smoothing the hair from her face, expecting at any time to see Claudia bolt from the truck.

It didn't happen. But what did was just as unexpected as the side trip had been.

Claudia's hair came away in her hands.

The blond, curly wig, the essence of Claudia the

waitress, now lay in the seat between them. With it removed, the wide red mouth suddenly fit the face. Dark red hair, bone-straight and shoulder length, framed a pair of bright green eyes that darkened with hate. And then Samantha saw the gun.

"I know you!" she gasped, and started to open the door, although it had simply been reflex. There was nowhere to go.

The shot went off, deafening from its closeness, and the suddenness with which it had been delivered.

"Of course you do. It's only fitting that you know the wife of the man you murdered."

Samantha was in shock. She'd finally been found. The hate on the woman's face was unmistakable. In spite of everything she and Johnny had done to stop it—as promised, her stalker had come. Heart pounding wildly, she tried to focus on something other than the gun barrel aimed in her face.

"Get out!" the woman shouted.

And when Samantha hesitated, another shot blasted past her ears and out the open window. This time it was much closer than the first, and left her in no doubt as to what her fate would be if she disobeyed.

She opened the door, stumbling as she got out. And as desperately as she tried to make herself quit shaking and concentrate on a plan of action, it didn't happen. The gun and the woman were too close and too real.

"Start walking!" she ordered.

Samantha complied while trying to make sense of the woman's wild accusations.

"Why, Desiree? Why me? I never did anything to either you or Donny. No one at the agency was sorrier than I was when we heard that he'd died. I know it's tragic when you lose someone you love. But to lose him to drugs has to be a difficult thing to bear. You should—"

"Shut up!" Desiree screamed. "You don't know what you're saying! Donny Adonis was a star. He was everything you're not and you were jealous! That's what! You were jealous! You gave away what should have been his part to that stupid television star who's losing his hair."

Her laughter was shrill and bordered on hysteria as she continued.

"Donny was perfect to play Casey Wilder. That part in Castle Rock's new film would have pulled him out of his slump. But no! You had to play God! You took away his pride and his faith in himself when you gave that part to someone else. The disappointment killed him!"

Shaking with the burst of adrenaline from the satisfaction of finally revealing her identity, she waved the gun in Samantha's face and sneered.

"Who did you screw to ruin Donny's life?"

The rude accusation made Samantha shudder. This woman was beyond reason and out of control. At any moment, she expected the gun Desiree was holding to go off. Yet when she started sobbing instead of shooting, Samantha began to pray for a way out. If Desiree was still able to shed tears, surely, she thought, there would be a way to reason with her. But hope died as swiftly as it was born when she jammed the gun up against Samantha's cheek and shrieked her words in a rush of hate and spittle.

"I hope it was good for you, bitch, because you humiliated Donny so badly that he committed suicide! Do you hear me? He killed himself! That means he'll burn in hell, and I'll never see any darling again."

As she took a step closer to Samantha, the fury in her voice went from rage to reason, frightening in itself by the instantaneous change.

"That's why you have to die, you see. I planned it for weeks afterward. Disguising my voice for the phone calls was easy. I have plenty of friends on the lots with all the technical equipment I needed. But implicating you was the best, don't you think?"

Her smile widened as she began to explain.

"I had a friend—I have lots of friends, you know. One of them let me in the office where you worked. I told them Donny's ring was missing, and I suspected he might have left it there during his last call. They let me look, and look, and look. While they were busy elsewhere, I used your typewriter to write the letters I sent to you. It was perfect, don't you see? That way the police would never help you look for me—because they wouldn't believe I existed."

As she laughed, she slapped her leg with the barrel of the gun. Samantha jerked in reflex from the sound of metal against flesh.

Then suddenly, all of Desiree's calm disappeared as she began to focus on the present instead of the past.

"You took Donny's life, so I'm going to take yours. But to get to hell with him, you have to die, too."

Samantha stumbled. *My God! The woman is beyond reasoning.* "Desiree, you have to let me explain."

Samantha's eyes were wide and frightened as she tried desperately to still the tremble in her voice. She couldn't let Desiree know that she was afraid. It might be all it took to send her over the edge.

The woman's entire body had undergone a transformation from the easygoing, giggling waitress to a tense, high-strung woman on the edge of madness. She was dry-eyed and panting, with her red mouth sliced into a snarl instead of a smile. She waved the gun back and forth in Samantha's direction as she ordered, "I don't have to do anything! Shut up and walk!

Samantha moved a few steps and then turned again, sensing that Desiree had a certain destination in mind and that when they got there, there would be no more time for talking. By then, she would be dead.

"You've got to listen to me, Desiree. Donny had a drug problem. He missed two auditions, and when he finally showed up, he was too messed up for the reading. I had no choice. It was my job to get someone trustworthy for the part. Donny was a good actor, but he couldn't remember his lines. He was always too strung out."

Samantha took a deep breath and then exhaled

slowly. She had to convince this woman of her innocence or it would be too late. "Donny didn't commit suicide, it was an accident. He overdosed. The coroner said so. It was in all the papers. Remember?"

Desiree staggered. Her eyes rolled back in her head, and for a moment Samantha thought she was going to have a seizure. She was poised on her toes for the chance to run, but it never came.

Desiree took a deep breath, straightened her shoulder, and screamed in Samantha's face: *"You're a liar! A filthy liar! Shut up! You just shut up!"*

But Samantha continued as if the interruption had never happened. "It wasn't the first time it had happened, was it, Desiree? But it was the last time, because this time he went too far and the doctors couldn't fix it. It wasn't his fault. It wasn't yours. And I swear to God, Desiree, it wasn't mine, either. Donny was sick and just couldn't get well."

"No! He's dead and it's all because of you!" Desiree screamed again.

Samantha didn't even see it coming.

Desiree kicked. Her foot came up and then out and hit Samantha squarely in the center of her stomach. Light exploded behind her eyelids as the breath was forced out of her lungs. She staggered backward from the impact, and then heard a loud crack, felt the ground sinking beneath her feet, and knew that she was falling. Breathless from the kick, she couldn't even scream.

Rotting boards that had been lying across the old well on the abandoned property gave way. As she fell, Samantha looked up and remembered thinking that Claudia/Desiree hadn't lied about one thing. She probably *did* have a black belt in karate. That kick felt authentic.

Desiree danced in a little circle of delight, shaking from exertion as well as exhilaration. She'd done it! Samantha Carlyle was gone. And then suddenly she had to see for herself, know for certain that where Samantha had gone, she couldn't get back.

Desiree leaned over and stared down into the dark, narrow shaft, then started to laugh. That smooth, pretty face was streaked with dirt and blood. The body that Sheriff Knight had so enjoyed lay crooked and crumpled in several inches of water.

As suddenly as it had appeared, Desiree's hysteria disappeared. She straightened slowly and began to look around, taking one last glance to ascertain that they had not been observed. A dangerous glitter sparkled in her eyes as she gauged their surroundings. The isolated location was perfect.

The gun hung heavily from her limp fingers. She looked down at the weight, surprised by its presence, and blinked twice, as if coming out of a trance.

"If he could see you now, he wouldn't be so quick bed you," Desiree said, her words coming out in ort, jerky hisses, and waved the gun back down ugh the opening to punctuate her statement.

Then suddenly, without warning, she braced her legs and pointed the gun into the well. Her finger twitched on the trigger, and yet she didn't squeeze. She realized that if Samantha died too fast she wouldn't have suffered enough. Donny had suffered. She must suffer too.

"No," Desiree said, in a conversational tone. "You don't get off that easy, Miss Samantha Carlyle. It's going to take you a long time to die. And while you're down there in misery and pain, crying for your lover and begging for mercy that no one hears, you'll remember what you did to my Donny. Then you'll be sorry."

She placed a couple of boards back across the hole, then turned and walked to her truck.

When she opened the door, she leaned inside and opened her purse, pulling out the note Samantha had intended for the sheriff. She wadded it up, tossed it down, then ground it into the dirt with the toe of her shoe. Satisfied that she was taking nothing of her enemy with her, she pulled a bag from behind the seat and quickly hid the gun between layers of clothing in it. Squinting her eyes against the glare of the overheard sun, she picked up the blond wig.

"Just one more time," she reminded herself, using the outside mirror on the door of the truck to make sure that none of the red strands of her hair were visible.

Without looking back at the scene of her crime, she started the truck and drove away. Less than thirty m utes later she was at the bus stop outside Marylee's Café waiting for the Greyhound bus bound for Dallas. From there she boarded a flight to L.A.

The blond curly wig and the gun in her bag found a final home in the women's rest room at DFW Airport just before Claudia got on the plane. There was no one and no way to connect Desiree Adonis of California to Claudia Smith of Texas, except Samantha Carlyle.

And bones didn't talk.

With consciousness came pain and thoughts of confusion. Why, Samantha wondered, did she feel wet and cold, and why was her bed suddenly so hard and lumpy? When she reached out, intent on pulling the covers back over her body, she groaned aloud as her hand bumped the side of the well instead. There was no way of stopping the chill that had invaded her bones.

"Johnny . . . I'm cold," she mumbled. But no one came and covered her up. No one took away the pain. She couldn't understand why her legs wouldn't stretch, or why she couldn't simply roll out of bed as she'd done this morning.

It was on the third aching breath that she remembered Desiree Adonis and jerked in reflex to the kick she hadn't seen coming. But it was too late. The kick had already come and gone and she was still in the well.

"Oh my God," she muttered. Reality surfaced as she became all too aware of her cramped and throbbing body when she tried to stand.

Movement made the ache in her back shoot straight up her spine, into the top of her head. The scream came without warning, bursting forth, echoing in an eerie refrain as it traveled against the narrow walls and then up and out of the opening above.

Tears flooded beneath her eyelids as she clapped a hand over her mouth in fear, terrified that Desiree might still be lurking somewhere above; afraid that her cry would alert the madwoman to the fact that she was still alive.

She had no way of knowing that Desiree Adonis was long gone. All she knew was that she was hurt and as alone as she'd ever been in her entire life.

"Oh God," she whispered, while tears made paths across the blood and dirt on her face. "Don't let me die. Not now. Not when I've just found Johnny."

She looked down at the water in which she was sitting and suddenly realized there was a good possibility she wasn't down here alone. Worrying about never being found or starving to death might be wasted if she'd fallen in the well with a cottonmouth. The water moccasin's deadly venom would simply finish what Desiree had started.

She sat for long painful moments, listening for sounds in the water and sounds from above. When she'd convinced herself that she was alone in her watery grave, she sighed with relief. It was a small thing for which to be thankful.

She said a prayer, took a deep breath, and once

again, began struggling to her feet—this time, much more slowly and carefully. Sweat mingled with tears as she tried to block out the shaft of pain that went up her leg.

"Oh God," she groaned when the walls around her began to move. She lowered her head between her arms and leaned against the dirt face of the well, ignoring the fact that the hairlike tendrils of roots extending out into the hole felt like webs against her skin. "Think of Johnny. Think of Johnny." Digging her fingers into the hard-packed walls of the old well, she took a slow, deep breath and thought about how to get out.

Somewhere in the back of her mind she could remember seeing a stunt man attempt to climb out of a crack inside a mountain. She closed her eyes and concentrated on the way that he'd inched himself up the opening.

"A chimney," she muttered. "He called the shaft a chimney," and she remembered that the climber had used his arms, back, and legs as braces against the narrow walls. She could almost hear his grunts as he'd push himself up with great effort, inches at a time.

"It has to work," she groaned, remembering how far they'd come off the main highway and how isolated the abandoned homestead was. "I will not die in this well."

She thought of the note she'd left for Johnny and a spurt of hope surfaced until she recalled Claudia gathering up the contents of her purse. She had a sudden horrible feeling that somehow, without her seeing it happen, Claudia had destroyed that note along with her life.

"God help me, because Johnny can't," she whispered, and put her back against the wall of the well.

At first, she thought it was going to work. Her legs were long, and a more than fair fit against the opposite side of the well. Her back was sore, but seemed able to support her weight as she began to move upward toward the sunlight taunting her from above.

Sweat popped out across her forehead, running down the middle of her spine and instantly soaking her shirt to her body. A short time into the climb, Samantha began to realize that it wasn't heat that was forming perspiration, it was pain.

With each movement of her leg, she felt as if red-hot needles were being poked into her knee. She looked down, expecting to see shards from the wood through which she'd fallen protruding through her jeans. Nothing was there but the fire spreading in her leg.

She looked up again. This time the hole moved above her, and then as if in a nightmare, the well began to spin. She threw her arms out in a futile effort to stop the motion, and fell back into the water.

She screamed in agony as the pain in her leg traveled up past her spine, clawing for a toehold inside sanity. This time it caught and held. Everything around her began to spin faster and faster as she fell off the edge of reality into oblivion.

Minutes, hours, even days, could have passed by the

time she came to again, and she would have been none the wiser. Daylight still made shadows on the edge of the well, but they were shorter, and she realized that however long she'd been down here, another day was about to end. Night was coming. And with it came fear. Unreasonable, impossible fear.

"Help! *Help!*" she screamed, shouting over and over until her throat went dry. "Someone, get me out! I'm down here! *I'm down here!*"

She looked up at the dwindling patch of daylight, holding her breath against the fear that Desiree might come back. When she could think with some reason, she came to the realization that Desiree Adonis was probably long gone from the scene of her crime. With the knowledge came fright. Samantha choked back a scream. There was no one left to tell the world what had happened to her.

Time passed.

Samantha shouted and screamed off and on for hours, standing when she did so in the odd belief that being that much closer to the opening above her head would make her voice easier to hear. But she knew in her heart it would take more than a miracle for that to happen.

Her aching knee suddenly gave way beneath her again, dropping her back into the cold, murky water with a rude plop. With nothing in her heart but a meager hope and a prayer, she leaned her forehead against her knees and finally gave way to more sobs of despair.

And night came.

*   *   *

The Cherokee County sheriff's office was in turmoil. Law officers from two surrounding counties, as well as a couple of Texas Rangers, compliments of Wheeler Joe Turner, were busy reading maps and marking off places to search. The local city police, as well as most of the able citizens from Cotton and Rusk, also filled the small rooms and spilled out into the streets.

Because Samantha Carlyle's disappearance was now officially being ruled a kidnapping, the FBI was en route, although John Thomas knew that no ransom note would come. He remembered the hate mail that Samantha had received in L.A. and knew that whatever the stalker wanted of Samantha, it wasn't money.

The locals were ready for war. The California Stalker had come and gone and taken one of their own right out from under their noses and they didn't like it. Search parties were being organized. Landowners had volunteered to guide the searchers over their properties in an effort to locate the missing woman. Road blocks had been put up at all the exits leading out of a three-county area surrounding Cherokee County. All efforts were being made to apprehend Claudia Smith in the hope that she would lead them to Samantha.

But none of the hubbub in the outer office made John Thomas one bit easier in his soul. He'd broken a promise to the only woman he'd ever loved when he'd failed to keep her safe.

His eyes narrowed as he leaned over his desk, staring uselessly at maps. *God help Claudia Smith if I ever get my hands on her.*

Carol Ann shouted from the other room. "Sheriff, Peter Meuller on line one."

John Thomas picked up the phone and mentally blocked out the noise beyond his office.

"This is Sheriff Knight."

"Hey, John Thomas. You remember that stranded motorist from California? The one with the Jaguar? I thought you might like to know that he lit a shuck out of here just before noon."

"Damn it. I warned him to let me know before he left. I guess that doesn't surprise me," John Thomas muttered. "He's been ready to leave since he got here."

"But you don't understand. The car was ready and waiting for him the day before yesterday."

"And he didn't leave until today?" John Thomas was surprised.

That didn't make sense. The man he and Monty had interrogated had seemed ready to leave Cotton since the day he'd been stranded. Why, when his car was fixed, had he suddenly chosen to wait? Did Claudia Smith have an accomplice? Had they read the situation all wrong?

"Thanks for the information, Pete. It might mean something after all."

"Sure, pal," Pete said, and hung up.

John Thomas yelled above the din. "Hey, Monty!"

Monty jumped up from his desk and waded through the lawmen and volunteers as he headed toward the sheriff's office.

"What's up, boss?" he asked.

"Give Carol Ann that information again on Aaron Reuben. Have them put out an APB on the man and the Jaguar. He left town. I want to make sure that he left alone."

"Yes sir," Monty said, and headed for the dispatch desk.

Less than an hour later the department was empty save for Carol Ann and Delmar. Both dispatchers had volunteered to stay round the clock until Samantha was found.

The radios were alive with traffic and static, as first one search party, then the other, called in to let them know they were at their starting point. And then, except for short, intermittent transmissions, the airwaves went silent. The search was on.

On the rougher terrain, the searchers used four-wheelers and horses. Where possible, they walked, searching every nook and cranny, every shallow pond and deep crevasse for evidence of recent entry. Each time they came to a place where the earth or the grasses looked disturbed, to a man they held their breath, hoping that they wouldn't be the one to find the lifeless body of the sheriff's lady.

Daylight disappeared, and they didn't even see it leave until they realized they were staring harder into shadows that hadn't been there earlier, and losing sight of one another as they moved across the land.

Within the hour, it became evident that a halt was imperative. Search parties were impotent without light by which to guide them. They were forced to stop and make camp until sunrise.

John Thomas stood beside a campfire, watching blindly as orange and yellow tongues licked into the wood. He was heartsick. All he could think was that he would give a year of his life to be able to start this day over.

She'd been safe up until the point that he got the call about the rustlers. After that, it was all a confusing collage of thoughts that played and replayed in his mind until he thought he would go mad. And yet he knew that would not bring Samantha back. He had to concentrate.

But he kept remembering what he'd promised her. Damn his soul to hell and back, he'd even crossed his heart and hoped to die that he would protect her. And he hadn't been able to do it. As far as he was concerned, living without her was no longer an option.

Some of the locals had gone home with promises to return at daylight, while others had opted to sleep at the point they'd ceased searching, anxious to be first on hand when daylight came.

Refusing the offers of food, coffee, and conversation, John Thomas retreated to a bedroll a distance away from the others. As he sat, he tried to remember

everything that had occurred from the moment he realized Samantha was gone, up until now. But no matter
how many times he replayed it in his mind, the only
clue they held to her whereabouts were the grasses that
he'd pulled from beneath Marylee's old black pickup
truck. Try as he might, he couldn't remember if there
was any particular significance to the varieties, not
even the berry vines that had pricked his hands.

He shifted uncomfortably on the sleeping bag, wondering where, and in what condition, Sam was trying
to sleep.

When I find her, please God, don't let it be too late.

His stomach grumbled. But the thought of food
made him sick. He didn't need to eat. What he needed
was Sam.

When he closed his eyes, the image surfaced again of
the grass and weeds that he'd pulled out from beneath
that old black truck. The answer had to be somewhere in
that drying bundle. It was there . . . it just had to be.

Instinct prodded him to go back to his car. He had a
sudden need to look at the evidence all over again.

The trunk light was dim, but it was enough to see
that the grasses and weeds were still where he'd tossed
them.

"Whatcha looking at?" one of the older men asked,
as he walked by the sheriff's car, then peered into the
trunk and tried to coax a smile from the sheriff by teasing, "Did you find yourself a marijuana plant?" He
laughed lightly at his own wit.

John Thomas sighed and stepped back. "No, just a clump of grass and weeds I pulled out from under Marylee's old truck." He tossed them inside the trunk and started to shut the lid.

"See you got yourself some dewberry vines in with it," the old man said.

John Thomas froze. Dewberry vines? He'd thought they were blackberry. It was a small distinction. Could it possibly mean something he'd overlooked earlier?

"As a rule, dewberries don't grow wild like blackberries, do they?" he asked.

"Nope." The old man scratched his head and leaned against the car, readying for a reminiscence. "My ma had a big old truck garden when I was a kid. Had two of the longest rows of dewberries you ever did see. Me and my younger brother had to pick them damned things ever year. The stickers were hell on fingers, but Ma's cobblers were fine on the stomach."

He patted the sheriff on the back and ambled away when he realized that storytelling wasn't what Sheriff Knight was after.

John Thomas's pulse kicked into second gear as his mind began to whirl. Exactly what did this mean to the investigation? There were commercial berry farms all over East Texas. But he couldn't imagine Claudia concealing Samantha on one of them. There were always too many people. The only thing that made sense was an abandoned farm and an overgrown dewberry patch that had once been part of someone's garden

And with that thought came another. Plenty of old, abandoned homesteads had an assortment of shrubs and bushes growing wild that their owners had once planted and nurtured with pride. But how many of them had a berry patch?

"Hey, Bud!"

The old man stopped and turned.

"You don't happen to know where there are any dewberry patches growing wild?"

The old man thought, and then shook his head. "But your deputy, Mike Lawler, might. He's a big one for hunting. I'd guess at one time or another he's walked over every square inch of East Texas."

John Thomas slammed the trunk down with a thud. Lawler was with another search party, but he had a sudden need to talk to him face-to-face.

"Tell the men I'll be back," John Thomas said as his deputy walked up.

Monty took one look at the sick, empty expression on his boss's face, crawled in beside him, and began to buckle his seat belt.

"What do you think you're doing?" John Thomas asked.

"Going with you."

John Thomas didn't argue.

Less than thirty minutes later he was in deep discussion with Mike Lawler, poring over a map of the area, while Mike related the location of every local hunting expedition he'd made within the last twenty years.

Hours later, John Thomas pulled up in front of his house and parked. Rebel came out from beneath the porch, wagging his tail and woofing a soft welcome.

"What are we doing here?" Monty asked.

"Getting some sleep, and when it gets daylight, getting my dog. I've got an idea that may or may not pan out. But I can't afford to ignore anything—especially gut instinct."

Monty nodded. "I'll take the couch."

"You may as well take a damn bed," John Thomas said gruffly. "I can't sleep in any of them. Not without . . ." He swallowed harshly, unable to finish his sentence.

"We'll find her, Sheriff," Monty said. "You can't give up hope."

You don't understand, boy, John Thomas thought. *Hope is all I have left.*

Sometime when Sam wasn't looking, night had come, shadowing the deep hole in which she was trapped to a frightening degree. In spite of the darkness sparkling with minute bits of starlight above her, she knew she must be sick. Only a fever would produce the psychedelic glitter she saw overhead.

She rubbed her knee and winced when it throbbed beneath her fingertips, hot to the touch even through the denim of her jeans. She was only vaguely aware of the consciousness that came and went at alarming intervals. But each time she came to, she knew that her

condition was deteriorating. Twice she thought she'd
heard John Thomas's voice. Each time she'd screamed
until she was hoarse, but he'd never answered.

The knowledge that she was seeing things—and
people—who weren't really there, frightened her more
than the hole she was in. She felt sick, shaky, and
weaker by the minute.

The wind rose, rustling the long grasses above her
just enough to make her think that something—or
someone—was up there. But each time she called, she
got no response. Her throat ached from continuous
shouting, and her lips were caked and dry, split from a
busted lip as well as lack of fluids.

At one point she slapped the flat of her hands into
the water in which she was sitting and groaned. "This
is a joke! I'm starving for a drink, and up to my ankles
in water I can't even stand to smell."

The thick, rank stuff had obviously been in the well
for ages. But she'd long since given up worrying
about what she might be sharing it with. Not even a
snake could survive down here for long. And with that
thought came a huge, ugly sob, tearing up her throat
and ripping out through her lips in a makeshift
scream.

Not even a snake could suvive.

A small, wispy cloud slid across the slice of quarter
moon, momentarily blotting out the weak glow from
its face. Samantha shuddered, closed her eyes, and
buried her face in her hands.

In seconds she was past misery and lost in a hallucination that saved her sanity.

She kept seeing her mother's face, hearing a young boy's voice from her childhood as he urged her to hurry, then feeling Johnny's arms around her, his hands on her face . . . on her body . . . just as he did when they made love.

She shifted in the water, trying to ease the ache in her leg and the throbbing behind her eyelids, but it was no use. The pain that came spiraled, sending her into blessed oblivion as fever claimed her body. The night passed and morning came without notice. Samantha was unconscious.

Desiree Adonis inserted her key in the lock and turned it, smiling to herself as it clicked sharply. The door swung open. She wrinkled her nose. The apartment smelled stale, but she would soon take care of that. She was back—for good! She turned on the light and locked the door behind her.

Tossing her bag onto the sofa with casual abandon, as if she'd just come in from a workout at the gym, she walked to her patio overlooking the pool. The security light reflected back from the water in a broken wave of refracted glitter. She leaned over the railing, staring down into the darkened end of the pool and imagined Samantha Carlyle below her in the well. She looked up at the stars, inhaled deeply, and walked back inside with a small smile in place.

The condo was in her maiden name, or it would have been sucked up with the rest of their assets that the courts had taken after Donny's death. But it was no matter. Up until now, money had been the farthest thing from her thoughts.

She walked into her bedroom. Without turning on the light, she stripped herself of her clothing, tossed it into a garbage bag, and made a mental note to put it out with the rest of the trash that had accumulated in her apartment. She needed no reminders of her accomplishments. The inner satisfaction was enough. Relishing the cool draft of air on her nudity, she walked slowly toward the bathroom, stepped into the shower, and turned on the taps.

The water spurted, jerking past the air pockets that had accumulated in the unused pipes, then ran fresh and clean onto her face, her hair, her skin. She'd done what she set out to do. The woman who had ruined her life was dead. Or she soon would be. Of that Desiree was certain. Now it was time to focus on the rest of her life.

And with that thought came the fear. What *was* left? Her entire life had been Donny. After his death, revenge had taken over her world. Now that it had been accomplished, she realized she had no direction. She felt lost and empty.

Fear overtook the rush of adrenaline that had carried her from Texas to California, replacing the success that she'd felt with another, more insidious emotion. Her hands flattened on either side of the shower as the water continued to pelt down upon her face.

Suddenly she began to laugh. Loud, jerky bellows of hilarity that changed into choked gasps for air. She dropped to her knees and buried her face in her hands, then yanked them away as the memories of what she had done surfaced.

Without turning off the water, she dashed from the shower and flung herself on the bed, ignoring the spots she was making on the satin comforter.

"She had it coming. She had it coming," she muttered, and rolled over on her back, staring blankly up at the shadows on the ceiling above the bed.

Midmorning of the next day, Desiree was at her dressing table, painting on a face to present to the world. She squinted her eyes as she traced a deep rose lipliner carefully across her upper lip, and then licked her little finger before running it across her mouth to soften the line that she'd drawn. Minutes later she'd put the finishing touches on her makeup, and was stepping into a subdued, but fashionable, black summer dress. She was, after all, still in mourning.

14

THE SUN WAS ONLY minutes away from the horizon when a car drove into the front yard of John Thomas's home. Rebel's baying was a second alert to the engine he had already heard.

Instead of sleeping, he'd spent all of last night going through the letters Samantha had received from the stalker, hoping to find a clue they might have missed. Nothing had surfaced other than the notion that when he found Samantha, it would be too late.

"Someone's outside," Monty said, as he came out of the bathroom with a towel in his hands.

"I heard them," John Thomas said. "Fresh coffee is in the kitchen. If you want any, make it to go. I'm leaving here in less than five minutes."

Monty hastened to comply as the sheriff went outside to greet his visitors.

"Sheriff Knight?"

The small, dapper man wearing a plain blue suit and a professional smile held out his hand.

"I'm Inspector Williams, FBI. Sorry my men and I couldn't get here sooner. I understand that the physical evidence the kidnapper sent is in your possession, and that you already have a search in progress. Mind filling me in on the details? After I hear the facts, it might be that some reorganization is necessary."

Neither his cool, dare-to-argue-with-me expression, nor the fact that he'd suggested changing plans in midstream, angered John Thomas. He didn't have time for one-upmanship over who had authority over whom. All he'd thought about last night was Samantha somewhere in the dark . . . alone . . . in pain.

"I don't think we're after a kidnapper," John Thomas said shortly. "Someone stalked Samantha Carlyle in California like a hunter after prey. We think it was a woman we knew as Claudia Smith who followed us when I brought Samantha out here. And when my goddamned back was turned she took her right out from under my nose." Anger was thick in John Thomas's voice when he finished. "There's been no ransom note, nor do I expect one."

Before the inspector could respond to his remarks, John Thomas yelled, "Monty! Bring me Sam's letters. Now!"

Seconds later Monty dashed out the front door with them clutched against his chest, looking wild-eyed and confused as to what was happening.

John Thomas all but thrust them in the agent's face, and then whistled for Rebel as he walked away.

In all of his years with the department, Inspector Williams had faced distrust, dismay, even disgust from lawmen who felt that their toes were being stepped on during an ongoing investigation. But this was the first time he'd had it all handed over without a word. In spite of the fact that he was now holding what he assumed to be all the physical evidence, he was certain that he'd just gotten a brush-off. It was the closest he'd ever come to being ignored. He didn't like it.

"Wait!" he ordered, as John Thomas began hooking the leash to Rebel's collar and loading him into the backseat of the squad car. "Where do you think you're going? We haven't had our meeting. I want to discuss—"

"Mike Lawler is one of my deputies. Find him. He'll talk to you."

"Where are you going?" Williams asked.

"To find Samantha Carlyle," John Thomas said. As far as he was concerned, there was nothing left to discuss.

Monty jumped into the car, slamming the door just as the car was put in reverse. John Thomas backed up, leaving the inspector standing in the yard wearing a frustrated expression to go with his three-piece suit. All the man could do was hold the letters he'd been given and soundly curse the independence of Texans.

A few miles down the road, the radio in the squad car

came to life as Carol Ann's voice reached out through the early morning air. Monty took one look at the distracted expression on his boss's face and answered. But they both listened intently to the dispatcher's message.

"Call came in early this morning for Sheriff Knight. He's to see the woman at 1222 Sunset in Cotton. Says she might have some information for you. Oh, and the APB we issued yesterday evening regarding the Jaguar and its driver, it's a negative. He was stopped on the interstate just this side of Dallas. The passenger he had with him was not Samantha Carlyle, just the maid who cleaned the motel rooms at the Texas Pig."

Monty grinned and whispered an aside to the sheriff that he didn't want going out over the air. "Now we know why Reuben spent an extra day in Cotton. He was beginning to appreciate the scenery."

"Ten-four," Monty said. "We'll be en route to Cotton. Over and out."

John Thomas turned on the lights and siren, then made a U-turn on the highway. Going back to Cotton, instead of the search party he'd abandoned last night, was the lesser of two evils.

He and Lawler had discussed berry vines and hunting locations until his head ached. The only conclusio they'd come to was to take Rebel and start a farm farm search of all the abandoned places Mike Law could remember having dewberry patches. Unf nately for John Thomas, his chances of finding S tha were fading. Mike Lawler had said there were many such locations.

The sirens screamed as he sailed past a car that had pulled over on the side of the road to let him pass. At this point, he needed a miracle. Maybe the lady in Cotton had better news. Anything would be better than what they had.

"Who are we going to see, boss?" Monty asked.

"If I remember my addresses correctly, I think it's the Baptist preacher's wife. And I hope she's got more to tell me than the fact that they said a prayer for the missing woman last night."

Monty nodded and rechecked his seat belt just for good measure. The scenery was passing in a blur of green.

"If I'd missed prayer meeting last night, I might not have known to call," Amanda Pruitt said, as she waved the sheriff and his deputy to a seat in her parlor.

"Yes, ma'am," John Thomas said, knowing it was going to take a miracle to get Amanda Pruitt to the point. She had a tendency to ramble. "About your call. Can you tell me anything about Samantha Carlyle's disappearance?" He held his breath, hoping against hope that it would be something useful. He wasn't disappointed.

"Won't you have some coffee cake? I just took it out oven. The reverend is real fond of my coffee

John Thomas shook his head, glaring at the wistful look Monty got on his face as she carried it back and set it on the sideboard out of reach.

"Now, about your news," John Thomas urged.

Amanda Pruitt nodded as she resumed her seat. "As I was saying, it wasn't until I got to church last night that I learned about the old black truck."

Please let this matter, John Thomas thought, and clenched his fists in his lap to keep from shaking the information out of her instead.

"Herman Simmons—you know Herman, his oldest boy is about your age, isn't he, Sheriff?"

John Thomas nodded and clenched his teeth, certain that this would never get said.

"Anyway, Herman told me that they thought the person who took her might have been driving an old black truck, is that right?"

"Yes, ma'am," John Thomas said. "It's what we think. Please, Mrs. Pruitt, why did you call me? Did you see Samantha?"

"Well, while I was outside watering my begonias, I know I saw an old black truck go through Cotton before noon. Must have been around 10:00, maybe 10:30."

John Thomas's heart lifted. The time frame fit.

"And," she continued, "I saw a blond woman dr[iv]ing it. The reason I noticed it at all was because it m[ade] so much noise." She giggled. "I mean, the truc[k] making noise, not the driver. It didn't have a m[

you know. It's against the law to drive without a muf-
fler, isn't it, sheriff?"

"Yes, ma'am, it is," he said. "As for the driver, you
said she was blond. Was she alone?"

"No she wasn't. But I didn't get a good look at the
passenger. Sun was in my eyes and all. I know he had
dark hair. That's all I can say for sure."

John Thomas's heart fell. He! That wasn't what he
wanted to hear.

"You sure it was a man?" he asked.

She squinted her eyes and thought. "Well, they had
the windows down. The driver had a lot of loose curls.
They were blowing in the wind. The other one had his
hair all slicked back. Didn't seem to be blowing like
that."

Monty suddenly jumped to his feet.

"Sheriff, remember yesterday morning when you
sent me after a change of your clothes? Samantha's
hair was in a braid. A long braid that hung down her
back. From a distance it might make her hair look
short, real short, if you can't see the braid."

Hope resumed as John Thomas continued.

"Mrs. Pruitt, is there anything else you can remember that might help us? Anything at all. Please try to
think. It's very important."

She shrugged. "Not really, I probably wouldn't have
even remembered that much except I saw it twice. Seeing things over and over is a good way to set them in
your memory, you know."

John Thomas jumped on her statement. "What do you mean, you saw it twice?"

"Oh that's right!" Amanda Pruitt cried, and clasped her hand to her breast in a gesture of dismay. "The truck, it went through Cotton, and less than thirty minutes later, it came back. One thing I know for sure, if the passenger wasn't lying down in the seat or something, that time the driver was alone."

"You're sure about this?" John Thomas couldn't hide his elation as he jumped to his feet.

"Yes, sir! I don't make mistakes like that. Besides, I was still outside watering my begonias. They need a lot of water this time of year and I—"

"Mrs. Pruitt, I can't thank you enough for this information," John Thomas said, and bolted for the door with Monty at his heels.

"You're welcome, I'm sure," she said, as she watched them running down the walk toward the police car. She shook her head and closed the door, satisfied with having done her civic duty.

"What do you think?" Monty asked, as they started north out of Cotton.

"I think we just got lucky," John Thomas said. "Start timing me. Marylee's old truck can't do more than fifty miles per hour. If we don't see something beforehand, tell me when ten minutes are up."

"You're right!" Monty said. "Wherever she went with Samantha she had to stop, get her out of the truck, dump the body—" His face turned white as a sheet as he realized what he'd just said. "Oh Jesus, boss, I didn't mean—"

"Save it," John Thomas said. "It's nothing I haven't thought of myself."

His features were stone-cold, the expression in his eyes darkening by the moment as his lips twisted, tasting the bitterness of the words pouring out of his mouth.

"It's just something I can't consider, not yet. Somehow I think Sam's still alive. I don't know why I think it. Maybe it's denial, maybe it's instinct. But I think I would know it if she wasn't. I can't explain—"

"You don't have to," Monty said, quietly. "I understand probably better than you think."

"Anyway, Claudia had to have time to do whatever with Sam, and then drive back the way she came. If Samantha was sitting up in the truck when they passed through Cotton, then that tells me she was still in the dark as to who she was with. And the Sam I know wouldn't go down without a fight."

"I'm timing you," Monty said. "Drive."

Rebel whined from the backseat, as if sensing his master's anxiety.

As he drove, John Thomas constantly searched the roadside for a sign of anything that might tell him they'd gone this way. But the farther he went, the more discouraged he became. Time was running out and if—

He slammed on his brakes, fishtailing the back end of the squad car wildly across the highway as he put the car in reverse and began backing up down the shoulder of the road.

"What in hell, boss?" Monty asked. "We're still two minutes shy of the allotted time."

"Look!"

John Thomas pointed and Monty saw an old, narrow road leading off the highway and across a pasture, then disappearing beyond the rise on the hill. And the overgrown ruts, well filled with grass and weeds, had a new trail up through the thick growth.

"I'll be damned," Monty said, as they started up the road. "Look how someone spun out on the grass. Dug it up real good before settling back into the ruts."

John Thomas bit the inside of his lip and tossed his sunglasses on the dash. He didn't want anything interfering with his vision, not even a shade between him and the morning sun. If there was a hope in heaven of finding Sam, he had to take it.

Rebel whined from the backseat, sensing the tension of the men inside the car, and then woofed once as John Thomas topped the rise and spooked a coyote on his way across the meadow.

"No coyotes today, boy," he cautioned. "We've got to find Sam. Remember, boy. We're gonna find Sam."

Rebel barked once, and then dropped back onto the seat. He understood "No," and he understood "Find." He would wait until he was given his orders.

*   *   *

There she was again, staring down at her and laughing like a banshee. Samantha sobbed and folded her arms across her knees, hiding her face from the woman above. She'd known all along that Desiree would come back.

She heard Desiree laugh and then cry, and then caught her breath, unable to tell which direction the crying came from as the sound swirled around her.

Maybe she's not crying. Maybe it's me!

She took a chance and looked up. A face wavered in and out of focus. It *was* her! Just as she'd feared. All that red hair kept changing into blond and back again. Sometimes her mouth would open so wide when she laughed that Samantha thought it would swallow her whole.

She put her hands over her ears and squeezed her eyes shut, fiercely trying to block out the vision. She had no way of knowing that what she saw wasn't really there.

"I won't tell," she muttered, unaware that insanity had finally taken over where the truth had ended. She swiped at the hair stuck to her face and neck. "I swear, Johnny . . . cross my heart and hope to die. I won't ever tell."

Lost with the ghosts in her mind, she didn't hear the sound of the car coming up the road, or hear a dog's excited yelp. All she could hear was the wind whistling down the well and the shrieks of Desiree Adonis's rage.

*   *   *

"Sheriff, look!"

Montgomery's excited shout drew John Thomas's attention to the right of the road where a large, brushy growth of berry vines had nearly overtaken the ground around it.

"A berry patch," he muttered, missing nothing of the skid marks that had cut across some of the longer vines and torn out part of the new growth. "We can't be this lucky."

"Hell, yes we can!" Monty shouted. "It's about time something good happened. Let's get the dog out of the backseat and see what happens. Want me to call in the other searchers?"

"Let's wait and see where this leads us," John Thomas said. "It might turn out to be nothing more than a wild goose chase. I don't want to relocate hundreds of searchers for nothing."

Monty nodded. "You're the boss, now let's get at it!"

They parked well away from the center of the clearing, unwilling to disturb what might be precious clues that Claudia Smith had left behind.

Rebel bounced out of the car with a loud bark. The sheriff stuffed Samantha's shoes beneath the dog's nose.

"Find Sam, boy! Search! Find Sam!"

The dog's nose went to ground like a furry vacuum as he began circling the area. Several times they lost sight of the dog in the tall grass, but never lost track of his presence. He was moving through the area like a whirlwind. A short time later he bayed, and began digging at the ground beneath his feet.

John Thomas ran forward, praying that he would not see bits of Samantha revealed beneath the earth. He breathed a sigh of relief as Rebel dug a paper from the grass instead.

"What did you find, boy?" he asked. The paper was wadded, and he held it only by the corners so as not to ruin whatever prints had been left on it. Carefully, he pulled out the worst of the creases until he could read what it said.

"My God!" he groaned softly, then motioned for Monty to come running. "Look! It's a note from Sam. She said she was going shopping in New Summerfield with Claudia."

He caught his breath against the tide of emotion that swamped him. His hand shook slightly as he carefully handed the paper to Monty. "Bag it as evidence. Sam probably never knew I didn't get it."

Monty slid it into a plastic bag. Every piece of evidence they garnered was one more knot in the rope they wanted to put around Claudia's neck.

"If anything has happened to Samantha, this is all the proof we need to show that Claudia Smith was in on it," Monty reminded him.

John Thomas turned away, unable to look at the undisguised sympathy on his deputy's face. "Search, Rebel. Find Sam."

The dog was still running, nose to the ground. At his master's insistent tone he increased his pace as if sensing the urgency of his task.

Except for the grass and trees, the homestead on which they had parked was dead, evidently abandoned long ago by its owners after too many years of bad luck. John Thomas stared intently beyond what was left of the fence row. But there was nothing to see other than the ever-present trees, knee-high grass, and the blue sky above.

Rebel's loud bay startled both men. Each turned from their individual search to look toward the dog who was near the dead tree, barking into the grass.

"Damn you, dog," John Thomas muttered. "If you're barking at anything four-legged and furry, I'll have your hide."

They converged on the area where Rebel had taken a stance. The closer John Thomas came, the more certain he was that Rebel was onto something. His heart began to pound and he began to run. Afraid to get closer and see Samantha's lifeless body lying bleeding and broken in the grass, afraid not to look for fear he'd miss the chance to save her.

"There's nothing here," Monty said, as he reached the area first. "I don't see a thing that—"

"Get back!" John Thomas yelled, as he knelt by his dog. "It's an old well. You just missed stepping on one of the covering boards. See?"

"Well, I'll be," Monty said, and took a step backward, aware of how close he'd come to walking on top of that board and falling through.

And then the same thought occurred to both men at the same time. Suddenly they were both on their knees, removing the scattered boards and brushing away the grasses at the edge of the well.

John Thomas took a deep breath and leaned over. It had to be done, and if anyone was going to find Sam, it was going to be him.

"Oh, Jesus!" he said, and nearly died on the spot. Even from here he could see the top of her head and the pale yellow blouse she was wearing. "Samantha! Sam, honey, can you hear me?"

But she didn't move, and the faint hope he'd had of finding her alive lessened with each beat of his heart.

"Go get the car," he yelled, pointing back to the squad car parked beyond the old yard. "Get the rope out of the trunk, and hurry!"

In less than a minute Monty was back, parked only a few feet away from the old well while John Thomas lay on his back beneath the front of the car, frantically tying the rope to the frame.

"I'm going down," he said, as he tied the other end of the rope around his waist. "Back up until the rope is taut between us. When I start inside, drive forward to lower me down. Go slow. When you hear me yell, you stop. I'll let you know when to pull us back up."

"Yes, sir," Monty said.

He could only marvel at the calmness with which

the sheriff was working, knowing how sick and afraid he must really be inside. It was at that moment that Montgomery Turner saw what made a good lawman. It was putting personal emotion aside to do what must be done.

"Deputy, when you get in the car, let them know we found her, and get me an ambulance here ASAP."

"Yes, sir," he said, and backed up the car until John Thomas waved his hand.

He watched as the sheriff tested the rope around his waist and then steeped toward the well. Monty held his breath as John Thomas disappeared into the hole. Then, remembering his other orders to call for help, he grabbed the radio as he put the car into gear and began to move.

"Sam, honey, can you hear me?" John Thomas's voice was rough and shaky, echoing within the small, enclosed space as he bounced and scooted his way down the shaft. But she didn't move, and wouldn't answer, and his hopes fell.

She heard his voice. But she'd heard it before and it hadn't been him. All during the night she'd heard him over and over, calling her name, but every time she looked up, expecting to see his face, there would be nothing above her but the night sky and a thousand glittering eyes. At the sight, Samantha had sobbed brokenheartedly. It had seemed to her as if all the eyes of Texas were looking down at her and still none could see her. It was going to be too late. No one could save her.

Later, she'd realized that it was stars she'd seen and not eyes, but even the stars had seemed faint, too distant to wish upon, too far away for dreams. Besides, she knew it was too late for wishes to come true. She'd come to terms with dying. It was her heart that kept having the problem. It didn't want to give up on Johnny Knight.

And Johnny Knight hadn't given up on her. When his feet suddenly bumped her shoulder, he scrambled to push himself away from the wall of the well, fearing that he'd land on her instead.

"Come on, Monty, a little lower, a little—*Stop!*" he yelled.

He found himself standing in several inches of water and straddling her legs.

With shaking hands, he reached down, touching the side of her face, half expecting to feel the chill of death beneath his fingers. But even though it was cold, supple flesh gave way beneath his touch.

Tears sprang to his eyes as he crouched in the cramped space, moving his hands frantically across her body in an effort to find her injuries. When he looked up to gauge the distance he'd come, he had no doubt that she had them. It was a long way to fall.

She moaned. The touch on her body was familiar. The voice that reverberated against her eardrums made her cry out in pain. She couldn't bear to be taunted with his ghost like this again. She closed her eyes, certain that once again, just like before, the image of John

Thomas would disappear and she'd come to only to find herself still hurt and alone . . . and dying.

"Don't try to move, darlin'," he said softly, as he lifted her to her feet. "Let me do all the work. You just keep breathing for me, Sam. Don't leave me now!"

He heard her gasp as her knee gave way, and he quickly slid his arms around her, letting his body bear all her weight as he prepared her for the trip out.

Monty was on all fours, peering down into the darkened well, trying to see past the sheriff to the woman in his arms.

"Sheriff?" he yelled down.

"She's alive, Monty. Thank the Lord, she's alive. Haul us up, man, and be easy. I can't tell how bad she's hurt."

The whoop came from Monty. The bark came from Rebel, who'd heard his master's voice from deep in the ground. In seconds the car was in reverse as Monty began a slow but constant pull on the rope.

John Thomas pressed her head firmly beneath his chin. With one hand against the back of her neck to keep her immobile, and his other arm wrapped as tightly around her as he dared to hold, they began the ascent. As the rope grew taut and the ride began, he locked his legs around the lower half of her body, using himself for the buffer needed to get them both up the narrow shaft.

Soon the earth gave up its prey as John Thomas's head appeared above the hole. His shoulders came next, and the hold he had on his lady would never have loosened had the ambulance not appeared at that moment, bouncing its way up the rough, uncharted path with several patrol cars leading the way.

"Thank God," John Thomas said, as he felt solid ground beneath him. He rolled onto his back with her on top, still using himself to keep her immobile.

"Sam, darlin', can you hear me?"

She didn't answer, and when the chill of her body began seeping into his own skin, he willed her some of his own warmth and strength. His hands shook as he traced the bloody paths across her face and arms, and he knew in that moment how fragile life was, and how dear she was to him.

He'd never wanted to kiss a woman so bad in his life, and never been so afraid to do so. There wasn't a place on her that looked safe to touch.

"I love you, Samantha Jean. Don't you leave me now," he whispered, and satisfied himself with the life he still held within his hands.

Samantha felt the warm, steady beat of a heart beneath her eardrum, heard the familiar rumble of his voice, and knew that if she'd died and gone to heaven it was okay, because Johnny was already there waiting for her. And if she hadn't, if Johnny had truly come, then he'd done as he promised. He'd saved her life. She would have to wait until later to know for sure. Right now there was a big black hole in her mind, just waiting for her to fall through.

She fell, just as the first of the rescue team got to her side.

"Is she alive?" the paramedic asked.

John Thomas had to take a deep breath before he could trust himself to answer.

"Yes, thank God."

When they started to roll her from his body onto the stretcher, his gaze connected once again with the medic's. "I don't know how she's still alive, but you've got to do your bit to keep her that way."

"We'll do all we know how, and then some, John Thomas. Now let her go."

Reluctantly, John Thomas gave her up.

He bolted to his feet as they strapped her down, then ran beside the stretcher as they carried her to the waiting ambulance. When they transferred her to the gurney and then into the ambulance, he beat the paramedics inside.

Monty was without orders, but he knew what had to be done. He whistled sharply. Rebel came running. Seconds later they, too, were on their way out.

Flashing lights and screaming sirens made a path through the denizens of the meadow. An armadillo made a run for his hole as a hawk took off from the highest branch of a tree in search of quieter hunting grounds. A jackrabbit bounded across the path of the lead squad car as a terrapin came to a rambling halt and pulled his head and feet into his shell, hoping for the best.

In minutes the abandoned homestead was nearly

silent, just as it had been before the arrival of man and the death that seemed always to follow. There was little to show of the drama that had unfolded upon it over the past twenty-four hours except a couple of men from the FBI who were gathering evidence. Slowly the grasses sprang back from the impact they'd suffered, pointing their long, slender stems toward the sun that was climbing to its zenith overhead.

Late that afternoon, as John Thomas sat watch by Samantha's bedside, waiting for a sign that would tell him she was on her way back to him, Montgomery Turner walked into the room.

John Thomas looked up at his stark white face and red-rimmed eyes, and suddenly remembered the dying fiancée.

"Sheriff." Monty kept swallowing over and over in an effort to get out his request without breaking down. "I'll need to be gone for a couple of days."

It was the pain in his eyes that told John Thomas the waiting was over for the young woman who'd been taken off of life support.

"Damn, Monty, I'm so sorry." He looked down at Samantha, lying still but alive beneath the covers, and felt sudden guilt for being happy.

"Don't think that way," Monty said quietly, sensing the path that the sheriff's thoughts had taken. "Some things are just meant to be." And then his mouth twisted as tears flooded his eyes. "In a way, it all seems right."

"What do you mean?" John Thomas asked.

"On the same day that my Lissa gave up on living, your lady did not. I guess it's true that the strong survive." He walked out of the room without looking back.

John Thomas sat down in his chair and lifted Samantha's limp hand to his cheek, curving it to fit around his face as if she were doing it herself.

"And you are strong, aren't you, Sam? Whatever hell she put you through was still not enough to make you quit. I'm so proud of you, darlin'. Do you hear me, girl? I'm so damned proud of you, I could cry."

And he did.

15

WHITE WALLS LACKED IMAGINATION. John Thomas cursed the hospital's lack of ingenuity, and wished for something abstract to occupy his thoughts. Anything but this flat, blank wall that mirrored his own mind too completely for comfort.

He paced the hallways of East Texas Medical, anxious for a verdict from the doctor. Earlier news had been unsatisfactory. He desperately needed a progress report that he could live with.

She had broken ribs. The thought made him sick to his stomach. Her concussion was serious but not life threatening. It gave him a headache just thinking about it. She'd just missed pneumonia, and it was the doctor's studied opinion that she would have been better off if she'd just broken her leg instead of the torn muscles and ligaments she'd suffered around her knee. John Thomas's teeth ached every time he took a step, thinking about the misery she'd suffered alone in that well.

"Damn that woman to hell," he muttered, thinking of Claudia Smith.

A nurse hustled by and glared at him. He flushed, embarrassed that he'd been overheard, yet unwilling to let go of his anger and frustration until Samantha woke up and at least acknowledged his existence. After that, he just might survive.

"Sheriff."

John Thomas spun, then all but pounced on the doctor who had just come out of Samantha's room.

"What is it, Doc? Is she worse? Did you get the results of her X rays? When will you know something?"

Doc Baker waited patiently for his "other patient" to calm down. If this one had as much consideration for a busy, overworked doctor as that little lady in the bed back there, he'd get a whole lot more accomplished. *She* hadn't argued with a thing he'd done. Of course, *she* still wasn't awake. Knowing women the way he did, the arguments would probably come later when she was given her restrictions.

"You ready to listen?" Doc Baker asked.

"I'm sorry," John Thomas said, and went limp against the wall, unaware of the curious gazes from the inhabitants in the room across the hall. "I'm listening."

"That'll be a first," the doctor said.

He'd delivered Johnny Knight. Seeing him grow from a troublemaker to a respected member of the community was satisfying. But there were obviously some personality traits that time would never change, and impatience was definitely one of them. But it was time to put him out of his misery.

"She's going to be fine," Doc Baker said. "All signs point toward a complete recovery."

"Thank God," John Thomas said, and hugged the doctor with unusual abandon.

"You save that stuff for the lady in there," Doc Baker said, grinning at the smile he put on the sheriff's face. "Now I'm not saying there won't be some tough days ahead for her. Even after the laser surgery we did on her knee, she's still got some rehabilitation to go through. And when she finally wakes up, she'll have a hell of a headache. But all in all, for someone who fell down a well, she's in real good shape."

"She didn't fall," John Thomas reminded him, his voice sharp, his eyes hard with anger. "Remember the shoe print in the middle of her shirt?"

The doctor nodded. He already knew that she'd been kicked in the stomach, and had in all probability fallen backward from the impact. It made him cringe. It was a wonder she'd survived.

"You can go back in," Doc Baker told him. "But you have to promise not to cause trouble. You sit and be quiet. Let the lady come back to you on her own."

The door was already swinging shut when Doc Baker realized he was standing in the hall talking to himself. He grinned and wiped a weary hand across his

face as he saw his nurse down the hall, waiting for him
outside the door of his next patient's room.

The curtains were shut. The room was cool and
dark. John Thomas sank down in the chair by
Samantha's bedside, resuming his post as diligently
as a soldier on guard, and slipped his fingers across
her hand, satisfied with the fact that he could actually reach out and touch her any time he chose.
Twenty-four hours ago he wouldn't have given a
plug nickel for the chances he'd have of ever being
able to do that again.

He stared at a point just above her chin where her
upper and lower lip met, and remembered how soft and
sweet it was to the touch, and how urgently she'd clung
to his kisses when they made love. Now it was swollen
and bruised. A cut was slowly healing on her lower lip
as was a large scrape beneath her chin.

She sighed. He sat upright, expecting at any minute
to see her eyes open. Then he'd know that she'd come
back to him. But the sigh was premature. And slowly
he sank back into the chair and resumed his watch. He
could wait. Right now, as long as he had Sam, he had
all the time in the world. And time passed.

She knew he was there long before she opened her eyes.
But she felt heavy, as if the blood in her body was flowing at a slower rate than normal, and the idea of moving
came and went so quickly it might never have been.

There was pain. But nothing like before. And the

bone-chilling cold and the smell of dank water were also missing. That had to mean something.

Finally there was nothing between her and daylight but the will to find it. She opened her eyes. It was then that she saw him, sitting in the chair beside her bed and staring out the window above it. Her fingers twitched and then clutched at his hand.

He jerked and looked down. He saw her slow, steady smile, and then after that everything was a blur.

She took a deep breath. "You came."

He couldn't resist leaning over her bed and placing a soft, baby kiss on her cheek. "I promised you, darlin', remember?" he said, and sank back into his chair.

A tear slid out of the corner of her eye. She inhaled slowly, and then moved her other hand tenderly across her rib cage.

"Everything hurts," she said, and looked to him for answers.

"Two broken ribs, and they fixed your knee," he said, and patted her hand, afraid to touch anything else that mattered.

She closed her eyes to signify she understood, and then they snapped open.

"Johnny."

"What, darlin'?" he asked, and wished with all his soul that he could pick her up and hold her.

"Desiree Adonis. Tell Pulaski. He'll know what to do."

John Thomas jumped. He'd been so focused on her

survival that he'd completely forgotten that with her consciousness would come answers.

"I will, Sam. I promise."

"Tell him now," she said, and then sighed, as if she'd used up all her strength. "You go. I want to sleep. Come back later and tell me it's done." She drifted back into semiconsciousness.

The hard look on his face was never more evident than when he exited the hospital room and started down the hall. She'd asked him for something he *could* fulfill. He looked down at his watch and realized that in California it was only 5A.M. Somehow he didn't think Pulaski would mind.

Pulaski rolled over in bed, cursing the loud, persistent ringing that had pulled him awake. But when he answered the phone, the frown on his face disappeared in seconds. He sat up on the edge of the bed, rubbing the sleep from his eyes as he listened to Knight's story.

"Hell, yes, I know who she is," he said, looking around the room for his pants. "Thanks for the information, John Thomas. I'll let you know when the deed is done."

He was referring to the imminent arrest of one Desiree Adonis, currently residing in Los Angeles, California.

"Who would have thought?" he muttered as the phone went dead in his ear. He shook the rest of the sleep from his brain and went to make some coffee. He had a long day ahead of him, but if all went well, for the first time since John Thomas Knight had entered his office, tonight he should be able to sleep without a guilty conscience.

The sun beamed down on the clay court as brown-skinned couples in white-bright, fashionably correct tennis attire volleyed in perfect form. The fuzzy white and fluorescent yellow balls flew back and forth across the nets like a swarm of giant bees. The steady thwack of the rackets as they connected on target, and the occasional grunt of a player as extra effort was added to the swing, made the scene picture perfect.

Mike Pulaski, escorted by club security and four other plainclothes detectives, made his way across the grounds toward the court at the far end.

Even from here she stood out in the crowd, her red hair a beacon against the stark white clothing, the vivid greens, and dark, clay red of the courts. Tanned to perfection, trim to the point of emaciation, she stretched up on her tiptoes as her arm shot up and out and caught the serve just before it sailed beyond reach. She sent the ball back across the net with a surge of elation.

"Ha!" she shouted, and then bounced back and forth on her toes as her opponent dashed to make the return.

The ball hit just inside the line.

"Game!" she shouted, and then laughed, and thrust her arms into the air, jubilant from the surge of pleasure that always came with winning.

The smile was still on her face when she saw the men coming across the grounds. The surge of panic and then anger that swept throughout her system was swiftly masked. There's no way, she kept telling herself. There's no way they can know.

Stifling whatever emotions their arrival brought, she waited, cool and composed for them to make the first serve. After all, she was the ultimate athlete, willing to give a lesser opponent first shot, but still a player who played to win.

"Desiree Adonis?"

Mike Pulaski's voice rumbled across her nerves. She noticed the man had a greasy spot on his tie. She frowned. Donny would never have gone out in public like that.

"Yes," she said, and smiled, offering her hand for the handshake that never came.

The gasp that came up her throat was as unexpected as the handcuffs that locked around her wrists.

"Desiree Adonis, you're under arrest for the attempted murder of Samantha Carlyle. You have the right to remain silent. If you . . ."

Everything he was saying faded except one word. *Attempted.* She couldn't have heard him right. There had to be a mistake.

But the look on the rumpled man's face was too fixed to ignore. She tried to smile, lifting her arms up and waving the cuffs around as if this were all a joke.

"I'm being arrested," she said, as her opponent

stood transfixed on the opposite side of the net, watching the entire proceedings. "Can you believe it? They think I murdered someone.

"Who did you say I'm supposed to have killed?" she asked, flashing her eyes at Pulaski and smiling in a way that had proved quite effective in the past. "And when did I do it? Between the bankruptcy proceedings, or my appointment at the hair dressers?"

Pulaski resisted the urge to put his fist in her mouth. And there was something about the look in her eyes that told him he had the right woman. The laughter was a little too hard and off-center. The glitter in those bright green eyes was too sharp, and the muscle jerking at the side of her mouth gave away her lie.

"I will repeat," he said slowly, as the detective beside him grabbed her by the arm and started leading her away. "You are being arrested for the attempted murder of Samantha Carlyle."

A jumbo jet flew overheard, suddenly drowning out the rest of what the detective was saying. But Desiree didn't need to hear any more. She'd heard enough to send her over the edge. Everything she'd been through since Donny's death—everything she'd planned, everything she'd done—it was all for nothing.

Her eyes rolled back in her head. Pulaski shouted and jerked as he grabbed her other arm, expecting her to try to make a break. He couldn't have been more wrong.

The shriek that came up her throat and out of her mouth made the hair at the back of his neck stand on end. She started to laugh, and then she began to cry. Sobs traded places with jerky coughs as she tried to talk. But nothing came out that made any sense. Tiny bits of spit frothed at the corner of her lip as they put her in the backseat of the patrol car.

The last sight Pulaski had of her was that bright red mouth, opened as wide as it would go, and the virulent curses and choking laughter spilling out of it and into the interior of the car like filth from a broken sewer.

He shuddered. Samantha Carlyle had endured much at that woman's hands. A wave of guilt hit him as he realized he'd inadvertently played right into the Adonis woman's plans. If only he'd believed Samantha Carlyle's story, some of this might have been averted. But Adonis had almost been too clever for them. And if it hadn't been for John Thomas Knight, she damned well might have won.

"I never said I was perfect," he muttered, as he crawled behind the wheel of his own car.

"What did you say, Pulaski?" his partner asked.

He shook his head. "Nothing," he answered, then put the car in gear and threaded his way back into the mainstream of traffic. It felt good to right a wrong.

"There he goes again," one of the nurses said, and elbowed her coworker, watching the sheriff exit the elevator and turn down the hallway toward Samantha Carlyle's room. For the last two weeks, his visits had been as regular as clockwork.

"Uh oh," the other nurse said. "He's been made. Weller caught him." They disappeared before they got caught in the head nurse's wrath.

"John Thomas!"

Dorothy Weller's voice was deep and full of authority. She stared long and hard at the small brown sack the sheriff held clutched against his chest, and tried to frown at him. It was hard to be firm with someone who ignored your very best glares.

"Hey there, Dorothy. How's business?" John Thomas asked, and winked.

"What do you have in that sack?" she asked, fully aware he was sneaking food into a patient's room, which was against hospital rules. Dorothy Weller was big on rules.

John Thomas got a stubborn look on his face and held the sack a little tighter.

"She doesn't like the soup," he said.

Nurse Weller rolled her eyes and then lowered her voice. "None of us likes the soup, John Thomas. But rules are rules. She's not supposed to have anything that's not on her diet."

He didn't answer and she wouldn't move. Long moments passed as John Thomas felt the sack in his hands starting to grow damp from the condensation forming on the outside of the cup.

"Are you going to be difficult?" she asked, and folded her arms across her ample bosom.

He sighed. "Yes, ma'am, I guess I am."

"Someone should have turned you over their knee years ago. Maybe you wouldn't have been such a menace today if they had."

"Are you offering?" he asked, and flashed a grin that sent a vivid red flush sweeping up her face. John Thomas decided that he'd probably pushed far enough.

"I'm going inside now," he said, and started past her.

"I did not see you come in with that, do you hear me?" she hissed, and hustled down the hall without looking back.

"Hey, Dorothy!"

In spite of instinct telling her to keep walking, something made her stop and turn.

John Thomas grinned, knowing this was really going to get her goat. "Did anyone ever tell you that you're real pretty when you're angry?"

Giggles swept through the hallway as Dorothy Weller turned several shades of a brighter red. And then to everyone's surprise, she answered.

"Actually, they have," she said, and smiled to herself as she finished her exit down the hall with a slight swagger.

John Thomas grinned and gave her a low wolf whistle before slipping into Samantha's room.

Samantha was grinning.

"I heard you," she said, holding out her hands for the sack in his arms. "You're shameless."

He leaned over and pressed his mouth across her smile, tasting it for texture and smoothness before handing over her smuggled treat.

"What did you bring me?" she asked, arranging her new, baby-pink nightgown that he'd brought her yesterday as a treat. It was as close to decent as sheer silk got, and he'd had a difficult time choosing the style at Monique's. Every salesclerk in sight had been offering tips on hospital attire. But he hadn't wanted prim, he'd wanted passionate pink. He got his wish. She looked good enough to eat.

"Among other things, a chocolate shake," he said, and sat down beside her on the bed. He took off the lid and handed her the straw and plastic spoon.

It was deliciously cold and went down in slow, smooth gulps as she diligently sucked on the straw, draining the shake down to is last sticky slurp.

"Thank you, Johnny," she said. "I've been thinking about that all afternoon."

She tossed the empty cup and straw into the trash can and then swung the bulky cast on her leg over the side of the bed so that she could sit up.

"Are you supposed to be doing that?" he asked, warily eyeing the way she'd maneuvered herself closer to where he was sitting. From here he could see the outline of her breasts through the sheer silk. It suddenly occurred to him that maybe he should have listened to the salesclerks' warnings a little closer.

"Doing what?" she asked, and leaned forward for a longer, better kiss than the one she'd gotten earlier.

He couldn't resist, and wouldn't have even if he could. She tasted of chocolate and temptation impossible to ignore.

"What are you trying to do, darlin'?" he asked softly, as he caught her hands about to slide below his belt. Knowing her, she could do serious damage to his already shaky reputation.

"I don't know what you mean," she said, and scooted a little closer.

"Look at me, Sam."

She did, willingly. Her gaze swept across his face, the beloved features so familiar, the seductive smile firmly in place. She looked her fill.

"I love you." He cupped her face in his hands and peppered her with kisses until she was aching and gasping for more. "I will never, can never, get enough of you. But if you don't stop teasing me into an ache we can't heal, then I'm going to have to slack off on the visits or they'll be redoing your surgery, and I'll be sending flowers from my own jail. Do you get my drift?"

"Are you trying to tell me that I'm causing you discomfort?" she asked, with a grin.

"I'm not trying to tell you. I *did* tell you. Now are you going to cooperate, or am I going to have to put the chair beneath the doorknob and pray no one comes knocking until I've wiped that smug look off your face?"

Her eyebrows arched as she contemplated the alternatives he'd just given her.

"I think if we hurry . . ."

He bolted off of the bed.

Seconds later an orderly walking past in the hallway outside heard a small thump, and then a giggle and a sigh. But he shrugged and continued on his way. He had a spill to mop up and no time to be checking for trouble he couldn't fix.

Nearly an hour had passed and it was time for temps and pressures to be taken. The door to Samantha's room swung open, and she turned over in bed and smiled at the woman who'd just entered her room.

John Thomas was sitting in his usual spot in the chair by her bed, using the underside of the frame for a footrest as he scanned an ancient and dog-eared *National Geographic* from the waiting room outside.

"You'll have to leave now," Nurse Weller said, eyeing the odd expression on the sheriff's face.

There was something about this man she couldn't quite trust. She didn't know what it was, but she'd bet her reputation it was there. One of these days, she'd figure out just what it was about him that made her nervous.

"Yes, ma'am," he said, and bent down to give Samantha a slow, lingering kiss.

Dorothy Weller fussed with the tray beside her patient's table, willing this man into the next county.

"Enough's enough," she said, and then saw the empty cup and the sack wadded and tossed in the trash can beside the bed. "So, did you enjoy your little treat?" she asked Samantha.

Sam grinned and looked straight into John Thomas's face.

"Oh, yes, ma'am," she said, a little too breathless for Nurse Weller's comfort. "It was the best thing I've had in weeks."

John Thomas laughed aloud, picked up his hat from the extra chair, and set it on his head at a jaunty angle.

"See you tomorrow?" Samantha asked, as she watched him almost swagger out of the room.

He turned and winked. "You up to it?" he asked.

"No, I think the question should be are *you* up to it?"

His laughter echoed down the hall, rich and vibrant with life. Nurse Weller frowned. There was more going on in here than she'd expected.

"Open your mouth," she said, and poked the thermometer carefully between Samantha's lips.

"Where have I heard that before?" Samantha asked, and then collapsed in a fit of giggles.

Visiting hours had come and gone long ago. The day had been difficult, the therapy intense and grueling. She should have been exhausted, and yet Samantha couldn't sleep.

She aimed the remote at the television, turned off the sound, and absently watched the antics of Laurel and Hardy as they romped through the scene of the vintage movie being shown on TV.

The door to her room opened a crack, just enough for whoever was on the other side to listen and see if the patient inside was awake or sleeping.

"Who is it?" Samantha asked softly.

The door swung back.

"I didn't mean to wake you," he said, and slipped inside the room and quickly shut the door.

Samantha was surprised to see Montgomery Turner in her room at this time of night.

"You didn't," she said, pointing toward the television. "I was just bored and couldn't sleep."

He nodded and came a little closer to her bed.

"I've been meaning to come sooner," he said, and then looked away as he worried the top of the little brown sack in his hands, unable to look for long at the dark hair spilled over the pillow and not remember another woman, with similar hair and features, who'd never come home.

"Come here," she said, and held out her arms. "Johnny told me what happened, and I would like a hug."

Monty shivered, knowing that her touch was going to give him pleasure, and at the same time pain. But he complied.

The hug was swift, but it was complete, right down to

a tender, brotherly kiss on the cheek. Monty stepped back
and tried to grin. The cocky look was gone. But Samantha knew that with time, most of it, if not all, would be
back. Time had a way of healing the worst of hurts.

"So, what's been going on at the department?" she
asked. "I hope old Pete and Wiley have made up their
differences."

He grinned, remembering the two elderly farmers
who'd duked it out in a fence row like two young studs.

"They're fine," he said. "Did the sheriff ever tell you
what caused it?"

She shook her head.

"Pete's bull got in Wiley's pasture and, if you'll par-
don the expression, had his way with two heifers Wiley
had been planning to sell. One thing led to another and
before they knew it, they were trading punches about
everything that had occurred since they were in school
together, right down to the fact that Wiley had stolen
Peter's fifth-grade sweetie and never apologized."

"Oh good grief," she said, and then smothered her
laughter so that they wouldn't discover her late-night
visitor.

"How did Johnny settle it?" she asked, remembering the two elderly wives who'd arrived on the scene as
she was leaving.

"He didn't, the wives did. They lit into those two old
men like wet settin' hens. Before we knew it, they had
them in their cars and on the way home. I never saw
two more down and out fellows in my life."

She laid her head down on the pillow and sighed, a smile still lurking around her lips.

"You're just what I needed tonight, Monty. Thank you for coming to see me."

He nodded, and then started to leave when he stopped. "I almost forgot why I came," he said, and handed her the sack he'd been holding.

"You didn't have to bring me anything," she said. "Your visit was more than enough." She opened the sack and reached inside.

The stuffed toy puppy was soft and brown, with big sad eyes and long, floppy ears. Except for the big red bow around its neck, it was nearly a replica of the sheriff's dog.

"It's precious," she said. "And it looks just like Rebel." She turned it over and over, marveling at the perfection of the droopy features and the huge, mournful eyes.

"That old dog did more than his part in helping us find you. Thought you might like it, just in case you're ever in need of another guard dog and we're not around."

"He's perfect," she said.

He smiled.

"Are you going to be all right?" she asked, changing the subject on him so fast he didn't have time to mask his emotions.

"With a boss like John Thomas Knight, and a grandfather like Wheeler Joe Turner, how could I not be?"

His mouth twisted, and tears shot to his eyes, but they didn't spill over. And the answer he'd given her had enough spirit and humor to tell her he meant what he said.

The door flew open. Nurse Weller glared at the man, the hat, and the gun in his holster, and balanced her tray of medication more carefully before she tore into him.

"I should have known it would be another lawman," she said, and started forward. "I suppose you have a real good reason why you're here when you shouldn't be."

Monty did a swift about-face. "Yes, ma'am. Official business. Just tying up a few loose ends."

He winked at Samantha and tipped his hat to the nurse as he hustled past her, then out of the door.

"Do you have anything to say for yourself?" Nurse Weller asked, and set her tray upon the table beside her patient's bed.

Samantha rolled over on her stomach, giving the nurse a clear target at her already overpunctured posterior, and sighed.

"Take your best shot."

Nurse Weller didn't miss.

16

JOHN THOMAS STOOD on the porch, waving as the preacher's wife drove away. He grinned slightly, watching as the dust settled on the grass at the sides of the road. Ever since Samantha had come home from the hospital, the stream of visitors coming to pay their respects had been constant and steady.

Although staying at the apartment in Rusk would have meant being closer to the doctor, as well as handier for John Thomas to check up on her during the day, she'd refused to go back. She'd stated loud and long that she wanted to go home. He had not had it in him to deny her another thing.

The pleasure he'd felt at knowing she considered his home hers was immeasurable. And all it had taken was her arms around his neck and the soft, breathless way she said "please," and they'd been on their way. He shivered, remembering that sweet sound against his neck, and then a lid banged against a pan inside the house and he frowned.

She must be in the kitchen again, even though she was supposed to be off her leg as much as possible. The broken ribs had healed, the surgery on her knee had come and gone, but everything about her was still weak and fragile, and just looking at her made a lump form in his throat.

He'd come so damned close to losing her that he still woke in a cold sweat in the middle of the night, thinking the nightmare wasn't over. Yet day by day, with her constant and reassuring presence, the panic in his eyes was slowly but surely disappearing.

Inside the house, Samantha stirred and poured, measured and chopped, satisfied that life had settled back into a more or less even course.

The first thing she had remembered when she came to herself in the hospital room was Johnny, sitting in a chair beside her bed, staring at her as if willing her to wake. And when she had, the relief on his face had been visible. She remembered seeing him shudder and try to speak. And when she had blinked, the tears he'd been holding back started a silent stream down his face. In all the years she'd known him, it was the first time she could remember seeing him cry.

After that, days became a blur. There were days of recovery and rehabilitation, days when she feared he would be fired for ignoring his duties, and days when she'd used up all her strength and leaned on him for everything. Those were the days most firmly locked in her memory.

There were the times after they were home when she would awaken in the middle of the night and know that, even in his sleep, he was clutching her to him in desperation. And during the day, she felt the way his gaze followed her every move as she hobbled from room to room. She worried that he would never be able to forget. As for her own fears, most of them were gone. Just knowing that Desiree Adonis was safely locked away was all that she needed for peace of mind.

And now that she was nearly healed, the constant caution in his look and touch was all she needed to know that she'd become the most important thing in his life.

It was good to know, but it was not enough. She wanted to hear him say the words. She needed to know that the decision she'd made to stay was not one-sided. And that was why she punched and prodded on a daily basis and dared him to explode.

The phone call she'd received today while he was gone had been, for her, the answer. It was all the spark she needed.

She thumped the lid another time or two just to let him know where she was, and then waited. It didn't take long.

The screen door banged behind him as he stomped toward the kitchen.

"You're not supposed to be doing that," he growled,

as he took the spoon from her hand, stuck it back in the pan, and lifted her off her feet.

Samantha's heart tugged as he carried her outdoors to the porch swing, and plopped her down in his lap. He didn't say a word, but the way he was holding her said it all.

She looked up at the shadows in those dark Texas eyes and then leaned forward and cupped his face, slipping small but apologetic kisses across his chin, cheek, and mouth until he groaned from the ache of her sitting so firmly against him when he so desperately wanted inside her instead.

She combed her fingers through his hair, loving the feel of the thick, springy strands filtering through her palms, as it glittered against the setting sun behind him, framing his obstinate expression and a go-to-hell chin.

"Are you through making fun of me?" he growled, and nuzzled the spot behind her ear that drove her wild.

"Only if you're through playing mother hen," Samantha said.

He shook his head and sighed. "But, Sam, if you only knew what nearly losing you did to me, you'd understand."

"I nearly lost you, too, Johnny," she said quietly. "But I'm here. Now, what exactly are you going to do about it? After all, I'm no longer in need of a bodyguard."

He went still. The swing stopped swinging about the same time his heart stopped beating.

"What are you trying to tell me?" he asked, as a new terror swamped him.

She shrugged. "My boss called me today. It seems I've become quite the item since Desiree's arrest. They would just *love* for me to come back, with a raise and a promotion of course."

Oh damn! How can I compete with Hollywood?

The sick look on his face drove her on. *He'll do something, say something, anytime now.* And then she thought, *Surely he won't just let me leave without a fight?*

"What did you tell them?" he asked, and looked over her head at the pasture beyond, staring without seeing what was in front of his face.

"Damn you, John Thomas," she said, and doubled up her fist and hit him on the arm. "You're going to make me do this all by myself, aren't you?"

He looked stunned. It was the first time she'd ever called him by his adult name. He started to speak, and then found that words wouldn't come. He could track criminals, stolen vehicles, and rustled cattle, but following the path her thoughts were taking was simply beyond his ability.

"Do what?" he asked. "You just up and told me you were leaving me. For the second time in our lives, I might add. What the hell did you expect me to do, wave a goddamned flag?"

By now he was yelling, and Samantha grunted and just caught herself from falling when he dumped her into the swing alone. He stomped off the porch, then walked across the yard, aiming for the fence on the other side of the road, needing to put space between himself and the pain.

She levered herself from the swing with a small, relieved sigh. Thank God. For a minute she thought he was ready to get rid of her.

She followed him across the yard. And when she came to the fence, she slipped between him and the railing, wrapping her arms around his waist, and forcing him to acknowledge her presence by staring until he complied by looking back.

"When are you leaving?" he asked, and swallowed a chunk of misery.

"Ummm, it can't be before next week because I promised Amanda Pruitt, the pastor's wife, that I'd be the cashier at the church bazaar."

He started to push her away, unable to stand and listen to this matter-of-fact destruction of his world. But she held on to him with firm persistence and continued to ramble.

"And I already promised Monty that he could come to dinner the first Sunday of October. It's his birthday."

John Thomas was starting to suspect he was being had, but the fear she'd instilled was too strong to disappear without a stronger promise than what she'd given him so far.

"And there's no way I can leave until after our children are grown and gone from home. I'm a firm believer in being with them as much as possible through their formative years."

"Children?"

She was grinning. The look on his face was priceless.

"You're not going to tell me after all the years I've known you that you don't like babies," Samantha said.

He shook his head. He wasn't about to tell her anything. He was too lost in hearing her say it all for the both of them.

"Well, thank goodness," she said. "I'd like two. It would be nice if we could have a boy and a girl, but it's nearly impossible to predict—"

His mouth covered her lips, putting a period to the end of her sentence before she was quite ready. But who was she to argue with such a persuasive technique? Especially when he picked her up, carried her across the road, and into the house with such panache.

And when he laid her down in the middle of his bed and began taking off her clothes, she knew it was time to put an end to her teasing.

"I will love you dearly, John Thomas, for the rest of our lives. I will warm your bed, cook your food, and clean your house. I will gladly bear your children and watch you grow old and bald. But you're going to have to say the words."

He grinned as the last of his clothes hit the floor and he slid into bed beside her.

"Just like a woman," he said, as his hands traced a familiar path across her body. "Can't come right out and say what's on her mind. Has to beat around the bush and scare the hell out of a man just to prove she can."

Samantha sighed as his body slid over and then he slid inside.

"Samantha Jean Carlyle, will you marry me?" he whispered.

"Ahh," she sighed, and arched her body to meet his. "Yes, Johnny, yes! But only if you promise to do something about this sudden need I have." She swayed lightly beneath him, just enough to remind him of where he was.

"I promise," he said, and started to move, slowly at first, and then with increasing speed until she thought her heart would burst from the pleasure.

"You swear," she gasped, and wrapped her arms around his neck as the end neared.

"Cross my heart and hope to die," he whispered.

And then the pleasure came, and after it came silence. Long minutes passed as peace overwhelmed them. But finally, John Thomas felt compelled to add, "I can't compete with all that glitter you'll be giving up," he said.

"I had it, Johnny. It wasn't all it's cracked up to be. Besides, I don't think I ever intended to stay in L.A." She turned and snuggled within the strength of his embrace. "I guess I was just taking the long way home."

* * *

Hours later, the sun slipped beyond the horizon and set a lone coyote to yipping as he started out on an early hunt. Rebel answered, marking his own territory with a long, deep bay. It was the end of another day in Cherokee County.

Elizabeth Lowell

HE **NEW YORK TIMES** *BESTSELLING AUTHOR*

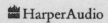